THE BROKEN FIXER

THE BROKEN FIXER

RALPH DENNIS

BRASH
BOOKS

ISBN: 1941298192
ISBN-13: 978-1941298190

Published by
Brash Books, LLC
12120 State Line #253
Leawood, Kansas 66209
www.brash-books.com

This is an edited and revised version of a book previously published in 1975 under the title *Atlanta*.

ATLANTA, 1975

CHAPTER ONE

The fog far out Peachtree Road was thin and wispy, blown here and there, as if the wind changed every few seconds, spinning around like some child's toy. At the Madrid Apartments, the night doorman stood outside long enough to smoke half a cigarette. He ground the coal out on the sole of his shoe and field-striped it. He watched the tobacco blow away, wadded up the paper and flipped it into the shrubs.

Back in the foyer, away from the chill, he stopped at the bank of television monitors. Nothing. The hallways and the elevators were empty. It was a long time before there'd be any movement in the building. By then he'd be off duty and gone, if his relief was on time. But that was still an hour away, at eight o'clock.

On the fifth floor, apartment 512, the Shooter was awake. It wasn't by choice. He was in the bathroom, still choking and gagging, watching himself in the mirror. The toilet was sucking and swishing and there went last night's supper and a lot of high-priced scotch. His stomach was empty now but the dry heaves wouldn't stop. Now and then it was like that.

He was a tall young man. Six foot six in his basketball shoes. He was nineteen years old and this was his first year away from home and away from Southeastern State, a small backwater college in North Carolina where he'd played basketball until the end of the season his junior year. Eleven months before, in March, he'd turned pro after being selected in the first round of the secret draft held by the A.B.A. His junior year he'd averaged 40.7 points a game and he'd passed up his final year of college ball when he'd

1

been offered a five-year, million-dollar contract. He had no second thoughts about it. It was too good to turn down, and there was always the chance that the two leagues might merge in the next year and take away his bargaining power.

The dry heaves stopped after a time, and the Shooter looked at himself in the mirror again. His eyes were red and watery, his skin gray, and there was the taste of vomit on his tongue. He rinsed his mouth with Listerine, and afterwards he brushed his teeth for five minutes. At the end of that he dropped the toothbrush in the trash can without looking at it.

He slept for another hour. It was a fitful sleep. He showered and shaved and dressed in dark slacks, a gray wool shirt and the Spanish leather jacket he'd bought on the last game trip to New York. He rode the elevator downstairs and waved at the day doorman on the way out. He walked across the parking lot to space No. 45 where his blue XKE was parked. He had the door open, about to step in, when a vague ghost of a thought floated up. He remembered something without remembering it at all.

He walked around to the front of the XKE and looked. The front left headlight was broken and shoved back and the fender was bent in, almost against the tire. The sickness got him again, and he decided he didn't want any breakfast after all.

"What now?" he said just under his breath. "What the hell now?"

Officer Ben Timmons and his partner Ralph Abse went off duty at eight in the morning. While Ralph cleaned out the patrol car and checked it over with the crew coming on, Ben took his citation book in and handed it to Martin, the watch sergeant.

Martin thumbed through the book and asked, "This the lot?"

Ben nodded. "There was one more maybe I should have given. Guess who I pulled last night, over the limit and smelling to high heavens?"

"Who?"

"The Shooter ... the kid, Eddie Simpson."

"Where was that?" Martin asked.

"Peachtree Road."

"When?"

"One-thirty, one-forty." Ben looked around the watch room. "He seemed like a nice kid. He said he'd park and take a cab home. So, I let him go."

Martin nodded. "No reason to make waves."

Ralph came in and Ben joined him and then went back to the locker room to shower and change clothes. As soon as they were gone, Martin left his desk and went into the watch captain's office and closed the door behind him. The watch captain was Noah French, a man on his way up in police politics, a young man who knew what move to make all the time ... the one that would get him the most brownie points.

"What time was that hit-and-run on Peachtree Road last night?" Martin asked.

"One forty-five or so," Noah French said. "Why?"

"I've got a bad feeling about this one," Martin said, and then he told Noah French about Ben Timmons stopping Eddie Simpson, better known as The Shooter, on Peachtree Road around that time.

"Speeding and drinking?"

Martin nodded.

"Shit," Noah said. He leaned back in his chair and stared at the ceiling for a minute or so. He tilted his head and looked at Martin. "I'll handle it. Sit on it unless I tell you otherwise."

Noah watched Martin return to his desk. He left his chair and walked around the room, stewing it over in his head. It was, of course, a long shot. More than likely it hadn't been the Shooter.

3

But he ought to check it and be sure. He sat on the edge of his desk and dialed Motor Vehicles. He got a car model, tag numbers, an address and left the station.

He drove out Peachtree Road to the Madrid Apartments, parked on the street and worked his way through the lot. He found the XKE without any trouble and matched the tag numbers. Then he circled the XKE and squatted to inspect the damage to the left front headlight and fender. When he straightened up, he left the parking lot, returned to his car and drove back to the station. He took it slowly because he was trying to figure what his best move would be.

It was a once-in-a-lifetime play and he wanted to look at it from all the angles. When he moved, it had to be the right move. And he had to decide what he wanted more than anything else.

Martin looked up at him when he re-entered the watch room.

"Ben Timmons still in the building?" Noah asked.

"I think so," Martin said.

"Didn't he request a transfer some time back? I vaguely remember ..."

"He wanted to go over to the stake-out squad."

"Okay it," Noah French said, "starting tomorrow night."

"What about his partner, Ralph Abse?"

"Move him to foot patrol down in tight squeeze."

"He's not going to like it," Martin said.

"Fuck him," Noah said.

Back in his office he closed the door and dialed the Grady Hospital number. He identified himself.

"That old wino got hit out on Peachtree Road ... what's his condition?" He nodded as the woman ticked them off for him: broken right leg, facial lacerations, probable concussion. "What's the outlook?"

"He's holding his own," the woman said, "but it's too early to say."

Noah thanked her and replaced the receiver. He leaned back in his chair and tried to steady his nerves. A lot went with this roll of the dice. It had to be done in the right way. And it was a shaky move because it meant going over the chief's head. That was not a healthy way for a captain to start the day or to end a watch.

Ben Timmons was standing alone by the coffee machine in the snack area when Martin found him. He'd had one cup of the awful stuff and he was trying to decide if he could stomach another.

"Watch captain wants to see you in five minutes," Martin said.

"What have I done wrong?"

"Nothing yet," Martin said.

"What's it about?"

"The stake-out squad job; it's yours. You start tomorrow night."

"That's good news," Ben said.

"I thought you'd think so." Martin turned away. "Five minutes then."

"Thanks." Five minutes. He fished out another dime and tried the coffee with double cream this time. It wasn't much better that way.

David Emmett Wardlaw awoke each morning at six. He didn't need an alarm clock. The clock was inside him. He awoke in the master bedroom of the penthouse apartment on the twentieth floor of the Mitchell Towers. It was a large, spacious bedroom with a glassed-in terrace that overlooked the northeast part of

Atlanta. He'd been living in the apartment for two years, since his wife Emily died. It had been a hard death, a grim one: cancer that would appear, be cut away and then reappear again without any warning. After her death, he'd sold the house on West Paces Ferry and moved into the apartment, which hadn't changed since he'd first moved in. The only things that he felt belonged to him were the clothes in the walk-in closet and his toilet articles in the bathroom. Nothing else had the stamp of his personality.

Everything from the West Paces Ferry home was now in storage. He seldom thought of the furniture and the paintings, except when his children Marty and Frances were in the apartment. But that was only during vacations. The storage charges were paid once a year. It was a transaction that his executive secretary, Helen Morris, handled for him.

Marty was in his second year at Yale and Frances was about midway through her first year at Smith. They'd both been in town during the Christmas holidays. The visits were never completely successful. No matter how hard he tried to arrange it, they seemed to be away when he was there. If David found an evening to spend at home, then Marty would have a date or Frances would be visiting an old high school friend. Sometimes, when it rankled him, he almost believed that the checks and money were the only bonds between them. But he knew that it hadn't always been that way. And perhaps it wasn't that way now.

Showered, shaved and dressed, he left the bedroom and cut through the living room. It was a huge, wide room, stark with its Danish furniture and the paintings and sculpture he never looked at. The table in the dining room seated twenty. At the far end, there was a large glass of orange juice and a cup of coffee. The *Constitution* was open to the financial page. This was the live-in chef's only duty of the morning—this single glass of freshly pressed orange juice, this cup of coffee made from Colombian coffee French-roasted and ground moments before it was made, and the paper turned to the financial page. The timetable was so exact that the juice was chilled and the coffee steaming when he entered the dining room. Most mornings David did not see John at all. That was the way he wanted it.

After David finished the juice and coffee and skimmed the financial page, he left the penthouse and rode the private elevator down to the lobby.

The doorman always said, "Good morning, Mr. Wardlaw," and opened the outer door for him. The black Continental was always parked directly outside the main entrance and his driver, Fred Masters, opened the passenger door when he was just two paces away.

Fred said, "Good morning, Mr. Wardlaw," and bowed him into the car and closed the door quietly after him.

There was another copy of the morning *Constitution* on the seat, and David read the front page and the editorial page on the fifteen-minute ride through the almost empty Atlanta streets. It was exactly 7:00 when David stepped into the Continental, and it was 7:15, give or take a minute, when he arrived at the Peachtree Investment Building. This morning, because of the fog, it was 7:20 when the Continental reached the closed entrance that led to the underground parking garage.

In the lobby upstairs, the security guard saw the Continental on the television monitor, and after checking the license plate, he touched the button that folded the door up and away. After the Continental was inside the garage, the guard touched a second button and the door unfolded and closed once more. Fred Masters parked the Continental at the space nearest to the elevator and went through the ritual of opening the door for David.

After David emerged, Fred closed the door and hurried past his boss and inserted a key in the slot to the left of the elevator. The doors opened and David stepped in and pressed a button.

Fred returned to the Continental. He got the *Constitution* from the back seat and carried it to the room where he waited. From the outside, the room looked like a broom closet. It was, in fact, much larger than that. There was a narrow cot, a chair and a desk; and on a waist-high shelf there was a two-burner hotplate he used to make coffee. The phone on the desk had no dial. It could not be used for outside calls. It connected directly with the phone on Wardlaw's desk.

Before Fred settled in with his newspaper and his cup of instant coffee, he got a soft cloth from the trunk of the Continental and wiped away the moisture and the dust that the car had picked up on the twenty-minute ride. That done, he returned to the small room, took off his cap and his jacket, and made his first cup of coffee for the day. He probably had a four-or-five-hour wait ahead of him, but with a man like David Wardlaw, he couldn't always be sure of that.

David Wardlaw rode the elevator to the twentieth floor. When he stepped out of it, he was in a short narrow hallway that led to his office. His executive secretary, Helen Morris, stood waiting for him at the corner of his desk. He said, "Good morning, Helen," and took off his topcoat.

"Good morning, Mr. Wardlaw." She took the topcoat from him and put it on a wooden hanger in the closet. When she returned he was seated behind his desk. "Would you like your coffee now?"

"Please."

There were two doors to Wardlaw's right as he sat at the desk. The door level with the desk led to his bathroom. The door forward and to his right was open: through it one could see the small but well-equipped kitchen. She returned a minute later with a cup of coffee, one sugar, no cream, and placed it at his right elbow.

"Why don't you have a cup with me, Helen?"

"I've had mine already," she said

Each morning he asked, and each morning she gave the same answer. It was, he supposed, the proper way for a secretary to act with her boss, but it bothered him anyway. They'd been together for twelve years and the reserve had never dropped. Helen was, he thought, thirty-two now, and she'd been around twenty when he'd picked her out of twelve applicants back in the old days of Asher, Spence and Wardlaw. No, "never" wasn't correct. There had been one time when he'd seen the reserve fall away. That was five years ago, when her marriage had broken up. Because he really didn't know her, he couldn't expect to understand why she'd married that particular man. Meeting him right after the marriage, David had felt his faith in her judgment shaken. He'd been a smalltime hustler, a man with the right glib things to say, a way of wearing clothes and the surface polish of a couple of years of college. The marriage lasted a year, and that was longer than he'd have given it. When the hustler left town, he left about $12,000 worth of debts behind him. David might not have known about these debts if the tailor hadn't called him. The tailor said that Helen had told him that she intended to pay off her husband's debts and he wanted to know if Helen's salary would allow that. David had said that he thought that Helen's word was good enough, and if there was any problem, he would underwrite payment himself.

Later that same day, David offered to pay the $12,000 in debts and let Helen pay him back over a period of several years. That was when he saw that spark in her, the hint of things behind that cool reserve. She'd said, "No...not from you," and there'd been such heat in the way she said it that he was surprised. He was puzzled as well, and he might have asked her why she especially underscored her refusal of help from him. But before he could, she recovered herself and explained that she did not think it was good business practice for a secretary to owe her employer.

In the end, without her approval, he did all that he could under the circumstances. He found out where the debts were lodged, he called each of the companies and, as he'd done with the tailor, he backed her pledge of payment. It took Helen almost three years to clear up the debts that her husband had contracted in a year. By the time the last one was paid off, the divorce was final and the husband, the last David heard of him, was somewhere in California selling cars.

Helen Morris was, at thirty-two, as beautiful as she'd been at twenty. Perhaps with maturity she was even more beautiful... soft brown hair worn shoulder length, dark eyes. She was tall for a woman, perhaps five-ten, and not rail-thin as most of the women around him seemed to be, influenced as they were by fashion models. No, she was molded to an older pattern from a time when full breasts and wide hips hadn't been something to be ashamed of. It was the same pattern from which his wife Emily had been cut. And as soon as he compared her to Emily, he caught himself and washed it out of his mind.

The coffee was the same Colombian French-roasted coffee he'd had in his empty dining room. Every two months, without ordering, a package arrived from the Schapira Coffee Company in New York. It contained nine pounds of coffee and the bill.

"Very good coffee, Helen," he said.

"Thank you."

David motioned at the neat stack of papers on the center of the desk. "Anything important here?"

"Loss figures on the Crackers."

David gave a mock shudder. For the last two years there'd hardly been a month in which the Crackers, the A.B.A. team David owned, hadn't lost money. "Any good news?"

"The report in the blue folder is the final draft of the study on office space in downtown Atlanta, the one you commissioned from Meyers and Whitman."

"Let's go back to the Crackers. Do you use the season tickets?"

"I've seen about twenty games," Helen said.

"And?"

Helen gave him a sad smile. "They're not very good. The Shooter is, though. He tries shots that Maravich wouldn't even think about."

"Does he make any of them?"

"I think he shoots close to fifty percent."

"I didn't know you were a basketball fan, Helen."

"I'm not sure that I am," she said.

"But you go?"

"You gave me the season tickets. I'd be foolish not to use them."

"Do you go alone?" As soon as he asked that he knew he'd stepped over the line and he wished that he hadn't. But it was too late.

"Of course not," Helen said. "Isn't that why you gave me two tickets? So I wouldn't have to?"

He nodded.

"Is there anything else, Mr. Wardlaw? More coffee?"

David said there wasn't. He watched her as she walked out of his office, the erect carriage now with the added stiffness that might have been anger. It had been, like most mornings, a bad beginning. He sensed a kind of frustration in himself and he wasn't even sure why it was there.

For ten years, since he'd set up his own real estate investment and development corporation after leaving Asher, Spence and Wardlaw, he'd been buying up acre after acre of slum land in the Boulevard section of Atlanta for a new development.

Two years ago, he bought the Jacksonville franchise in the American Basketball Association and moved the team to Atlanta. Like Tom Cousins had done with the Hawks before him, Wardlaw's team played that first year at Alexander Memorial at Georgia Tech. During that year, Wardlaw cleared the first of the Boulevard slum land and put up a geodesic dome stadium. The new team, in a contest, was named the Atlanta Crackers in honor of the Southern Association baseball team that had been Atlanta's pride before the Braves moved to town. The first year the Crackers had a hard time drawing against the Hawks of the N.B.A., and Coach Bill Thorn had insisted that they draft Eddie "the Shooter" Simpson in the secret draft. Thorn believed that the Shooter could battle Pistol Pete and the rest of the Hawks for the ticket dollar and perhaps hold his own. The Shooter, according to Thorn, was more mature as a player than Maravich had been when he finished his career at L.S.U. And, Thorn argued, the Shooter had the advantage of not being coached by his father.

Wardlaw had gone along with Coach Thorn and signed the Shooter to a five-year, million-dollar contract. The A.D.A., when it was possible, tried to schedule the Cracker games at home when the Hawks were on the road. Even when this wasn't possible, the Crackers, with the Shooter, were holding their own. And everywhere you went in the city you would see kids wearing t-shirts with "Shooter" on them in big red letters.

Acquisition of the land had been the first step. That had been slow and careful, lot by lot, block by block, the buying done through ghosts so that his interest in the area wouldn't be known. At first he bought the Boulevard land at $15,000 a quarter acre. Later, when rumors of large-scale buying began to circulate, the price moved upward. But, in all, the land hadn't cost him much over an average of $85,000 an acre. He'd spent a bit over $2.5 million and he controlled a fan-shaped block of a fraction more than thirty acres.

The morning the story appeared on the front page of the *Constitution* that Wardlaw had bought the Jacksonville Flyers of the A.B.A., that he would move them to Atlanta and that he planned to build an indoor stadium on the Boulevard land he owned, the asking price of land around his fan-shaped block doubled. It was to go even higher when ground was broken on the geodesic stadium. And there was another spurt upward when the stadium was completed and the Crackers began playing their home games there the previous October.

To this point, what David had done was an exercise in taking slum land and, by placing the stadium near the center of it, artificially tripling the land values. A lesser man might have been content to take his profit and move on.

David Wardlaw was not that kind of man.

There was one more element that would assure the success of the Boulevard project. He'd heard the first whisper of it almost twelve years before. It came from the downtown merchants, hurt as they were by the proliferation of outlying shopping malls. Atlanta needed a Convention Center, the merchants said. It would bring in new money, a weekly cascade of it, and it would be good for the city.

When the whispers shifted to outward talk and discussion, the concept developed of a state-and-city-owned Convention Center. The state would appropriate from $35 to $40 million for the construction of the Center. A joint state and city commission would administer the Center, and the city would be responsible for the funding for the staff that would run it.

Location of the Convention Center on the Boulevard site would be the final piece fitted into the project. With the Center there, land sales for hotels, motels, restaurants, bars, shops and stores might total as much as $75 or $80 million.

There were other proposed sites for the Convention Center. There was a block of land near the rundown section of Whitehall that was mentioned often. Some people supported a site a block or so away from the Civic Center. And there was, of course, Wardlaw's Boulevard location.

Each of the land owners had offered the state a parcel of land large enough for the Convention Center at no cost. Wardlaw had been the first to make this offer, and the others had followed his lead. Now the site selection was bogged down in a study committee that had been established by the General Assembly. The waiting was almost over. The committee would announce its decision in the next day or two.

The intercom buzzed. It was Helen. "Mr. Wardlaw, there's a Noah French from the Police Department here. He says it's urgent."

"I don't think I know…"

"He says it's about Eddie Simpson. He's in some kind of trouble."

Twenty minutes later, Noah French left Wardlaw's office. David followed him to the outer office and shook his hand. He stood in the doorway and watched French until one of the outer-area secretaries led him down the hallway and out of sight toward the elevator.

"Miss Morris," he said. Helen followed him into the office and closed the door behind her. "I want you to find Vince Gorman for me."

"I think he's off today," she said.

"Find him anyway."

"Yes, sir."

"I want him in this office in an hour," he said.

After Helen left, he sat at his desk and closed his eyes. It was not going to be a good day. It was already going bad. The selection of the Convention Center was a delicate thing, and almost anything could tip it this way or that. Now, after listening to Noah French, he knew that the noise he heard in his head was the sound of $75 million going down the drain. Unless he could plug it up.

CHAPTER TWO

Vince Gorman rode the elevator from the sixth floor of the Sheraton Biltmore down to the lobby. The Sheraton corporation had spent a large round sum on renovation but they'd kept the old-style lobby. It was, perhaps, an attempt to leave some of the personality of the old hotel intact. As he did each time, Vince wondered if the visiting businessmen and vacationers appreciated it.

He was a tall man, almost six-two, and, with his effortless walk, he moved like an athlete. This morning he was shaky. Too much scotch and too many cigarettes had done that and the time in bed hadn't rested him. The lady from Charlotte hadn't let him sleep as much as he'd wanted.

Whatever her name was.

Carol, that was it.

In profile, his face was hawk-like. It took a person by surprise. It had the sharp lines of the blade of an axe. The tan was deep, but this morning, close up, there was a pale tint under the tan.

He was thirty-two, and this morning he felt as old as God.

To the people in the lobby, he must have looked like any other visiting businessman on the way to whatever meeting or whatever appointment he had for ten o'clock. Though he'd showered and shaved off part of his stubble with the leg razor he'd found in the bathroom, his underwear felt clammy and rank. The skin under the collar of last night's shirt itched. He was a lot of things—but nothing less than neat—and these mornings-after bothered him.

At the rear door of the hotel, the doorman looked at Vince and he nodded. The doorman waved a cab up from the waiting line. Vince palmed a one and passed it to the doorman as the cab door swung open for him. He gave the driver his address in Ansley Park, put his head back and closed his eyes.

The phone was ringing when Vince entered his apartment. He stood over the phone and let it ring another twenty times or so. When it was obvious that it was going to ring on and on he picked up the receiver.

Helen Morris was on the other end. "Mr. Wardlaw wants to see you in his office right away, Vince."

He knew it wouldn't do any good to protest that it was his day off. It would be wasted breath. "I'll be there in twenty-five or thirty minutes." Even as he said this, he was yanking off his tie and beginning to unbutton his shirt.

When Vince Gorman finished Duke Law School seven years before he'd felt like the whole world was open to him. He could do with it what he wanted to, he could put in both his hands and rip out as much as he could. That had been the young man's dream. It hadn't worked out that way. He'd passed the Georgia Bar and found a position with one of the middle-range law firms, one that didn't have an ex-governor of Georgia as a law partner. He hadn't lasted very long. He found that he had a taste for long nights in bars and that women liked him for his ruthless look and his lean body. The long nights and drinking sapped him, and he wasn't especially surprised when he found himself on probation with the law firm. And six months later, when probation was over, he found himself without a job.

That was almost six years ago. He had trouble finding another position, and when he thought of what happened next, he wasn't sure whether it had been good luck or bad. He'd answered an ad in the *Constitution* and found himself being interviewed by David Emmett Wardlaw. Before the interview, and as he sat in the outer office, he'd considered all the lies he might use to mitigate the bad effect his dismissal from the law firm might have upon his application. In the end, he looked into the hard eyes of

Wardlaw and told the truth. To his surprise that hadn't hurt him at all. Within two days, he received a call from Helen Morris, and another appointment was arranged with Wardlaw. At that meeting, a job was offered him with one proviso: he could drink and wench as much as he wanted to, as long as he could get as much as seven hours' sleep before each working day. The first day he came to work shaky and red-eyed, his final check would be drawn within the hour and he'd be back on the street.

It was hard talk. Perhaps it was what he needed. For the first year, he worked under Benjamin Spencer in Contracts and Leases. It was dull and sometimes frustrating work. But he kept his bargain with Wardlaw, and at the end of the year, Helen Morris called for Mr. Wardlaw one morning and asked Vince if he had plans for lunch. Without thinking he said no, he didn't. For the next three hours he tried to assess the year with Wardlaw. He had a bad feeling about the lunch appointment. There was always the chance that this was Wardlaw's way of firing him: taking him to lunch, talking to him and then telling him that he hadn't worked out.

It was an uneasy first hour. The lunch was at the Midi, a small French restaurant near Lennox Square. Careful of his image, Vince had refused a cocktail and asked for sherry instead. He thought, as he took his first sip of sherry, that he caught a glimpse of a smile on Wardlaw's face. But it was gone so quickly that he wasn't sure that he'd seen it at all. It might have been, he thought, a reaction to the gin in the martini Wardlaw was drinking.

The talk was of this and that, a kind of sparring. What Vince thought of the political situation in the city. Did he follow sports at all? Was he interested in national politics?

At the end of the meal, when the dark rich coffee came, Wardlaw smiled at him and said, "Vincent, I think I understand virtue as well as anyone, but after a year, I think we can weaken a bit." And before he could answer, Wardlaw told the waiter to bring his bottle of fifty-year-old cognac and two glasses.

Over the mellow burn of the cognac, Vince began to have second thoughts about the purpose of the lunch. It didn't seem, after all, that the axe was going to fall.

"How are things in Contracts and Leases?" Wardlaw asked.

"Fine."

"But dull?"

"I think you could say that," Vince agreed.

"Ready to move on?"

He misunderstood the question. He thought the axe was out again. "I'm happy with the company," he said.

Wardlaw looked at him with the same even face, a face that didn't tell him anything. "A year ago, I hired you because you didn't try to gloss over what had happened at Mays, Winters and Spector. Maybe you'd better tell me what you think we're talking about."

"Didn't you bring me here to fire me?"

Wardlaw laughed. It was the first time Vince had ever seen him laugh. It was shocking. At the same time, he felt himself relaxing for the first time since he'd received the call from Helen Morris. The axe was back in its cover.

"Honesty then," Vince said. "You've hardly noticed me for the whole year. Now I get the full treatment. I don't know what I was supposed to think."

Wardlaw held the belled glass in his hand, warming the cognac. "I needed to be sure about you. I needed to know if you could keep your bargain for a year. You have and now it's time for a move."

"What move?"

"To a position as my executive assistant." He lifted the glass and sipped at the cognac. "It's a fancy title for what can occasionally be a nasty job."

"I'll take it," Vince said.

"Without knowing what the job is?"

Vince nodded. He rolled a small swallow of the cognac around on his tongue.

"I think I ought to be honest as well," Wardlaw said. "I don't want to mislead you. Do you have any idea why I've chosen you?"

"Not really, unless it's the law degree, the background in legal matters."

Wardlaw shook his head slowly. "I think there's a ruthlessness in you. That's the part of you I want."

Helen closed the door and, still holding the knob, put her back against it. She looked at David Wardlaw. His head was back, his eyes closed. He wasn't, she thought, sleeping. With his face in repose he looked five or six years older than his forty-three years. There were long lines, like knife scars, around his mouth and a deep, sunken cleft in his chin. His hair was a little longer this year and that seemed to accent the gray fringes in the sideburns and at the temples.

He opened his eyes and looked at her. That was it, the eyes. The eyes looked out at a person with a kind of memory of innocence. "Yes, Helen?"

"I found Vince," she said stepping away from the door. "He'll be here in half an hour."

"Did he argue?"

"Not this time," she said.

"Where was he?"

"I don't know where he'd been. I finally found him at his apartment."

"He sound all right?"

"Better than I expected," she said. "Is this something I should know about, Mr. Wardlaw?"

He closed his eyes. "I'd rather you didn't, Helen."

"Then I won't ask about it," she said. Even though she tried to fight against it, she knew the sense of hurt was in her voice.

"Helen." He sat up, his elbows on his desk. "I don't think that came out the way I meant it to."

"I understand," she said.

"It's messy, very messy," he said, "and I'm not sure what I ought to do."

"There have been problems before."

"Not like this one." His sad smile touched her. "My reasons might be self-serving. I might not want you to know what I'm really capable of."

She shook her head. It didn't make sense.

"I'll put a question to you," he said. "You know what a wino is. You've seen them on the streets, passed out or stumbling and staggering around."

"Yes." A few times, out on the street after work she'd been frightened when they'd come up to her to ask for some change.

"What's the life of a wino worth?"

"I can't answer that," she said.

"I can't either," he said. "You'd help me if you could."

Puzzled, not sure what it was all about, she waited to see if he'd add something more that would clear it up for her. He didn't, so she said she'd send Vince in as soon as he arrived.

Helen Morris had been born in Sumter, South Carolina, and while her grades in high school had been good enough for entrance into most colleges, she'd known there wasn't going to be money for college. She passed up the college preparation courses and majored in the business area. She took all the typing, shorthand and bookkeeping courses that were available to her, and three afternoons she worked for a lawyer on Law Range next to the court house.

The day she graduated from Edmunds High School was the same day she graduated from Crosswell Orphanage. And two days later, though the lawyer wanted her to work full time and there were several other offers through the Business Club advisor, she left for Atlanta by bus. The first year in Atlanta, she lived at the Church Home for Business Girls on Ponce de Leon, a bleak and cheerless place crowded with girls waiting for marriage or beginning to settle for less. She worked as a typist for a downtown lawbook publishing company, one of ten girls in a long narrow room. It was spirit-killing work, typing and correcting the manuscript that would be fed into the computer downstairs. After ten months, she knew she'd had enough. She spent April and May using her forty-five-minute lunch break filling out applications and doing interviews. She kept telling herself that it might take months and months to find the right job. She set herself up for a long wait, and then her chance came the day she arrived at Asher, Spence and Wardlaw for her interview. For some reason she never understood, though the company was large enough to have a personnel manager, she was interviewed by David Wardlaw.

He took a long time over her application. At first that puzzled her and then she realized, with a sudden warm feeling, that he was giving her time to steady herself.

His first question surprised her. Usually if it was asked at all it came near the end of the interview.

"Why are you leaving the job you have now?" He put the application aside. "The pay scale is slightly higher there than it is here."

"It's not that," she said.

He waited, his blue eyes seeming to see her for the first time.

"I don't want to be a machine," she said. "I feel like a machine there and I don't like the feeling."

That appeared to stun him. "I've never thought of it that way."

She wanted the words to be the right ones. She wanted him to know what eight hours of typing legal language felt like. "There it's like I get turned on at the same time the typewriter gets turned on. Then I type for four hours and then I turn the IBM off and somebody turns me off and I go to lunch and when I come back I turn the typewriter on and somebody turns me on and we both run for another four hours."

"And you think it might be different here?"

"Would it?" she asked.

He smiled. "I think you're interviewing me, Miss Morris."

"I'm sorry."

"Don't be." He shook his head. "Maybe a good interview should be that. Let me ask you this. How many other places have you made application?"

"Twelve," she said.

"And how many have offered you jobs?"

"Twelve."

"You seem to be hard to please, Miss Morris."

"I guess I am," she admitted.

"I need a personal secretary," he said. "It won't be tea dances and holiday trips … if that's what you're looking for. It might be more exciting than typing lawbooks and there might be more variety in the work."

"I'll need to give them two weeks' notice," she said.

"That's fine," he said. "I've just given my secretary her two weeks' notice."

When the partnership of Asher, Spence and Wardlaw broke up, she moved to the new offices of Wardlaw Properties. She'd been with Wardlaw for twelve years and she'd loved him for eleven of those years. Two years ago, Emily Wardlaw died and she'd cried then, partly for the pain she knew he felt and partly for herself—for the selfishness and the need she saw in herself.

"I don't like it," Vince Gorman said when the meeting was over.

"You don't have to like it," Wardlaw said. "To tell the truth, I don't like it either."

Vince headed for the door that led to the outer office. "I never liked that smart-assed kid."

Wardlaw stood behind his desk. "I remember you saying so at the time."

It was right after the secret A.B.A. draft. Wardlaw had gone along with Coach Thorn to draft the Shooter, and he'd sent Vince up to North Carolina the next day to sign him. After an afternoon of conversation with Eddie Simpson, Vince hired a secretary who worked for a downtown lawyer, and he drew up the contract. Later that same night, when it came time to sign, the Shooter hesitated. It was all there in the contract, all that the Shooter had said he wanted. Still he hesitated.

"I want a woman," he said.

"I'm not a pimp." Vince reached across the table and picked up the copies of the contracts. He was folding them and heading for the door when the Shooter stopped him.

"Sheeet, man," he said, "don't you know a joke when you hear one?"

"When I hear one," Vince said.

And then the Shooter signed the contracts, witnessed by a couple of basketball players the Shooter called from down the hall. After the witnesses left, Vince took the envelop from his suit coat pocket and handed it to the Shooter. It contained 10,000 in unreported under-the-table money. Vince left while the Shooter was still counting it.

"But you don't know the name of the wino?" Vince said.

Wardlaw shook his head. "It ought to be easy to find him. The one hit on Peachtree Road early this morning."

"I like it less and less," Vince said.

Vince parked twenty minutes later in a space three cars down from the Shooter's XKE. On his way past it, he circled around to the front and looked at the dented fender and the smashed headlight. Sure enough, he'd hit something.

The doorman came back from making the call and said the Shooter would see him. "It's on the fifth floor, apartment…"

"I know," Vince said, getting into the elevator. He should, because he'd found the apartment for Eddie Simpson and he'd sent over an interior decorator who did some designing for Wardlaw Properties. The man had been a little light-footed and he had done the work under protest. He told Vince that what the Shooter wanted was a design in jock-strap gray.

The Shooter met him at the door and Vince followed him into the kitchen. The Shooter was having a Bloody Mary, with the vodka, the bottle of tomato juice and the Tabasco on the table next to his half-filled glass.

"Want one?" the Shooter asked.

He did. His body fairly screamed for one, but he shook his head. "You got any coffee?" Without waiting for an answer, he found a jar of instant coffee in the cabinet. When the kettle had a flame under it, he turned and looked at the Shooter. The Shooter was sipping his Bloody Mary and looking past him toward the living room.

"You tore it this time," Vince said.

"Honest to God, I don't remember anything."

"You remember being stopped by a patrol car? A cop who recognized you and let you go on your promise you'd park and take a cab home?"

The Shooter blinked and shook his head.

"As far as we know, that cop hasn't put it together yet. Maybe he won't."

"Maybe I didn't hit anyone," the Shooter said. "I might have hit a phone pole or a parked car."

That was clutching at straws.

"It's easy enough to find out," Vince said. "You call the police and they'll come over and get the XKE and take it over to the police garage. A lab man will go over it and see if they can find any blood or tissue—either on the headlight or the underside of the car."

The Shooter didn't say anything. He stared down into his glass.

"You want that?" Vince asked.

"No."

The water stirred in the kettle. Vince made a cup of coffee and put it on the table across from the Shooter. He left the kitchen and passed through the living room and into the bedroom. The bed was rumpled and unmade. Both pillows had "Shooter" embroidered on them in red. Red was the Cracker color. In the bathroom, Vince ran the basin full of cold water and dunked his face into it several times. Done, he backed away from the basin with his eyes closed and felt along the towel rack. He found a towel and dried his face. Before he put the towel back, he looked at it. "Shooter" was embroidered on it also. He checked a linen shelf in one corner and found that all the towels, hand towels and wash cloths had been given the same showy lettering.

"Jesus," he said under his breath, "the kid doesn't even know what his real name is."

Back in the kitchen, he drank his coffee. "Game here last night?"

"Yeah, we lost the game, but I scored thirty-eight."

"What time was the game over?"

"Nine-thirty or so," the Shooter said.

"What time did you leave the Dome?"

"Ten or a few minutes after that."

"Alone or with somebody?" Vince said.

"Alone," the Shooter said. "I asked a couple of guys, but nobody wanted a drink."

Not with you, Vince thought. "Where'd you go?"

"Five-ninety West. That's the top of Stouffer's, the twenty-sixth floor."

"How long?"

"An hour or so."

"After that?"

"I cruised around some. A drink at five or six places."

"People see you that knew you?" Vince asked.

"People always know me," the Shooter said, his pride flaring up.

"In this situation, that's not something to be proud of."

"I guess not."

"What's the last you remember?"

"It started getting hazy at this place near Pershing Point. I'd never been there before, and I don't know the name of it. There was this girl there and she was interested, but her stud didn't like it and he wanted to make trouble. The manager threw the both of them out." He gave Vince a weak smile. "I guess that means they knew who I was too."

"What time was that?"

"A bit after midnight. I don't know for sure."

"You in training, Shooter?" He couldn't resist the sarcasm.

"There's no game today. Next game's tomorrow night when the Squires come in."

"The word we got was the cop stopped you at one-forty or so. There's an hour missing there somewhere." Vince stood up and put the coffee cup in the sink. He returned to the table and placed his car key in front of the Shooter. "If you need to go out, use the black Ford that's parked three spaces down from where your XKE was. Give me your key."

The Shooter dug out his key ring and unclipped the key. "You going to get rid of it?"

"I ought to." He shook his head. The concern on the Shooter's face was comic. "I'll get it fixed and have it back in a day or two."

"Thanks, Mr. Gorman."

At the doorway that led to the living room he couldn't resist it. "You sure you don't want me to get you a woman, Shooter?"

The Shooter remembered and closed his eyes, his face flushed.

⚜ ⚜ ⚜

Vince drove the XKE to Wilt Mason's Garage. It was a place he'd used a time or two before. Mason came out and met him. He was wiping his hands on a red rag and looking down at the headlight and the fender.

"Got troubles, Mr. Gorman?"

"Got sideswiped last night while I was in a bar."

Mason pursed his mouth. "This an insurance job?"

"I'm in a big hurry," Vince said, shaking his head. "You got somebody can get on it right away?"

"We're busy right now. Might be able to get to it tomorrow."

Vince dug out his wad of cash and, flipping through it, he fished out two fifties. "I can't wait that long."

"If it's important…" Mason crushed the two fifties and shoved them into the greasy coverall pocket. "I'll get a body man on it right away."

"In a minute," Vince said. "First I want to steam off the engine."

"We'll do it for you," Mason said.

"Get the body man," Vince said. "I'll do the steaming myself."

Mason went into the garage. Vince moved the XKE over closer to the steam hose. He steamed off the engine first and then he squatted and pushed the hose under the front of the car. He ran the steam for a long time, moving it back and forth and from side to side. When he stood up and withdrew the hose he turned and saw Wilt Mason watching him through the dirty front window.

CHAPTER THREE

Vince Gorman's cab dropped him at the entrance to the Peachtree Investment Building. He rode the front elevator up to the twentieth floor. Usually, if a person came to Wardlaw Properties without an appointment he had to pass through five secretaries, all very polite and very friendly, to reach the inner office of David Wardlaw. At each level the probing was more direct, more exact. Helen Morris had the final yes or no decision.

Vince was an exception.

The secretary at the desk that faced the elevator knew Vince and pressed the buzzer that unlocked the door straight ahead. He nodded at her and went through.

Wardlaw was at the large table to the right as Vince entered. The new model of the Boulevard development was displayed there, the drapes open behind the model and the weak winter light coming in.

At the center of the model was the only real building, the only one that had been constructed so far. That was the geodesic dome, the indoor stadium where the Crackers played their home games. In the five months the Dome had been open they'd been competing for bookings with the Omni for rock shows and other attractions. David Wardlaw had put out the word: undercut the Civic Center, the Omni, and the Municipal Auditorium. Go below cost if you have to. And the booking war was on.

When the stadium was under construction, a creative team from Abel, Tenner and Shipman had been brought in to name it. The names they came up with all sounded like variations on the names of already existing sports arenas. After an especially frustrating session Vince said, "Shit, just call it the Dome."

And they had.

One big problem was the neighborhood. It was still transitional, mainly black. Cars got broken into during games, and there had been several muggings as the fans left the Dome. Wardlaw had exerted all the pressure he could for an increased patrol in the area. So far, the pressure had only resulted in promises. It would take a serious injury or a murder to get anything done. It was a kind of pressure that neither David Wardlaw nor Vince Gorman wanted.

Around the model of the Dome were the tall, narrow shafts of three modernistic hotels. There was one large shopping center, a mall with rows of shops and a movie theatre and a couple of restaurants. Spotted here and there were the small dots that represented bars and nightclubs. The model maker had taken a lot of trouble with details. He'd made a doll's world of an inner city.

And there, near the center, a half block from the Dome, was the only unshaped, undetailed building. It was just a square block, but it was the important one. On that block, in large letters, it said, "Convention Center."

Wardlaw turned from the model. "Did you fix it?"

"You know I always fix everything," Vince said.

Wardlaw put his back to the model and walked across to his desk. "You don't sound very happy in your work, Vince."

Vince followed him and stopped across the desk from him. "I tried to con a garage owner who knew better. And I spent some time steaming off blood and maybe tissue and God knows what else from under the Shooter's toy."

"You know a better way?"

"We could say the Shooter parked the XKE and took a cab home. That would mean buying ourselves a cab driver. Then it would look like somebody stole the XKE and ran over the wino. It's been done a time or two."

"Too risky." Wardlaw shook his head. "I can't run it right now with the Convention Center coming to a vote." He sat behind the desk. "Sorry I ruined your day, Vince."

"You don't know how much." Vince slumped into the chair at the left corner of the desk. "I'm going to be straight about this. I think I can find another job if I have to. I've done all I want to cover that kid. That straight, that simple." When Wardlaw didn't say anything right away Vince added, "The XKE ought to be ready in the morning —all straightened out, the headlight replaced and the fender hammered out and repainted. I'll buy some silence and I'll take it back to the Shooter. After that, I'm done."

"What's left to do?"

"It's hard to figure right now. Maybe nothing. Maybe a hell of a lot. For one thing, there's that wino over at Grady Hospital. We might not want to turn the Shooter in, but we probably owe him the best medical treatment that's available."

Wardlaw nodded. "I'll handle that myself … and anything else that comes up. But I have to say I'm a little surprised at you."

"I'm surprised at myself," Vince said.

"What'll you be doing the rest of the day?"

"If I'm not fired, I thought I might spend the rest of the day looking into what's going on down in the tight squeeze area, around Colony Square. I got a rumor something's happening. A couple of realtors who own about twenty percent of the property down there are playing some games."

"What kind of games?"

"They didn't say." Vince got out a cigarette and lit it with the desk lighter. "How much do you control down there … say from Fifth and Peachtree to Pershing Point?"

"I'd have to check it to be sure," Wardlaw said, "but I'd guess about twenty houses and fifteen or so assorted buildings ... apartments and office buildings."

Vince took a deep breath and stood up. "My first stop's City Hall. I need a tax plat that covers the whole area, and then I'm going to do some asking around and visiting."

"You know who're playing the games?"

"From what I heard, your old friends, Asher and Spence, and the Temple Brothers."

Wardlaw dropped a note pad in front of him and scribbled on it for a couple of minutes. He tore off the sheet and passed it to Vince. "If it's something tricky, the tax maps won't tell you all you need to know."

Vince looked at the heavy, bold writing. Under the major heading, Wardlaw had written down four companies he'd never heard of: Peach State, Harpur Inc., Northend Realty and Schaffer and George. "Fronts for Asher and Spence?"

"You could call them that. They're companies where Asher and Spence are on the Board of Directors. These are the ones I know. By now there might be others."

Vince folded the sheet of paper. "I need a car. I left mine with the Shooter."

"Use the company one downstairs."

"I'd rather not," Vince said. "The company name on the panel won't help in what I'll be doing."

Wardlaw pressed down the intercom button. "Helen, would you come in for a minute?"

A few minutes later, Vince left the office with Helen's car keys. She'd called down to the parking-lot attendant, and the 1972 blue Impala was waiting for him.

He drove to the Fulton County Courthouse on Pryor and bought copies of the tax plats that covered about a fifteen-block area from Fifth Street to Pershing Point.

❖   ❖   ❖

"And if you think today was bad," Hap Seaver said, "wait until tomorrow."

Harley Brisker and Hap Seaver were having lunch in the Tap Room, and it was a measure of how far the blacks in Atlanta had come in the last ten years that nobody paid any special attention to them. Ten years ago, neither of them would have been seated or served. That was what Martin Luther King, Jr. and the movement had accomplished.

For nine months of the year, Harley was vice president of the downtown branch of The Georgia National Trust Bank on Forsyth Street. The other three months of the year he was a member of the House, the lower chamber of the General Assembly. The pay wasn't much, but the bank was glad to see him in the House and his pay continued during this period. On all matters that affected banking he voted in the interest of banks and banking. On all other matters he was his own man.

At least he was until the Governor had appointed him to the Convention Center study committee over the summer. A more experienced or a less dedicated man might have tried to avoid the appointment. For seven months, the pressure had been building. It wasn't an easy task. It wasn't a matter of saying "Yes, the state needs a Convention Center" and "Yes, the state should finance it." The eight-man committee was to recommend where the Center should be built. That was the hard one, and he found he had more "friends" than he knew and more enemies than he ever wanted.

One of them was Hap Seaver, the black state senator from the southeast part of the state. He was light-skinned and polished in manners as only an Ivy school education would do for a man. It rankled Harley that Hap came from the monied black class and he'd never had to struggle for anything. During the civil rights movement, when Harley was in the front ranks, Hap had remained back in the shadows. He never marched and he never put himself in the way of the white anger. He had, however, donated thousands to the SCLC and, when it was possible for a black man to take advantage of the changing social winds, he'd used his money and his influence to unseat a KKK man in his district. His was a district where blacks outnumbered whites three-to-one and the only problem had been to make sure that enough of the three-to-one advantage registered and voted.

The Convention Center study committee had just finished its morning meeting. The lines were drawn, and it looked like the selection of a site was going to be a dog fight right down to the end. The Governor had chosen the committee members carefully. Of the eight members, only Harley Brisker and Senator Robert Mast were from the Atlanta area. The other six, three state senators and three representatives, were from districts far removed from the concerns of the city. While Harley and Senator Mast might be expected to support one site or the other for strong political reasons, the other six were supposed to weigh other considerations. After all, it was state money that was to be spent—some $35 or $40 million—and the Governor wanted the rest of the state to feel that it had a major voice in how it would be spent.

So far, the committee was in a deadlock and it didn't look like it was going to break. Three members, including Senator Mast, voted this morning for the downtown Whitehall site. Harley Brisker and Hap Seaver stood behind the Boulevard site that was controlled by Wardlaw Properties. Of the remaining three members, two had voted for the site near the Civic Center. Jim Sims was the spokesman for the Civic Center location.

One member, Senator Johnson, hadn't voted yet. He'd abstained. He was an opportunist, a redneck from up in the mountains. He appeared to be waiting, holding back, until he decided where his vote would benefit him the most. He expected a shift, and when the shift came he would move with the power.

Harley Brisker had made his choice in the interest of the black landowners in the Boulevard area. Already, with the completion of the Dome, he'd seen land values rising and some new wealth pouring into the area.

Hap Seaver had gone along with Harley's argument. It wouldn't hurt him with the black voters back home when they knew he was all for black capitalism. It might be worth a few more votes.

"It can't get any worse," Harley said.

"Wait," Hap said. "Somebody's going to crack. It might be Jim Sims."

"What makes you think so?"

"Just a feeling," Hap said. "He's got nothing to lose. Back in his district, they don't care one way or the other. If anything, they don't like the state spending the money at all."

"And if he breaks?"

"It's going to be like it was when the power went off at the cathouse. You're not going to know which one is in which bed."

"All except us," Harley said.

"Of course," Hap Seaver said. And then he ordered a slice of pecan pie to go with his second cup of coffee.

At exactly 1:00 p.m. David Wardlaw stepped out of the elevator on the twenty-sixth floor of the Oglethorpe Building. Only one elevator went as far as the twenty-sixth floor and it was an express. The button was over-large and had "Founders Club" printed on it.

As soon as Wardlaw was two steps away from the elevator, the club steward met him. "May I help you, sir?"

"I'm expected by Judge Tate."

The steward turned to the guest log on its perch and ran his finger down the open page. "Mr. Wardlaw?"

"Yes."

The steward nodded to the maitre d'.

It was a large room, gleaming with starched white tablecloths. What David noticed each time he entered the Founders Club was the wide spacing between the tables. In a restaurant open to the public, this huge, daylight-lit room might have accommodated a hundred tables. Instead, there were no more than fifty. It was, David assumed, one way of giving the members a certain degree of privacy.

The Founders Club was chartered with the state in 1892. There were originally fifty members. Forty-eight were landowners or successful businessmen in the city. The other two members were the pastor of the Marthasville Baptist Church and the headmaster of the Whitehall Academy. These were the concessions the Club made to religion and culture. There were no others. The business of the city was business, and it was natural that they thought of themselves as the only real founders of the city.

In time, the club's constitution was amended to allow expansion of the membership to one hundred. That was in 1920. All further attempts to expand the membership had failed.

Some years before, after David received his first invitation to lunch at the Club, he sent a secretary to the Carnegie Library to research it. She returned with a sheaf of xeroxed papers, the constitution, the bylaws and the application for a charter. There was nothing else available on the Club. What interested David was the second paragraph in the application for the charter. It was dated April 4, 1892.

Second. The purposes of such incorporation are not for direct or indirect monetary profit, trade or gain, but the formation of a social organization to promote felicity, kind feelings and the culture of its members.

It was amusing, looking back over that first lunch at the Club. The only discussion that afternoon concerned itself with the feasibility of the construction of an office park some miles outside of

Atlanta. David ate the Club's best and appreciated the wine from the cellar, but he declined to join in the venture. The office park was constructed without him and the last David heard of it there was a struggle to keep it at 25 percent occupancy.

Judge Tate had a table against the east window. It was one of the choice tables. As soon as the judge saw David, he pushed back his chair and grasped his walking cane, as if to rise. David hurried to him and put out his hand, saying, "Please don't stand, Judge."

The maitre d' remained just long enough to ease the judge's chair in once more.

"You're on time," Judge Tate said.

"It's good to see you again, sir."

"I must say I'm amazed at the number of young men who think a one o'clock appointment means one-fifteen or one-thirty."

Judge Tate, as far as David could determine, was almost eighty years old. He came from an old Atlanta family. He'd been educated at Harvard, and he received his law degree from the University of Virginia. That was before it was essential that a political figure in the state attend the University of Georgia Law School.

In the years that followed, he'd worked his way up to a partnership with a law firm, sat for several terms in the General Assembly, and once sought the Democratic nomination for Governor in the primary. It had been a close, bitter fight and the judge, when he lost, was enough of a good politician to throw his support behind the winner. Some months later, when there was a vacancy, he was appointed to the district federal bench. He remained on the bench for twenty years, and at the end of that time he resigned and rejoined his old law firm. Five years before, at the age of around seventy-five, he retired. But he'd kept his ties with the party, and he found himself the grand old man of politics in the state.

David Wardlaw met him three years before he retired. There'd been a problem with the title to the tract of land that was in the center of a block David was assembling for a project. Judge Tate cut through the red tape and the clouds on the title in a matter of days. Following that, David used the judge's law firm from time-to-time, and after his retirement the judge had a way of dropping into David's life every few weeks. There was always some good reason, a question about the value of a certain piece of property or some advice about a proposed business venture. It didn't take David long to see through the judge's excuses. He realized that Judge Tate, his wife dead twenty years ago and his only son killed in World War II, was a lonely old man. With this understanding, David began to drop by the judge's house once-a-week to talk for an hour or two. When Emily had been alive, the judge had been a frequent guest at David's Paces Ferry home and the judge had charmed Emily with his old world courtly manners.

At first David thought of his relationship with the judge as an investment in time that might bring indirect returns some-day. But that had changed. He liked the crusty old man, and he'd never had to ask a favor from him or go to him for help. It was, he thought, probably one of the reasons that the judge seemed to appreciate his company.

Judge Tate nodded toward the chilled silver bowl of relishes. "You won't find any black olives in there, David. I ate all of them."

David reached in and got a radish rose. "That seems fair enough. I'll do the same to you the next time I invite you to lunch."

"I bet you would."

"You know I will," David said.

A waitress stopped at their table. She wore the uniform the Club insisted upon: a severe white blouse with long sleeves and a black skirt that reached down to a point halfway between the knees and the ankles. The uniform had a way of making even an attractive girl look over forty.

David ordered a vodka martini. The waitress turned to Judge Tate. "Would you like another drink, sir?"

The judge looked her up and down with a hard eye. "Young lady, that is not the proper way to ask me that question. You do not ask me if I want *another* drink. You ask if I want a drink."

David saw the girl's hand tremble. "Yes, sir."

"If you ask me if I want *another* drink, you are revealing too much of my private business."

"Yes, sir," the waitress said.

"I'd like a Wild Turkey bourbon on the rocks," Judge Tate said.

The waitress scurried away. The judge looked after her and shook his head slowly. "I wonder what happened to the manners people used to have thirty or forty years ago."

"Gone," David said. "Atlanta's too big for manners now."

"I think I'll speak to the steward on the way out." He turned and looked out the window. "Do you realize this is considered a choice table? I inherited it by outliving some very good men."

David leaned toward the window and looked down. The Oglethorpe Building was new and it overlooked an older section of town, an area of flat two and three story buildings.

"Someday," Judge Tate said, "we're going to have to do something about the skyline of Atlanta. It lacks something when it's compared to San Francisco and New York. And there is something depressing about looking down on the tops of buildings where dresses are made to be sold in dime stores."

"It'll come in time," David said.

"Not in my time."

"You'll outlive me by ten years," David said.

"That would be a tiresome thing to do. I'm not sure that's a worthwhile ambition. At eighty, all I have left are some memories and a taste for good food and good bourbon."

"Good memories?" David asked, smiling.

"Some of them," the judge said.

The waitress brought their drinks and hurried away.

"If I lived to eighty, I don't think I could ask for more than that," David said.

"You wouldn't try to fox a senile old man, would you?"

"Only if I thought I could get away with it," David said. He lifted his martini and sipped at it. It was the temperature of ice and a good blend. The bar and the wine cellar, according to the judge, had held up over the last few years. The kitchen had become ordinary. The judge explained that the younger members just didn't care enough about food.

Over squab and rice—"frozen," the judge said— there was little talk. The judge did like his food, and he ate with the gusto that would have fitted a much younger man. After the waitress cleared the plates away, and the coffee and Benedictine were brought, the judge looked around the room for a few moments. "How is the Convention Center coming along?"

"You probably know more than I do," David said.

"Are you asking me, David?"

"No. I think I could. But it might change our relationship and I wouldn't want that."

"I'd regret that," Judge Tate said.

"I don't think we ought to talk about it then."

"Forty million dollars in state money, that's a large investment."

"Quite large," David agreed.

The judge sipped his Benedictine and followed it with a gulp of black coffee. "What happens to the Boulevard land if the Center is awarded to one of the other sites?"

"The same thing that happens to the other land if I get the Center. The *coup* is off. And I might have to become a slum landlord until the next chance comes along."

"I don't like to think of you as a ghetto rent collector," the judge said.

David shook his head. "I wasn't serious about that. There's always an alternate plan, a plan B, and sometimes even a plan C."

"Which are?"

"Medium-level inner-city housing. That's plan B."

"And plan C?" the judge asked.

"That's plan B with frills. Inner city housing with a shopping mall—a city within a city."

"Do the others have a plan B and a plan C?"

"I suspect they do," David said.

"But the real *coup* is the Convention Center?"

"That's the whole ball game," David said.

The judge nodded. He lowered his voice. "It's still up in the air. The lines are drawn now, the factions establishing themselves. It's so delicately balanced that anything could throw it one way or the other."

"I didn't ask you, Judge."

"That's why I told you." The waitress leaned over them and refilled their coffee cups. The judge waited until she moved to another table. "I'm an old man, David, and I don't have many friends. When I first met you, I thought you might be like the rest of them, the hustlers, the ones who wanted something out of me. You get accustomed to those and you give them what it doesn't hurt you to give." He smiled at David. "I have to admit I was pleasantly surprised when it turned out you didn't want anything from me. At least nothing that involved influence or my connections."

"I'd be less than honest if I said I'd never thought of using our relationship," David said. "So far, I've never wanted anything enough to ask you for it."

Judge Tate's eyes looked damp and he turned slowly and looked down at the building tops.

David excused himself and went to the men's room. He remained there long enough to let Judge Tate recover his composure. When he returned, the judge was gruff, but not unfriendly, and they left the dining room together a few minutes later. David stood beside the elevator while the judge talked to the steward.

The conversation was short and low-voiced. The steward nodded and made a few notes on a pad.

"Nothing will come of it," the judge said in the elevator.

During the ride back to his office, David thought of the Shooter and the problems he had caused with his drinking and driving. The wino in the hospital, the hit-and-run—that could tip the delicate balance the judge had mentioned. He could feel the anger growing deep in him, and it was all he could do to shake it by the time he reached the underground garage and entered the elevator that took him up to his office.

CHAPTER FOUR

"I don't think I know anybody named Melinda," the Shooter said.

"She says otherwise." The voice was that of the doorman security guard downstairs "Says she met you at the Mouse Trap last Monday night."

"What does she look like?"

"About five-three or four, short dark hair, green eyes... and pretty."

Maybe he did know her. He had been in the Mouse Trap Monday night and there'd been such a fog of girls there anybody'd have trouble keeping them apart. "Sure, I remember her," he said. "Send her on up."

He stood in the doorway to his apartment and waited until the doors of the elevator swept apart and she stepped out. Added to what the doorman said, she had good legs and what was probably a sun-lamp tan. Looked good but looked very young.

Melinda lifted her head and saw him. "Hello, Eddie."

"Call me Shooter," he said. When she reached the entrance to the apartment, he put his back to the door frame and motioned her inside with a mock bow.

"I didn't think you'd remember me," she said.

"How could I forget you?"

"You must meet a lot of girls." She stopped in the center of the deep white rug and looked around. Her eyes remained longest on the blow-up of the *Sports Illustrated* cover, the one from two Octobers before. It was a bust shot of the Shooter. He was holding a basketball on each shoulder and chewing on a long piece of hay straw. In thick black print over the picture was the headline, "The Shooter's Back."

"I don't know that many girls," the Shooter said. "Those stories get exaggerated."

"But you do remember me?"

"Sure, I do." He walked around her and stood next to the sofa. At first, when the doorman had called, he'd been irritated. A lot of the girls who came by were just high school kids and they were more trouble than it was worth. Looking at Melinda, he was glad he'd acted on the impulse to let her in. Hangovers put the horn on him, and having her around might take the edge off and make the afternoon a pleasant one. If she knew the score. "Have a seat and I'll mix us a drink."

"It's early for me," Melinda said. "Do you have a Coke?"

"No Cokes in my bar," he said. "Scotch, gin and vodka."

"A gin and tonic?"

He mixed himself a scotch over the rocks and poured her a massive shot of gin and topped it with tonic. After he handed the drink to her and watched her take a tentative sip he asked, "How'd you know where I live?"

"This." She opened her purse and brought out the card. It was one he'd had printed a couple of months after he moved to Atlanta. He'd treated it as a joke and he thought he'd stopped giving them out a long time ago.

Eddie "the Shooter" Simpson
Come up and see me sometime.
Madrid Apts.
Peachtree Road

"I gave this to you at the Mouse Trap?"

"Monday night," she said, nodding.

"I must have been impressed," he said.

"Then you don't remember me?"

"It's coming back to me," the Shooter said. "I'd had a few drinks at the time."

"Me too," she said, "but I remembered you."

"You got me there. But now that you're here what are we going to do?"

"Talk, I guess," she said.

"Or play chess."

"I don't know how," she said, "but you could teach me."

"Or play cards."

"I know how to play rummy and ..."

"Or we could go to bed," the Shooter said.

His leg was against hers and he felt the muscles go tight, as if with surprise. "I don't think we ought to."

"Act your age," the Shooter said. "You didn't come up here after my autograph."

"I'm sure I couldn't tell you why I came," Melinda said.

"Look at it this way. If it's not going to happen today, then it'll probably happen tomorrow. But if it's going to happen anyway, why waste a whole day?"

"I never thought you'd be so cold about it. I mean, you haven't kissed me or touched me or anything."

"I can take care of that easy enough," he said. He took her drink from her hand and put it on the coffee table. He turned her and kissed her, feeling her mouth close to his tongue. He held the kiss a long time and ran his hands along her sides, brushing her breasts. When he ended the kiss, and leaned away from her, he said, "The bedroom's in there."

"I guess that must be the price of admission," she said.

"What?"

"It doesn't matter." She got up and walked past him into the bedroom. He gave her a minute and then took up their drinks and followed her in.

⚜ ⚜ ⚜

"The card … you didn't give it to me," she said.

"You said …" He felt himself pulled back from the half-dozing that followed their lovemaking.

"You gave it to my sister Elaine. She's three years older than I am and she has platinum blonde hair."

That was it. That was the one he remembered from Monday night at the Mouse Trap. A big fleshy blonde with breasts that came around a corner about a minute before she did. And a big proud rump rounded like an orange.

"She said she wasn't sure she liked you," Melinda said.

"Why?"

"Too cocky."

He laughed and looked down at himself. "Well, that's what it's about."

"No, she meant you acted too sure of yourself."

"Why shouldn't I be?" he said. "You know any other nineteen-year-old millionaires? I mean ones that didn't inherit it from somebody?"

"I don't know any other millionaires at all," she said.

"You know one," he said.

"I'm not as thrilled as I thought I'd be," she said. She turned away from him and curled up in a ball.

"Fuck you too," he said.

All through high school the Shooter didn't have much time for girls. Or, when he was interested, they seemed not to have time for him. At Thacker High, the girls liked basketball players during basketball season and appeared less interested after the season was over. Players who spent too much time with girls ran head on against Coach Maple's training rules. The coach didn't believe in what he called "dissipating" during basketball season, and when he saw a player dogging it on the court, he always figured that the player had left his good energy in the back seat of a car.

Eddie lived close to the training rules, and the few dates he had after the season was over hadn't been too successful. He really didn't know what to talk about to the girls; they didn't seem to know much about basketball, and that was all he really knew anything about.

At Southeastern State it was different. Almost from the first, the publicity department started booming the Shooter for All-America, and it was as though the girls started lining up. And when that was too much trouble there were the jock groupies, the coeds who just wanted to ball a star athlete. They were the ones you'd just call up at the dorm. They'd meet you in front of the dorm; and you'd just drive out into the woods, screw all you wanted to and then take them back to the dorm—without having to say more than five or six words to them.

When he left Southeastern State and moved down to Atlanta it was spring. The regular season was over and he had time on his hands until the early fall workouts. On the advice of Coach Bill Thorn, he joined the informal summer league where most of the pros in town played away the off-season. It was a kind of church league, and he got to try himself against some of the Hawk and Cracker players and some of the pros from other teams who lived in Atlanta. The league was a way of keeping in some kind of shape and keeping the shooting touch.

It started then. He'd play a part of a game and do some of the fancy crap, and after the game the girls would stand around looking at him. And sometimes they'd pass him a note with a name and a phone number on it or a line or two asking if he'd like to meet them outside.

The first few times he didn't do anything at all about the notes. He was confused and he wasn't sure how he was supposed to act. Bert Saunders straightened him out on it. Bert was a big white forward from the University of Georgia. He'd had good press there, and the last two years he'd tried to make the Hawks—only to be cut each time late in the exhibition season. Not enough muscle around the boards and not mean enough to take the licks.

One night, back in the locker room after they'd showered and dressed, he showed Bert his latest collection of notes.

"Shit, man," Bert said, "take all they offer you."

"I thought it might be the money."

"Naw, man, they're just jock-sniffing girls. No hassle in that. Just want to screw a name ballplayer so they can tell their girl-friends about it, maybe lying a little as they tell it. How this star player chased them all over town and begged to get in their rank drawers."

"I might try it," the Shooter said.

"See if one of them's got a friend," Bert said.

A couple of times he played it that way. He'd have the girl get a friend for Bert and they'd double for part of the evening. When he realized Bert was right about the girls, he started going it alone.

Even after the season, started it kept up. On the road, in Denver, New York and Dallas, some how they'd find out where the team was staying and they'd call from downstairs in the lobby. He'd go down and meet them and if they didn't turn him on, he'd buy them a drink and brush them. If he liked what they had, it was up to his room or off to an apartment.

And most of them seemed damned grateful, like he'd done them a favor. Not like Melinda with that shit about not being as thrilled as she thought she'd be.

She was gone when he awoke an hour or so later. He looked for her in the bathroom and the kitchen. Nothing. Not even a note.

Over lunch at Eng's on Tenth and Peachtree, Vince spread out the tax plat maps. He used the salt and pepper shakers and the duck sauce and hot mustard bowls at the corners to keep the maps from rolling up. He ate the beef with Chinese vegetables and washed it down with three bottles of beer.

Checking both companies, the Temple Brothers and Asher and Spence, would take more than a single afternoon. He put the Temple Brothers aside for the moment and concentrated on Asher and Spence and the list of front companies that Wardlaw had suggested they might be using to cover up their real-estate transactions.

The pattern, when he found it, didn't mean anything to him. He was on the third plat, the one that covered the area around the huge Colony Square development, when he found his first large cluster of Asher and Spence-owned houses. Within one solid block, more than half the houses were controlled by either Asher and Spence or their related companies. The others, except for two owned by Wardlaw, appeared to be private homes. Of course, the tax plats weren't always up-to-date and some of the property might have changed hands since the plats were drawn up.

He marked that map and put it aside. He rolled the others up and wrapped a rubber band around them. He leaned back in his chair and drank the last of his third beer. Over a final cigarette, he waited to see how his system would react to the food and the beer after the ravages of the night before. When nothing happened, he left Eng's and drove over to the block he'd marked on the plat map.

He parked midway in the block. He got the first hint then. It was a large house of three stories. He'd parked next to it and sat in the car looking it over and checking it on the map. Owned by Asher and Spence. From the outside, it seemed to be a functional dwelling, the shell and the porch in good shape. Woodwork and trim looked solid enough. Needed some paint and the gutters and downspouts could use a cleaning.

The good ended there. Three motorcycles perched on what had once been the lawn. The lawn was rutted and torn up, grooved by tires. On the front porch, he saw a dozen or so open paper bags of garbage that hadn't been put out on the street for collection. Dogs or cats had been into the bags, tipping some over and rooting around in them. It was a good thing it was winter or there'd have been a million flies swarming about the porch.

Vince stepped over some of the garbage and went inside. More garbage and a motorcycle that partially dismantled and being worked on. The smell of gas and oil was strong in the heated hallway. He made a circuit of the three apartments on the first floor to get a feel for the tenants. The first one was rented by the motorcyclists, hard-looking and with very little to say when he asked if there was an empty apartment in the building. Three hippie girls were in the second apartment. It smelled of old grease and incense and, if it wasn't his imagination, the wood-chip smell of hashish somebody'd been smoking. Two homosexuals had the third apartment, the kind who used eye makeup and teased their hair and carried shoulder bags.

In the next hour, he went through five more houses controlled either by Asher and Spence or the front companies. The same as the first one. Vince had the feeling that whoever handled the rentals went out of the way to find as many freaks as they could. In a fanciful moment, Vince almost believed that they'd been carted in from out of town.

His last stop, when he decided he'd seen enough, was a small house that was locked in on both sides by rundown houses. It was a neat house, lawn well kept, leaves raked away, the trees pruned and the shrubs covered by plastic. According to the map, it was owned by Henry R. Christian. He stopped on the porch and looked across the street. Two apartment houses there, both owned by Wardlaw and maintained far above minimum standards.

A frail little woman with blue-gray hair answered the doorbell. Vince gave her his card and said he was with Wardlaw Properties. She peered down at the card and her mouth tightened.

"We're still not going to sell," she said.

"I think you've misunderstood me," he said. "My company owns property across the street. There and there."

She watched as he pointed out the two apartment buildings.

"I'd like to talk to you about what's happening on the street," he said. "Is Mr. Christian in?"

She opened the door. "He's in the kitchen. Come in."

Vince talked with them for half-an-hour in the kitchen. Mr. Christian was retired, and they'd finished paying for their home five years before. It had been a thirty-year labor of love and now they could see there wasn't much they could do about the neighborhood. They spoke with bitterness about loud music at all hours and the motorcycles and loud shouting late at night.

"You sure of this?" Wardlaw looked down at the map in his office.

"It's all there." Vince leaned over the map and touched the two *x*'s he made after his talk forty minutes ago with the Christians. "In the past six months these two gave up and sold out."

"They as bad as you say?"

"Worse," Vince said.

"Slums on purpose," Wardlaw said. "I've heard of it, but I've never seen it. It's hard to believe."

"Not really." Vince put his hand on the corner of Fourteenth and Peachtree, the Colony Square site. "This is the hub. The impact's all around. These houses will go anyway. It won't matter how rundown they are when the wreckers do their sweep."

"And none of them had leases?"

"Not any I talked to. They seemed happy about it. Couldn't have been prouder." Vince backed away from the desk and sat down. "You can see how it's shaking the old residents. It used to be a good neighborhood. Many of the owners are old people, people near retirement or retired. They don't want the hassle that goes with it. And they can see the investment going down the drain, the land values dropping. So they sell out and move into an apartment somewhere."

Wardlaw reached for the intercom. "I'll talk to the building inspectors."

Vince shook his head. "Go higher. The Christians tried that and got the runaround."

"Helen," David said into the intercom, "get me the county commissioner at his office."

Vince eased out of his chair. He gave a brief wave. "I'll be in my office if you need me." He left the office and stopped next to Helen Morris's desk.

As soon as she'd put through the call to the county commissioner, she looked up at him and smiled. "Dent any of my fenders?"

"Not a single one. And to show I appreciate the loan, I'll buy you a drink after work."

Her smile wobbled, but she was still amused. "Worked your way through the typing pool already?"

"That's not friendly."

"But truthful," she said. "I've heard the girls talking in the powder room."

"Good things, I hope."

"It's according to what interests you," she said.

He leaned over her. "What interests you, Helen? I keep meaning to ask."

"You keep forgetting?"

"I'm going to tell David on you. Disrespect or impudence or something like that."

"Threatened with that," she said, "I'll take the drink."

"I thought you might," he said. "It works every time in the typing pool."

He gave her his best grin and went to his office and closed the door behind him. He put his head down on the blotter and closed his eyes. He was just getting loose enough to nap when the phone rang.

Helen said, "A call for you, Vince. It's a lady, so I guess we have to put off our drink."

"Not a chance," he said. "See you at five." He waited for her to put the call through.

"Vincent, it's Joyce."

That tore it. Now it was a bad day. "How are you, Joyce?"

"I'm fine. I know you're busy and I know I shouldn't call you at the office, but I wanted to remind you about tomorrow."

"What's tomorrow?"

"Timmy's birthday."

"I haven't forgotten," he lied.

"Then you'll come?"

"Of course," he said. "I'll be there between twelve and one."

"You won't forget?" He could feel the hesitation in her voice, as if she wanted to add "this time."

"I'll be there with a present."

"I'll see you. Again, I'm sorry..."

"It's all right," he said.

After he put down the phone he tried to nap again, but the moment had passed and he was wide awake. It was just as well. At 4:30 Wardlaw called and wanted him.

"This is Mr. Wyman," David said, indicating a huge man who overflowed the chair to the right of his desk.

Vince shook hands with him and took the other chair.

"Mr. Wyman is an independent insurance agent. He's been kind enough to agree to help us with the matter of the old man who was the hit-and-run victim on Peachtree Road last night."

"It's irregular," Mr. Wyman said, "but I think we can work out something."

"It turns out that the old gentleman—his name is Todd Barker—has an accident and hospitalization policy with Mr. Wyman," Wardlaw said.

Mr. Wyman smiled. "It goes back two years."

"Mr. Barker is lucky," Vince said.

"The policy will pay all his hospital expenses and a thousand dollars when he leaves the hospital."

"It's quite a good policy," Mr. Wyman said.

David looked at Vince and Vince gave his nod. It seemed as good a way as any. The wino wouldn't question it and Wyman looked like the type who'd do anything for a dollar.

Vince left them to work out the details. It wasn't his concern anymore.

CHAPTER FIVE

During the General Assembly, Harley wasn't expected to drop by his desk in the main offices of the Georgia National Trust Bank on Forsyth Street, but the Friday afternoon session was usually short, so the out-of-town legislature members could get a jump on the weekend. He arrived at the bank a bit after three, and by the time the door was locked at four, he'd dictated five letters and had cleared the "In" file on his desk. His topcoat was over his arm and he was ready to leave when John Franklin, president of the bank, stopped by his desk.

"Have you got a minute, Harley?"

"I've got more than a minute," Harley said. He followed Franklin into the president's office and closed the door behind him. It was a large office. There were no windows, but there was a skylight directly above the ten-foot curved desk that was the central feature of the room. The skylight was in the open position now, though the winter light was dim. In the closed position a thick steel shield covered the skylight and a special alarm was activated. The skylight was John Franklin's idea and he was especially proud of it. He'd had it installed even though it posed a problem for bank security.

"How is it going, Harley?"

Harley didn't have to ask what the "it" was. He knew Franklin meant the Convention Center committee and more particularly the site selection problem. "Slow," Harley said, "and we're meeting again tomorrow afternoon."

"Time's running out."

"The Governor says that too. He wants us to meet tomorrow as long as it takes—until he has a decision he can take to the Senate and the House on Monday."

John Franklin nodded. He was a sleek, pampered-looking man in his mid-forties. He'd been lured away from Chase Manhattan ten years before, and Harley, during the time he'd been at the bank, had watched his accent soften until it was the cultivated, Southern speech of a lifelong resident. In the bank, Harley was considered "his" man, and Harley knew he owed his advancement to him. In realistic moments, Harley knew that his promotion was a concession to the increasing black wealth and that major accounts of a number of black businessmen had switched to Georgia National in the last few months. And it bothered him to realize that he was pointed out as an example of what was possible for a black man in the new South.

"But no site has the five votes yet?" John Franklin said.

"Not yet. Hap Seaver thinks that Jim Sims will weaken and pull away from the Civic Center site. I don't see any signs of it, but it's possible. Senator Johnson—the one from the mountains—he's still on the fence as far as I can tell."

"What are our chances?"

It was the first time Harley knew for sure what he'd suspected for the last few months. Franklin's use of "our" confirmed it. The day after Harley's appointment to the Convention Center committee, Franklin took him to lunch and asked which possible site Harley would back. When Harley said that it would be the Boulevard site, and gave his reasons, Franklin had nodded. In the time since then, Harley, with his new insight into the bank's business, had learned that much of David Wardlaw's financing had been arranged through Georgia National and there was reason to believe that development of the Boulevard land would further benefit the bank.

It just happened that Harley's position on the site had coincided with the interests of Georgia National and Wardlaw. But if it hadn't, would they have pressured him to change? Would he have given in, though it was counter to his beliefs? He wasn't sure. And he was glad he hadn't had to make that choice.

"If we could move Sims toward us, another vote might follow him. Then we'd have to see how Senator Johnson leaps."

"But Sims might go to the Whitehall site," Franklin said.

"That would be the ballgame," Harley said. "Sims would give the Whitehall area their fourth vote and Johnson might make it five."

Franklin looked up at the skylight. His gaze became vague and distant. "We wouldn't want that to happen."

"I've done my best …" Harley began.

"Of course you have." The vague and distant look vanished from Franklin's face. He put an arm around Harley's shoulders. "You've done fine work, and we couldn't be prouder of you."

"I could try to talk to Sims."

Franklin shook his head. "It might be better if the pressure didn't come from you because of your connection with the bank." He dropped his arm from Harley's shoulders. "How's Ethel Ann?"

"Fine and frisky," Harley said. And with that he knew that the interview was over. He said his good-night and left. He was only steps away from the office when he heard the motor running that closed the metal shield over the skylight.

The house was the same one that Harley Brisker had been paying on for the last ten years. And only twenty more years to go before it belonged to him. Ethel Ann was teaching English at G. W. Carver when he married her and they'd lived in an apartment the first year. Paying rent didn't make sense to either of them, so they'd found this house in a transitional neighborhood in southwest Atlanta. Harley was the second black to buy a home on the street, and right after that, the "For Sale" signs went up down the length of the street. For the last four years, Ethel Ann had been campaigning for a move into a better section of town. Other areas were opening up, and she spent part of her time driving through the Morningside part of Atlanta, watching for the "For Sale" signs. So far Harley had refused to make the move. He thought the blacks who'd elected him might think he was deserting them, setting himself above them. But Ethel Ann wanted a better home, and Harley knew he might have to give in just to keep his marriage from becoming a nightmare.

He found a note on the kitchen table.

"It's my hospital day. I won't be home until six. If you're hungry there are cold cuts in the refrig."

Harley grunted to himself and balled up the note. He tossed it toward the trash can. It hit the lip and fell in. At least one thing had gone right so far. He couldn't hope for much more.

He found a bottle of Michelob in the refrigerator. On the shelf below the beer there was a plate of cold cuts and cheese, plastic-wrapped and arranged like a flower display. Maybe some of the afternoon meetings were devoted to demonstrations of how to arrange cold cuts on a plate so the husbands wouldn't starve while they had more and more meetings.

He uncapped the Michelob and sat down at the kitchen table. It was a long way from teaching math at G. W. Carver School, an all-black school in southwest Atlanta. Back in those days, trying to live on low teacher pay, trying to teach math to students who didn't care and never would, he'd known his share of frustrations. Still, in some ways, he'd felt freer.

And then, in 1963 he met Martin Luther King, Jr. and his world changed.

Harley hadn't been at the Lorraine Motel in Memphis that late afternoon. That Thursday, April 4. He'd seen Martin that morning at breakfast, and, after an early afternoon with some of the strikers, he'd flown back to Atlanta. The march was being put off until

Monday and he was to try to organize a train of buses that would leave Atlanta on Sunday, bringing another 500 or 1,000 people to support the strikers and march. He didn't hear about the murder of Martin until he was getting off the plane in Atlanta. He was standing in the main concourse of Hartsfield Airport, stunned, tears running down his face, when an AP photographer, on his way to catch a flight to Memphis, saw him and snapped his picture just on reflex. At the time the AP photographer thought of it as just one more picture, one more reaction shot. But in the days that followed, the shock and the grief on Harley's face, looking out from the newspapers and magazines across the country, came to represent what the death of Martin had meant to people everywhere. And an obscure black math teacher became a known man. He hadn't tried to use this new recognition, but he found that other people were willing to use it for him. It led to his election to the General Assembly, and it eventually led him away from G. W. Carver School to Georgia National.

Halfway through the beer he returned to the refrigerator and took out the plate of cold cuts. He wasn't hungry, but it wouldn't do to hurt Ethel Ann's feelings. Dutifully he ate two slices of roast beef and a slice of Swiss cheese. He rewrapped the plate and put it back in the refrigerator. He finished the Michelob, opened another and carried it into the living room. It was time for the early local news.

"Let's be tourists tonight," Vince said. He was driving Helen's Impala and they'd just passed out of the underground garage and into the steady flow of the afternoon rush traffic.

"I don't remember that as one of your opening lines," Helen said.

"The girls in the typing pool talk too much."

"Don't men?" Helen said.

"That sounds like women's lib," Vince said, "but I see you haven't burned your bra."

"Only because I need it," Helen said.

"Tourists?"

"Tourists," Helen said.

Vince found a table near the window. They were at 590 West, the bar on the twenty-sixth floor of the new Stouffer's Inn. It was a little too new, without character or any kind of personality.

The waitress, wearing a swallow-tailed coat over hot pants, took their order. A Bloody Mary for Helen and a vodka martini for Vince.

"I don't remember you bringing any of those other girls up here."

"I wouldn't," Vince said. "Tiny minds need a fancy atmosphere to impress them. Something that'll dazzle them. Make them think they're living over their heads."

"And you're not trying to impress me?"

"It wouldn't work. My old daddy told me to know my limitations."

"What does that mean?" Helen asked.

"It means you can relax. I'm not going to put my hand on your knee."

Helen smiled. "I'm not sure whether to be pleased or disappointed."

The waitress brought the drinks. Vince waited until she moved away. "Monday, in the powder room, you can say I made a pass and you put me down so hard it chipped my tailbone."

"I think I'll be disappointed."

"Be pleased," Vince said.

"After all those stories I've heard?" Helen nibbled at the celery stirrer in her Bloody Mary.

"What stories?"

"About how suave and charming you can be…and how overpowering."

"Lies," Vince said, "just lies."

The sky over Atlanta was darkening. Car headlights outlined the shape of streets below and in the distance. In some of the buildings they'd left a pattern of lights on, perhaps to give the city some kind of skyline. Lord, but Georgia Power must love them.

"The sad hour," Vince said. "The drinker's hour. The time you remember other places and other people."

"Have you ever considered AA?"

"Once each morning," Vince said.

"Are we joking now?"

"I thought we were. All those rumors are attempts to make a romantic figure out of me."

A waitress passed their table, carrying a tray on which a dozen snails bubbled and hissed, the waves of garlic trailing behind it.

"Interested in some escargots?"

"Remember my humble birth," Helen said. "Even as humble as it was, we never got that hungry."

"Know Betty Nickerson?"

"Yes," Helen said.

"She said she just loved escargots. After eating two or three she spent half an hour in the ladies room … throwing up, I think."

"Poor thing," Helen said.

"Her?"

"No, you. You waste yourself on the unworthy ones."

"That's true," Vince said. "But they're the ones who screw because they think that's something they're also supposed to do besides ordering the right drink and saying the right things."

"So that part isn't exaggerated?"

"Not much," he said.

Night fell, but nobody was hurt. He remembered that as one of the titles used in a silent film he saw at the Duke film society. Or would it have been better to say that everyone was hurt? He looked at the still darkening sky. Night was only minutes away and he could see the evening unfolding in front of him. Drinks and some music, some women. Dinner if he didn't forget about it. Where? Maybe the Midnight Sun or the Abbey.

"I can't help thinking I must be missing something," Helen said.

"Not you," he said. "You made your choice about ten years ago."

"You mean Edmund? That wasn't ten years ago."

"I don't mean Edmund," he said. Edmund had been the short-time husband, the bastard in her woodpile. "I was talking about David Emmett Wardlaw."

Blood flushed her face and she blinked. "That's below the belt, Vince."

He couldn't keep the hard edge out of his voice. "You've been talking about the way I live like it's something you watch under a microscope. I thought I'd put both of us under there. So, it's not under the belt, it's equal time."

He thought she'd leave. It was there, in the way she finished off her drink and put it aside, the look she gave to make certain where her purse was, feet back and braced under her, ready to rise. And as quickly as it came it went away. "Where's the powder room?"

Watching Helen return a few minutes later he saw how men at the other tables looked at her. She was a damned handsome woman. It was all there, waiting for some man with the right key. So far nobody had tried who mattered. But something was changing in her and changing in him too and, he decided, without forcing it, to let it become what it would—like the Eskimo ivory carver who held the piece of ivory in his hand and talked to it, saying, "What little animal are you in there?" and then made his first cut in the ivory and let the animal reveal itself.

When the waitress brought another drink, without asking Helen, Vince ordered a dozen snails, shrimp and oysters on the shell. She could choose what she wanted. It was, he decided, an interesting way to approach an evening. Not pushing, not structuring it or planning it. Instead, riding with it.

It was getting dark in the room and he noticed that the lights had been turned up a notch or two. It was dark down in the streets and they'd turned the animals loose. Far back in the mind's ear, you could hear the bellow and the roar.

David Wardlaw didn't leave his office until after six. The conversation with the county commissioner hadn't been what he'd expected. The commissioner had hemmed and hawed and David had been polite and heard him out. How there weren't that many violations of the housing code in the area or he'd have heard about it. That there was so much to inspect and not enough housing inspectors. "But," he'd said, "as soon as we can, we'll look into the questions you've raised."

"Those aren't questions," David said then. "They're facts."

Under that kind of pressure, the commissioner retreated. He said he'd send out a team the first thing Monday morning.

David thanked him and hung up.

At no time had there been talk of votes or support in the previous election and there'd been no talk of funds for the next one. Still, stated or not, it was there. And it wasn't a comfortable time for the commissioner. He was whipsawed between Asher and Spence on one side and Wardlaw on the other. He couldn't move and he couldn't stand still. It was going to be a weekend that might produce the first faint tracings of ulcers.

And just to be sure, as soon as he closed out his conversation with the commissioner, David placed a call to "Red" Winston, the former chairman of the Democratic party in the state. "Red" operated somewhat back in the shadows now, but he had a strong voice that everyone from the Governor down listened to. He was as country as grits and fatback, but he was shrewd enough to know when a big contributor felt he'd been burned. He heard David out. There wasn't a threat or a promise made. When David finished, "Red" said he'd call the commissioner later in the evening. He was not against a favor now and then, he seemed to be saying, but an elected official ought to know where the top of the favor list was. And Wardlaw was definitely up there at the top.

David said he'd appreciate what "Red" could do. And before he closed out the call, he told "Red" to keep in touch with him. He was certainly interested in the selection and election of the next Governor.

It was a promise and an interest that "Red" could understand.

Ethel Ann had hardly taken off her coat and kissed him before the phone rang. "It's for you, Harley."

Harley took the receiver from her and stroked her hip as she moved away. She whirled and smiled at him. "Harley, it's Jim Sims here."

"How are you, Jim?"

"Confused," Sims said. "I thought we might have a few words if you can get away for an hour or so."

Harley turned and looked at Ethel Ann. She moved about the living room, straightening up, emptying the ash tray he'd used, taking out his empty beer bottle. For a woman almost forty, she kept herself up pretty well. He knew that was from dieting and morning workouts at one of the spas.

"I don't know," Harley said. "We spent all morning together and nothing came of it."

"A quiet, off-the-record talk might do some good," Sims said. "This between you and me … or will there be others there?"

"Senator Johnson."

"Wait a minute," Harley said. "I'll have to talk to Ethel Ann."

"I'll hold," Sims said.

Harley put the receiver down and went down the long hallway to the bedroom. Ethel Ann was undressing, down to her bra and half-slip. "I might have to go out for an hour or so. It's some bargaining about the Convention Center site."

"I always wonder about those sessions."

"Why?"

"All those stories you hear about the three B's— booze, broads and bribes."

"Not anymore," Harley said. "I've never been offered more than a drink or two."

"That's your fault." She stood on her tiptoes and kissed him. "You're too honest and they know it would be a waste of booze, broads and bribes."

"Nice of you to think so," he said.

"Of course I think so."

"I'll tell you what. While I'm gone you make a reservation for a late dinner. The sky's the limit."

"I've always wanted to go to the Midnight Sun."

"It's yours," he said. Back at the phone he said, "Sorry it took so long. Had to do some bargaining of my own. It's going to cost me a late dinner at the Midnight Sun."

"It might be worth it."

"Where do we meet?" Harley asked.

"I'm at the Executive Motor Hotel near Baker and Peachtree, room 21."

"I'll be there in twenty minutes or so."

It was 7:15 when Harley knocked on the door of room 21. It was dark and windy out on the narrow walkway, the wind gaining velocity as it swung through the U-shaped motel courtyard.

On the second knock, Jim Sims opened the door. "Come in, Harley."

Past the shoulder of Sims, Harley could see the heavy, lumpy form of Senator Alvin Johnson. He was at a bar set up in the far right corner of the room. In contrast with Johnson, Jim Sims seemed youthful and trim. He'd been an Air Force ace in the Korean War and he never let you forget it. He still wore his hair in a bristle-brush flattop and his face was deeply tanned.

"I was telling Al you'd be here on the minute hand, and here you are," Sims said, backing into the room and letting Harley pass.

Harley peeled off his topcoat and handed it to Sims. While he put the coat in the closet, Harley and Senator Johnson looked at each other. He knew that Johnson didn't like him, that Johnson couldn't get past his age-old prejudice against the blacks. Most of the time he covered it well, and there was even a story that he'd been seen at lunch with two blacks once when he'd been campaigning for a bill he wanted passed.

"Glad you could come, Harley," Johnson said. "I think we've got an idea that might be worth listening to."

"I'm here," Harley said.

Sims returned from the closet. "What are you drinking?"

"Scotch and water."

"That's what I heard." Sims went to the bar and opened a bottle of Red Label. "I think it was Hap Seaver who said you were getting expensive tastes," Sims said as he made the drink.

"It's not expensive if you're drinking somebody else's whiskey," Harley said.

"Now you're talking," Senator Johnson said, taking a big swallow.

Jim Sims brought Harley the drink and nodded toward a seat on the sofa. Sims remained standing while Senator Johnson waddled over and sat in the easy chair that faced the sofa.

Harley sipped his scotch and said, "Who starts it?"

"I think Al ought to," Sims said. "It's partly his idea and partly mine."

"All the dogshit and lace aside, this is how I see it." Senator Johnson put aside his drink and got a cigar from a pack in his jacket pocket. He licked it all over and lit it. "We got too god-damn many possible sites. So, we got a three-way split going. And everybody locked in tight as a virgin's knees." He took the cigar from his mouth and pointed the wet end at Harley. "Like you. You're for the Boulevard site and that one's got as much chance as I have of pissing bourbon." He turned and nodded at Sims. "Jim here's backing the site near the Civic Center. That's got about a whore's chance of heaven too. Now me, I've been sitting around and listening to the shit and the talk fly. If words weighed a pound each, that meeting room'd have dropped four floors to the street a long time ago. So, I got to thinking. Three men banded together could make the difference. They could swing the whole thing by the tail. They could stand it on its head and shake the pocket out."

"You mean the three of us?"

Senator Johnson nodded. "You got it."

"Not really," Harley said. "It's vague around the edges."

"Let me jump in here," Sims said.

"Be my guest," Johnson said. He stood up and waddled over to the bar. "This talking makes me thirsty anyway."

Sims stood over Harley. "It's this way. We become a compro-mise group. We swing the weight this way or that."

"According to what's in it for us?"

"I wish you hadn't put it that way," Sims said. "It sounds somehow dishonest."

"Sorry," Harley said. It had to be held down. He wanted to hear the rest of it. "Go on, Jim."

"Between now and tomorrow afternoon, we do the bargain-ing. We let it be known we can pick the site and deliver it. Then we see what happens."

Senator Johnson turned from the bar. "What you think, Harley?"

"It won't work. Say we go to Wardlaw and say we can swing it. We'd be lying. Hap Seaver and I make two votes and you two make two more. That's four and we're still short of the five Wardlaw's site needs. It's the same with the Civic Center site. Jim Sims and Frank Clawson make two and Senator Johnson and I make two more. That's still four and not enough." Harley stood up and walked over to the bar. He added another ice cube and a splash of scotch. "The Whitehall site is the only one that would be a sure thing, but since they already have three votes, you two could swing it without me. You don't need me at all."

"I told you," Senator Johnson said. "You can't slide a curve past him."

"Never more right," Sims said.

"There's more then?" Harley asked.

"Maybe," Sims said. "Hap Seaver might come over if you do. That would give us four votes to bargain with."

"You talk to him about this?"

"It wasn't much of a talk," Sims said. "He heard us out and said he'd do what you did."

It was there, the soft center he thought he'd seen in Hap Seaver. He was ready to shift, but he wouldn't unless Harley did. Otherwise, he might find himself under attack.

"If Hap and I come in this we still couldn't bargain with Wardlaw. We'd be writing off the Boulevard site altogether … unless you've got somebody else hidden in the closet."

Jim Sims shook his head.

"I don't know if I can explain a shift from Boulevard this late."

"You might not have to," Jim Sims said. "Let's assume Wardlaw offers the best bargain. We have four votes for him and we hold firm. We might break somebody if we hold out long enough."

"On the other hand," Senator Johnson said, "we could push the Whitehall site over the edge. Or, we could handle the Civic Center the same way we'd do Boulevard. Hold out and hope somebody breaks."

"I'm still not sure I could explain a shift," Harley said.

"Don't worry about it," Senator John said. He reached two fingers in his mouth and brought out a long shred of tobacco. "We'll see to it that you get some heavy praise for making the compromise that allows the Center to get built. We'll force a deal so more black labor gets used in the building of it." He winked at Harley. "That's just two possibilities and there must be another dozen or so we could work out."

"We'll see you're covered," Sims said.

Harley put his glass on the bar. "I've got to talk to Hap Seaver."

"There's a phone in the bedroom," Sims said. "I think he said he'd be at home for another hour or so."

"In person," Harley said.

"What good would that do?" Senator Johnson asked.

"The same good it did talking to me in person rather than on the phone." He kept it easy. He wanted them to think that he was leaning, getting close to buying it. "I got to talk all the angles over with him."

"But you're interested?" Senator Johnson insisted.

"Some," Harley said. "But I've got to be sure I'm covered. I can't cut my throat with my district or with Georgia National."

They understood that. They knew you always protected yourself no matter what the rewards were. Sometimes you had to deal and shave a corner here and there, but you never dealt yourself into a corner where you couldn't see the daylight.

"Have another short one," Jim Sims said. "I'll call Hap and tell him you're coming by." Sims went into the bedroom and closed the door behind him. Senator Johnson got Harley's glass and mixed him another drink. Harley sat on the sofa and sipped it. A couple of minutes later, Jim Sims came out of the bedroom and nodded at Senator Johnson. After he fixed himself another drink. he came over and stood across from Harley. "Now this is what I call a hard bargaining session."

There was a knock at the door. Sims gave Senator Johnson a puzzled look. "We expecting anybody?"

"Not that I know of."

The knocking got louder. Sims reached the door and swung it open. Four shivering girls lunged into the room. "This is where the party is, isn't it?" one of the girls said.

"Are we having a party?" Sims asked of Johnson.

"It might be fun," Johnson said, "Especially after all that hard work we've been doing."

Harley stood up as the girls entered. It wasn't because it was the gentlemanly thing to do. He wanted to make a run for the door. He knew they were the hundred-dollar girls as soon as he saw them. They got the hundred-dollar base pay and whatever else they could make during the party. And all four girls were white, and Harley knew that this was their way of trying to trap him. With a cynicism that went past their prejudice, they'd decided he wouldn't be able to resist white meat if it was offered him.

As Sims began the introductions, Harley headed for the closet for his coat. He got the door open before Sims saw him. He jerked his topcoat from the hanger and turned.

"Hey, Harley," Jim Sims said, "I forgot to tell you that Hap's going to meet us here."

"He can call me at home. I'll be there in twenty minutes."

One of the girls, one with a huge platinum blonde wig, moved on a nod from Senator Johnson. She reached Harley and caught his arm. "Stay around, huh? We'll have ourselves a party like you never had before, and that's a promise."

"Sorry." Harley pulled his arm free. He turned to Jim Sims. "I told you I had to promise my wife a night out, just to come over here in the first place."

"Hell, she'll wait."

"You don't know my wife." He started to say "Ethel Ann," but he didn't want to use her name. He reached the door and swung it open. "Have Hap call me."

As he closed the door behind him, he heard Senator Johnson say, "You didn't tell me he was queer, Jim."

A few blocks from the Motor Hotel, Harley stopped at an open service station and made a call to John Franklin, the President of Georgia National, at his home.

"It looks bad," Franklin said, after Harley explained the meeting with Sims and Johnson. "I think I might need to talk to Mr. Wardlaw."

"Are you at home?"

"I'll be there in ten or fifteen minutes."

"I'll call you there," Franklin said.

Harley drove slowly home. The anger burned in him, against Sims and Johnson who thought he could be bought by a piece of white ass, and against Hap Seaver, who'd shifted and wanted him to shift too.

When he reached his house, he parked and stood out in the dark yard for a couple of minutes until he'd calmed himself. He didn't want to carry the anger into the house where Ethel Ann might begin to make her guesses.

At the end of Harley's telling of it, Wardlaw stood up and walked to the tray in his living room where the decanter and the two glasses were. "I have some excellent brandy here, Mr. Brisker."

"A small one, thank you," Harley said. He pushed his cuff back and checked the time. "Until this came up, I was supposed to take my wife out to dinner. I still have hopes."

Wardlaw smiled and nodded. He poured two short shots, kept one glass and passed the other to Harley. "What do you think I ought to do?"

"If I thought it was your kind of move, I'd suggest you tip the vice squad and see if they couldn't catch some of them with their pants down in room 21." Harley looked down at his hands. "I think I'm still a little mad about the way it was set up over there."

"And now you'd like to see all their names in the morning paper?" Wardlaw smiled, as if he understood how Harley felt. "I suspect the party ended as soon as you left."

Harley noticed that Wardlaw hadn't been insulted by the suggestion the room be raided. He'd rejected it only as an unworkable possibility. "You might be right. I don't think they had anything to celebrate."

"Any other way to handle it?"

"I don't think Hap Seaver will shift unless I go with him," Harley said.

"So it's a two-man block."

"They could still deal with the Whitehall block...if they remain together."

"You don't think they will," Wardlaw said.

"I think they can be split. I don't know what Jim Sims wants but Senator Johnson can be bought."

"I think I know what Jim Sims wants," Wardlaw said. He looked at Harley's glass and saw that he'd hardly touched the brandy. "He's got some illusions about high public office." He poured another splash of brandy into his glass. "Of course, even if we split Sims and Johnson, I don't see how that puts us any closer to putting the Convention on the Boulevard site."

"That's true enough." For the first time, Harley saw the Wardlaw he expected, the way he cut through Harley's anger and resentment and kept his mind upon the primary concern.

"Would you feel uncomfortable with Sims and Johnson in your camp, supporting the Boulevard location?"

"Politics and strange bedfellows," Harley said. "And that was almost literal tonight."

"I'll give it some thought and I'd like to call you in the morning."

"Any time after eight," Harley said. He sipped a bit more of the brandy and stood up. "Thank you for seeing me."

"I'm glad I met you at last," Wardlaw said. He led Harley to the outside door. "I have one question, Mr. Brisker. I hope it won't insult you. What do you want out of the Boulevard site?"

"A fair shake for the blacks there."

"And that's all?"

"That's all," Harley said.

"I'm used to hearing selfless things in public but hardly ever in private."

"I'm sorry if I disappointed you."

"No," Wardlaw said, "I'm far from disappointed."

CHAPTER SIX

"I'm not going in there," Helen said.

"Remember, we're tourists."

They were on the sidewalk in front of the Schooner Bar on West Peachtree, bathed in a kind of neon flutter. A large-scale model of an old schooner reached out above the sidewalk and was attached to the model on which was printed: "All Topless Revue."

"Women don't go into places like that," Helen said.

"How do you know?" Vince took her arm, and when she didn't pull it away, he guided her from the windy cold into the bar. A heavyset man was standing at the far end of the bar, next to the entrance into the large room beyond. There was a sign next to him that read: "Admission, $1.00."

Vince led Helen past the bar and handed the man two ones.

He picked a table directly in front of the stage. As soon as they were seated, a waitress appeared. She wore a sheer blouse that was like wearing nothing at all. Vince ordered a cognac for himself and a Bloody Mary for Helen. On the stage a short, red-haired girl with firm, hard breasts was finishing a set. The breasts looked as solid as stone.

Helen looked at the dancer and leaned toward him. "Are those real?"

"I guess so."

"Couldn't they be silicone?"

"I'll ask," Vince said.

"No, Vince, it doesn't matter ...."

"Of course it matters." The waitress brought their drinks. Vince paid for them and added another dollar. "The red-haired girl up there … are those real?"

"Marie? Sure, she says they are."

"Not silicone?"

"I asked her. She says they aren't."

Vince thanked her. He turned to Helen. "Blushing again? It's almost worth it."

"Damn you, Vince."

"Don't you know? I already am. At least that's the word from some quarters."

"Why are you damned?" she asked.

They finished the one drink at the Schooner, and now they were driving back toward the main part of town.

"Can't do the devil's work without some of the brimstone rubbing off on you."

"The devil's helper," Helen said. "That's an interesting and somewhat sad way to think of yourself."

He grinned at her. "Isn't it, though?"

"And David … Mr. Wardlaw … is the devil?"

"He doesn't mean to be," Vince said. "The level he's at, I'm not even sure he's aware of what he's doing. Money is abstract because who ever saw ten or twenty or thirty million dollars? The malls and shopping centers and office buildings are abstract because nobody ever knows the people who shop there or rent the space." He stopped for the light at Baker and West Peachtree. "Sometimes I even think people are abstract too, a good idea that doesn't quite work off the planning board."

"I think you're being too harsh," Helen said.

He shrugged and put the car in motion again as the light changed. "Take you, for example. Do you think he really sees you as a person?"

"I don't want to talk about myself."

"That's okay," he said. "I'll talk about you instead. You won't have to say a word."

"I'd rather you didn't, Vince."

"I'm drunk. Can't hold what a drunk does against him. Have to be understanding. Now you, you've been in love with David Emmett Wardlaw for eight or ten years. Almost from the beginning." He pressed in the cigarette lighter and got a cigarette from a crushed pack on the seat between them. "And you know, I bet he's never wondered what kind of underwear you wear."

"That doesn't mean anything. You're not making any sense."

"Sure, I am." He lit his cigarette and puffed at it for a long moment. "Just as you know that I always wonder at least once-a-day what kind of underwear it is. Functional and conservative or lacy and daring."

"Save that for the typing pool," she said.

"I don't wonder about those girls," he said. "I always know."

They were on Peachtree headed for Five Points. "Where are we going now?"

"There's this brothel I know where..."

"No," she said, "I think I've been a tourist long enough."

"A nightcap then?"

"I'd like that," she said.

"To tell the truth," Vince said, "I can't remember whether we had dinner or not."

"Lots of nourishment in tomato juice," she said.

It was 10:30 when Vince parked the Impala in the Ball Park parking lot. The lot was almost full. That meant the bar would be straining at the seams.

The Ball Park went back to the year when the Braves first moved to town from Milwaukee. One of the over-the-hill pitchers opened the bar to give him an off-season way to make a living. After one year, the pitcher was traded away and the bar went into other hands. The name remained the same, and it was now a hang-out for the young pro jocks, their camp followers and the other people in town who liked to rub elbows and shoulders with the Hawks, the Crackers, the Falcons, the Braves and now the Flames, the new hockey team.

In the doorway Vince said, "I really ought to have a small bloody steak."

"I'll watch you," she said.

In the lobby, they turned left and went into the small restaurant. The bar was straight ahead, dark and full of smoke and a jukebox that shook the building. The walls in the lobby behind them were given over to displays of bats and gloves donated by players, as well as autographed pictures of members of the Braves squad.

The pictures that lined the walls in the bar were of players in the other sports, basketball and football and hockey.

Vince took the table in the far left corner of the restaurant. When the waiter came, he waved the menu away and ordered the small steak rare and a green salad. Helen shook her head and said, "I'll have one more Bloody Mary and that's my last one for the night."

"You always drink this much?"

"That's supposed to be my question." After she looked around the small room she added, "I've had more to drink tonight than I've had in years."

"What do you do with your times?"

"Read, do needlework, go to movies, watch TV."

"That doesn't sound like much fun," he said. "No men in there anywhere?"

"Nothing serious," she said.

"That's a waste of a great natural resource."

"I have a feeling you're picking on me," she said.

"You're right. I am picking on you."

"Stop it then," she said.

"I could, but what I'm trying to figure out is the why."

The waiter brought Helen's Bloody Mary and a coffee for Vince. Helen sipped her drink. "The why is the easy part. You made an impulsive offer of a drink and you got stuck for the whole evening. Now it's going toward midnight and you've still got an empty bed."

"And I'm angry because of that?"

"Yes."

"That's odd," he said. "I don't feel angry at all. I feel very relaxed. I might even say happy."

"Then you're crazy."

The waiter brought Vince's steak and salad. The steak was still sizzling on the metal plate. Vince cut the first wedge from the center and offered it on the fork to Helen. "Have a taste. It's doped."

After she chewed and swallowed the cut of steak she said, "Good."

"Of course," he said. "And now that you are under my power, tell me, what kind of underwear are you wearing tonight?"

The Shooter left his apartment at nine and drove to the downtown club area, the one around Luckie Street. Just driving the Ford that Vince Gorman left him kept the angry burn going. After the XKE, it was like trying to manhandle a big boat in rough waters.

Thought he was so fucking smart, that Vince Gorman. He was just Wardlaw's flunky and ass-wiper. If Mr. Wardlaw had to choose between Gorman and the Shooter, he would damn well choose the Shooter and that was the straight word and no crook in that.

He spent an hour head-hunting. It was what Ab Slaton, the other first year guard on the Crackers, called it. Cruising had been taken over by the fags. So, head-hunting. But there wasn't much out to hunt. In one place there was a grade-A who was giving him the eye, but the stud with her looked like a hood who might give some bruises. And there might be a hassle if he tried to walk off with her. A few nights ago, it might have been worth a try. Not now. He had to give Wardlaw's flunky time to cover it up. Not that he believed for a minute that he really hit that old wino. Hell, the road out there was full of cars that time of night and any one of them could have hit him. His XKE had probably hit nothing more alive than a telephone pole or the rear end of some parked car.

A bit after ten, he drove over to the Ball Park. He wasn't sure he wanted to go there. Some of the other Crackers went there most nights and they didn't seem to like him much. The only one he could call a friend was Ab Slaton. The rest of them seemed to be angry because he made more money than they did. Besides the Shooter, the next highest paid player on the Crackers was Brewster, and he wasn't making a third what the Shooter was.

Still, since the Ball Park was a jock hang-out, young stuff dropped in all the time. Ready to pig and grunt for it. Not that he needed it that much tonight. The jock-groupie—Melinda, or whatever her name was— had taken the edge off. Now he could wait and make the good choice.

Ab Slaton was back in the bar. He'd come out of a small college in Texas, one the Shooter had never heard of, and he was happy just to be playing. He and Shooter got along well. Ab was willing to pass up his shots until the Shooter got his twenty-five or twenty-six, and then he'd remember that he had to make a few points too. So, he'd get his ten or twelve a game on hustle or by taking his free shots when the Shooter was on the bench getting a blow.

Ab saw him and patted the empty bar stool next to him. "Sit, Shooter."

He took the offered seat and nodded at the bartender. The bartender brought over scotch over the rocks. "How's head-hunting?" he asked Ab.

"Not too good. A couple back at the back booth. One grade-A and one C-minus."

The Shooter swung around in his bar stool and took a look. "You got a taste for a C-minus?"

"She's probably got a good mind or a great personality."

"I'll see." He took his drink and walked down the aisle back toward the last booth. On the way past two or three guys spoke to him and he nodded and said, "How's it going?" without breaking stride. When he was even with the booth, he didn't look at the two girls. He was looking at his own signed photo. Still not seeming to notice the girls, he leaned into the booth and brushed the shoulder of the girl on his right. "Excuse me," he said, leaning back.

He got his look at the girls then. The one on his left was the grade-A. Small blonde girl with a tan and a pretty face and, from what he could see of it, the body to go with the rest of her. At least the breasts looked real.

He grinned at the girls. "Somebody told me they'd taken my picture down. I was just checking."

"It's a good likeness," the blonde girl said.

"You think so?" He squinted at it. "Now that Pistol Pete's got a mustache, I thought about growing one."

"Why not?" the other girl said.

He took his look at her then. She was tall for a girl, maybe as tall as five-ten. Dark hair worn shoulder length. A thin face but nice features. Maybe Ab had overstated it. She might be a C-plus or a B-minus. "How do you mean that?"

"You do all the other Maravich things. Why not grow his mustache too?"

"You talk dirty," the Shooter said. He turned to the little blonde. "You ever watch me play?"

"All the time," she said. "We both do. Edna's stubborn and never says what she's supposed to say."

"Is that right?"

"I think she tries to shock people," the blonde said.

"Well, she's young and she might grow up yet." He nodded down the bar. "I'm with Ab Slaton, the other guard. You know him, don't you?"

"Sure."

"How about Ab and me joining you for a drink?"

"I'd like that," the blonde said.

"I've been out-voted," the dark-haired girl, Edna, said.

The Shooter waved down the bar at Ab, and Ab came over smiling and stood in the aisle for the introductions. The blonde girl, it turned out, was named Greta. Within minutes after he sat next to her, he could feel her leg next to his, a trembling in the thigh. One ready, he said to himself.

But he had to eat something, he knew that. If he'd been going home in the next hour or so, he'd have passed it up and had something at home. But it looked like it might be a good evening and he didn't want to spoil it because he'd been drinking on an empty stomach.

"You girls had supper yet?"

"Supper," the dark-haired girl said. "Isn't that quaint?"

"We've eaten," Greta said.

"You mind going with us into the dining room?" the Shooter said. "I've got fairly good table manners."

"Been taking lessons since you moved to Atlanta?" Edna asked.

He ignored her. But he noticed, with a little heat, that Ab Slaton had laughed.

"Can we take our drinks?" Greta asked.

"Sure," the Shooter said, "and we can have another while we're there." He eased out of the booth and led the way through the lobby and into the dining room. At the doorway he bowed them into the room and he remained bent over for a few seconds looking at the pert hard rump on Greta and liking it. When he straightened up, he saw Vince Gorman at a table in the far corner of the room. He was there with some woman. The sight of him got the angry burn going. He didn't wait for the hostess. He motioned Ab and the two girls to a table in the center of the room. "Got to say a few words to a friend," he said.

Behind him Ab said, "Sure thing, Shooter," and then he was walking across the room toward Vince and the woman.

Vince didn't see the Shooter at first. He was adding sugar to his fresh cup of coffee when Helen said, "Look who's here, Vince."

He lifted his head and saw the Shooter wobbling his way through the tables, smiling. God knows why he was smiling. If he has half a brain, he'd be thinking about that old man at Grady Hospital.

The Shooter stopped near the table and grinned. "It sure is good running into you, Mr. Gorman."

"Hello, Shooter."

The Shooter turned his head and looked down at Helen. "I don't think I've met this lady."

"Helen Morris ... Eddie Simpson." Vince pushed his coffee away. "Miss Morris is Mr. Wardlaw's secretary."

"It must be great working for a great guy like him," the Shooter said.

Helen nodded. "And I'm one of your biggest fans."

"Gee, that's great."

Vince watched the Shooter go into his act. It was the one he'd developed for the lunch meetings with the booster clubs and the talks with the boys' clubs. It was all modesty and gee whiz, the unspoiled country boy, the same as he was before the new money, the instant wealth.

"I was at the game last night," Helen said. "Isn't that Ab Slaton with you?"

The Shooter pulled out a chair and sat down. "Yeah, that's Ab. He's a great guy. The best." The Shooter put his elbows on the table and gave Helen his boyish grin. "It's not every night you meet a real fan."

The waiter brought over a menu. The Shooter ordered the Hoof and Horn Special. "And have my friends order anything they want. I'll take my order over there after I've visited a few minutes with my friends here."

The waiter nodded and went away.

"I bet you didn't know that Vince and I were such great friends, did you?" the Shooter said. "Like, for example, he loaned me his own car today. Just like that. He knew my car was being repaired so he offered me his. Now, what do you think of a favor like that?"

Helen looked at Vince. "I knew you didn't have a car but ..."

"See?" the Shooter said. "Does his Boy Scout deed and doesn't tell anybody about it."

"It was business," Vince said.

"What happened to your car?" Helen asked.

"Somebody brushed it in a parking lot." The Shooter watched Vince's face. "Creamed a headlight and tore a fender and didn't stay around to report it."

"That's the way it looks," Vince said.

"You file a damage claim for me?" the Shooter asked Vince.

"I thought you'd better do that for yourself," Vince said.

"Hell, you work for me, don't you?"

Vince shook his head. "I work for Wardlaw Properties."

"I'm a property," the Shooter said.

"We'll talk about it tomorrow," Vince said.

"No," the Shooter said, "I'm a damned important property and you better start acting like it."

Vince took a deep breath and let it out slowly. "Shooter, I think your friends miss you."

"That sounds like you want me to leave." The Shooter turned to Helen. "I'll leave if the lady wants me to."

Helen looked stunned. The conversation had gone from out-wardly friendly to the edge of violence in just a matter of seconds. "Vince, Shooter, I think…"

"It's these old guys," the Shooter said. "Always getting their backs up just because I make some friendly talk with their girls." The Shooter pushed his chair back and stood up. "Like the flunky here. He thinks I'm trying to make time with you. And all the time I was just being sociable." He waved an unsteady arm toward the table where Ab Slaton and the two girls were. "Shit, I got mine waiting over there."

"Good-night, Shooter," Vince said.

"You think you're so goddamn smart," the Shooter said.

"We'll talk about it in the morning. This isn't getting us anywhere."

"Please, Shooter," Helen said.

"Worried I'm going to hurt the flunky here?" The Shooter edged toward the table. "And I damn well might."

Vince knew it was coming. He braced his legs and waited for it. When the Shooter took his wild swing, Vince ducked under it and, coming up out of the chair, caught his shoulder and turned him. He put a lock on the Shooter's neck. "Take it easy now. I'm going to turn you loose and you walk back over to your table."

"All right," the Shooter said.

But when Vince released him and started to step away, the Shooter threw an elbow that hit Vince in the pit of his stomach and pushed the breath out of him. Vince sagged and the Shooter turned and swung again. It wasn't a good punch, but it caught him in the neck and staggered him.

Away from them, in another part of the room the hostess was yelling for someone named Arnold. It was a high-pitched voice, somewhere close to a scream. The Shooter was still swing-ing and mostly missing. Vince found himself backed up against a wall. He said, "Call it off, Eddie," and the Shooter said, "Like shit I will." He swung again, and Vince decided that he'd been the punching bag long enough. He pushed away from the wall and moved in close. He took one punch on the shoulder and then he swung a low short right that hit the Shooter in the groin and took the fight out of him. The Shooter's mouth dropped open and his knees buckled. Vince caught him and pushed him down into a chair. The Shooter sat there stunned and gulping for breath. It was over.

That was when Ab Slaton came out of nowhere and let loose a roundhouse right that struck Vince flush on the chin and dropped him. He wasn't completely out, but he couldn't move and Ab stepped toward him and kicked him in the ribs a couple of times.

Helen screamed. He heard that just before he blacked out.

CHAPTER SEVEN

Helen handled it all. By the time the manager, Arnold, arrived she was over the shock of the violence and she'd pushed Ab Slaton away and yelled at him to stand still. To Arnold, she identified herself as David Wardlaw's executive secretary. The name meant enough to him, and he pointed out the way to the club office. The Shooter, gray-faced and shaken, followed her, steadied by Ab Slaton.

Arnold helped Vince to the men's room and tried to help him clean up. He'd taken one or two bad punches in the head but the ribs were giving him most of his trouble. He couldn't straighten up.

In the office, Helen looked at the Shooter and Ab and pointed to chairs. "Sit down."

"I'm not through with that shithead in there," the Shooter said.

"Whatever you say," Ab Slaton said.

"You two are going to be charged with assault and battery. And if Vince Gorman doesn't file the charges, if he's not well enough, I'll file them for him." She kept it short and conversational, but she saw that it drew them up short.

"You work for Mr. Wardlaw," the Shooter said. "He wouldn't let you do that."

"Wouldn't he?"

"I'm too important to him," the Shooter said.

"Not the way you acted in there." She took her time, taking the pack of cigarettes from her purse and selecting one. Ab Slaton tried to light it for her, but she ignored him and lit it herself. "In terms of who's important to Mr. Wardlaw, Vince Gorman is worth ten of you. If Mr. Wardlaw had to make a choice, he wouldn't choose you."

"I don't believe that."

"A year in jail might convince you," Helen said. Moving around the desk, she punched a button on the phone for an outside line and dialed David Wardlaw's home number. When there was no answer, she opened a small notebook and dialed another number.

"I'd like to speak to Mr. David Wardlaw," she said.

There was a short wait. When Wardlaw came on the line, with an economy of a few words, she told him about what she'd witnessed in the dining room. At the end she said, "Yes, Mr. Wardlaw." She looked across the desk at the Shooter. "He'd like to speak to you."

She handed him the receiver and stepped away. She watched his face. He said very little, a "yes, sir" or two. Mostly he listened. When he replaced the receiver, he remained for a long moment, staring down at it.

"Do you believe me now?" Helen asked.

"He said ... he said he'd suspend me for a year. Just drop me off the team."

"Without pay," Helen said. "I've seen the contract, and I think there's a clause in it that covers what happened out there."

"I'll get a lawyer," the Shooter said. "I'll jump leagues."

She waved that aside impatiently. "I know a man who says that if money can buy justice, it can also buy injustice."

"He wants to see me at his office in the morning."

"I'd be there on time." She turned to Ab Slaton. "And if I were you, I wouldn't send out any laundry in the next day or two."

The Shooter and Ab Slaton got their coats from the girl in the checkroom in the lobby. Before they left, Ab looked in the bar, but he didn't see either of the girls. When he returned and reported that to the Shooter, he said, "I guess they got scared."

"Dumb cunts," the Shooter said. But he regretted it. The blonde, Greta, had been getting to him, and now he wasn't sure he could find her again. That was bad luck. And, with the white heat of the anger gone, he realized that he still hadn't eaten. Back there somewhere was his steak-and-lobster-tail dinner.

Ab Slaton was hanging onto the Shooter. "You think I could go with you in the morning when you go to see Mr. Wardlaw?"

"If he'd wanted to see you, he'd have said so."

"But, Shooter, I could explain it to him. How I thought you might get hurt and I went over there just to help you."

"I'll tell him for you," the Shooter said.

"You will?" Relief washed over Ab. "That would be great of you, Shooter. It really would. You're right what you said back there. They're not going to do anything to you. Hell, you're the whole team. He's not going to suspend you. But *me*. Shit, he could brush me off and not miss me. And that's what he might do if you don't speak for me."

"I'll speak up for you," the Shooter said.

They were out in the parking lot.

"How about another drink? The Mouse Trap or Uncle Sam's?"

"Not tonight, Ab. I'm tired." He patted Ab on the shoulder. "You know what time he wants to see me? Eight fucking o'clock in the morning."

"See you at the morning workout then?"

"Sure thing," the Shooter said.

"And thanks ahead of time for speaking up for me." Ab waved and walked toward his old Mustang in the far end of the parking lot.

Like hell, the Shooter thought. Oh, he'd try if he got a chance. If he saw that Wardlaw wasn't after his hide, if he saw that Wardlaw just wanted to throw a scare into him, he could afford to make a pitch for Ab. Ab might be country stupid, but he knew where his paycheck came from. And it wasn't just from Wardlaw Properties. It came from playing in the back court with the Shooter. From playing twice as much defense and trying to get the ball to the Shooter so he'd have a free and open shot. A couple of the veteran guards on the team didn't feel that way. And that was why the Shooter had contrived to make Ab look good all through the exhibition season. He wanted Ab as the other guard. And, if possible, he'd save Ab's ass. But only after he'd saved his own.

As soon as he opened the door to Gorman's Ford, he smelled the perfume. And then his surprise when he saw which girl it was sitting there. It wasn't the blonde, Greta. It was the tall, dark-haired one, the one who'd acted like he was dirt the whole time he'd been with them. Edna.

"Where's Greta?"

"She got scared and left. I stayed."

"I see that," he said. "Why?"

"I wanted a ride home."

"Where do you live?"

"No," Edna said, "to your home."

He was driving through downtown Atlanta, passing Peachtree Center, before he asked his next question. "I thought you didn't like me. That right?"

"That's right."

"Why then?"

"I might tell you later. I might not."

He took the West Peachtree part of the fork at Baker. "What do you do?"

"Nothing," she said.

"How do you manage that?"

"My family doesn't want me to work. Greta works. She's a secretary, types and knows shorthand. I don't think my family would approve of her at all."

"Your family wouldn't approve of me either," the Shooter said.

"Not a bit. They have an attitude that's really sort of dated, sort of Renaissance."

"That went past me," the Shooter said.

"A gentleman is supposed to do any number of things well. Athletic things, literary ones. But he's not supposed to make money from them. If you were an excellent tennis player, they'd admire you for it—as long as you didn't turn professional and make money from it."

"That's silly."

"They call athletes jocks, don't they? Well, you're not only new money, but you're also jock money. If they knew I was out with you, they might do one of those things parents did back around the turn of the century. They'd pack me off to Europe."

"You're not serious."

"Yes, I am. It's the way they think, these first families. They're not very realistic. If they bothered to look back and see how they became first families in Atlanta, they'd find that some great-great grandfather was a redneck who bought land near where Peachtree and Cain are now when it cost about a hundred and thirty dollars a lot. That redneck farmed it or put up a grocery store or a boarding house. Or some relative came in later and bought that lot that had sold for a hundred and thirty dollars for three or four thousand. And now that lot is worth about a million dollars some hundred and twenty-five years later."

"You belong to the Piedmont Driving Club?"

"Yes."

"I never understood. What's so important about it anyway?"

"Nothing," she said. "Nothing at all."

"You've been talking about your family. I don't think you told me your last name."

"I told you," Edna said, "but you weren't listening."

"No second chances?"

"You were too interested in Greta," she said.

"You were giving me shit."

"Wasn't I, though?"

They passed Pershing Point where the two Peachtrees merged into Peachtree Road. "I didn't get my supper. I've got to find a place where I can get a bite of something."

"Why bother? I can fix you something if you've got all the basics."

"I've got a full pantry." Like the ex-poor boy he was, he'd spent a fortune at Cloudt's, the fancy-food store on Peachtree Road. The shelves in his pantry looked like grocery-store shelves. He'd bought almost everything in sight, but he'd never had the nerve to try some of it.

"Trust me not to poison you?" she asked.

"Yes."

"You're too trusting."

Helen wanted to take him straight to the emergency room at Grady, but Vince wouldn't have anything to do with that. He said he wouldn't mind seeing a doctor, but he'd be damned if he'd sit all evening in the waiting room with the drunks with the DT's and the rednecks with the cuts.

It was a stubborn stand. He was having trouble moving, and his ribs hurt when he breathed. His jaw, while he didn't think it was broken, felt swollen and oversized.

"I'll see about a doctor who makes house calls," Helen said.

"You've got to be kidding."

On the way out of the Ball Park, he waited while she talked another minute or two with the manager, Arnold. He assumed she was giving him a card and telling him to send a bill for the damages to Wardlaw Properties. And he made his guess that she was making whatever effort she could to assure that the brawl wouldn't get into the papers.

It didn't do any good to worry about the newspapers. The Ball Park was crowded, and it wouldn't remain a secret very long.

If it didn't get in the morning paper, the *Constitution,* you could make bets that it would be in the *Journal.*

"Where are you taking me?"

"To my place," she said.

"I'm afraid you picked a bad evening to answer my question about your underwear."

"It's not that at all," she said, laughing. "I'm going to find a doctor who'll answer my question about your underwear ... and your ribs and your jaw."

"I can answer part of it," he said. "They're boxer shorts, size 32, and they're puce colored."

"Puce?"

"Stunning, huh?"

"I bet you don't even know what color puce really is," Helen said.

"Flea-colored," he said. "The color of a flea that's been drinking blood."

"Uuugh."

"I thought you'd feel that way."

It surprised him, the apartment where she lived. He'd expected one of the new apartments in a complex on the outskirts of Atlanta. The ones with the clubhouse and the swimming pool and the tennis courts. Instead, she had the top half of an old Tudor-style house in the Morningside section of town. There was a large front lawn and a flagstone walk. Upstairs, she had a large living room that was about half of the floor and beyond that two bedrooms and two baths and a large open, old-style kitchen. And, though he couldn't see it, he suspected there was a wooded backyard for summer and spring living.

Wardlaw called while she was helping him take off his topcoat. Vince got the last arm out while she answered it.

"I've been trying to reach you," David said. "How is Vince?"

"I think he's all right," she said. "I'm just about to start the long process of looking for a doctor who'll make a house call."

"Vince is with you?"

"He didn't want the emergency ward."

"I'll make the call for you," he said. "I'll have a doctor there within the hour."

"Thank you, David."

"David?"

"I forgot myself, Mr. Wardlaw," she said.

"I don't mind," he said, and then he said good-night.

"David? That's a breakthrough." Vince was hunched over in an easy chair, trying to straighten up. The muscles in his chest and his stomach seemed shorter, balled up. "Where's your liquor cabinet?"

"Do you really need another drink?"

"In the movies, the hero always gets a drink before the doctor cuts out the bullet or sets the broken leg."

"I'll get you one."

When she returned with a scotch on the rocks he was standing, one arm braced on the mantelpiece above the fireplace. He took the drink and nodded down at the fireplace. "This work?"

"Yes. And now you want a fire in it?"

"It's romantic," he said, "and I need all the help I can get."

He stepped aside while she moved the fire screen and used a wadded-up newspaper and some kindling to get the fire started. When she replaced the screen, flames were beginning to lick away at the log.

"Satisfied?"

He nodded. "And now if you will kiss my wounds and make them well."

"That's for your mother to do." She left him looking down into the thin ribbons of flame and went into the kitchen. She came back a minute later with a cup of tea. She stood beside the fireplace and dunked her teabag.

"Well, you see my mother would do it for me, except that I'm an orphan, a poor lost child."

"That's strange," she said, "I'm an orphan too."

"What?"

"Nothing." She drew the teabag out and stored it on the side of the saucer. "Vince, you might be a nice guy. I really don't know. But you're strange. Like now. You're hurt and probably a little drunk; you're tired…and you keep right on trying."

"The Lord hates a quitter. When the going gets tough, the tough get going. Nice guys finish last."

"You don't have the least bit of interest in me. It's all reflex now. You punch a button in your side and you run on by the hour, like a spool of tape."

Vince looked down into the flames and shook his head slowly. "I've always been misunderstood. All my life, ever since I was a kid."

"That sounds like the number you did on Marcie," Helen said.

"It does, doesn't it?" He grinned at her and then wiped the grin away and replaced it with the sad look. "Of course, I drink. Why shouldn't I? It's the only way I can kill the pain. You'll never know in a hundred years what that woman did to me."

"Mary, the girl in Payroll," Helen said.

"It could be," Vince admitted. "I forget."

"Aren't you ashamed of yourself?"

"Not really. Let me tell you something." He held out his empty glass. "I need another drink."

She took the glass. "Is that what you want to tell me?"

"No, something else—as soon as I have a bit more fuel."

She was gone for a few minutes. She returned with an ice bucket and about half a bottle of J&B. She mixed him a stiff drink. "This ought to knock you down, right after you tell me whatever you want to tell me."

"Ready?"

She lifted her cup of tea and nodded.

"Women don't believe lines. They never did. They're amused by them. I wish I could have been in the powder room and heard them discussing me. God, how they must have laughed."

"They were amused," Helen said.

"So, I'm as outrageous as I can be. Really absurd. But I don't use the same line on two of the girls. I feel each one deserves a line of her own, even if it's one of the old standard lines."

"Principles?"

"Did Peggy tell you the line I lavished on her?"

"I don't think so," Helen said.

"Probably too embarrassed to admit it. I told that child I was impotent and that this was the aftermath of being kidnapped and repeatedly raped at the age of fifteen by a sex-crazed librarian named Miss Boggs."

"Vince... Vince..."

"You'd be surprised how sympathetic Peggy was."

"And she tried to make you feel... normal again?"

"And succeeded," Vince said.

"Do you match the lines to the girls?"

"Sometimes," he said.

"Someday," she said, "I'd like to know what line you'd use on me."

"I'd talk about your underwear," he said.

"No, the real one."

The doorbell rang.

"Saved by the doctor," Vince said.

"Isn't that what he's supposed to do?" Helen asked from the doorway before she went down to let the doctor in.

The doctor didn't stay long. He said Vince's jaw wasn't broken, and his ribs, though they'd be painful for a few days, didn't need taping. The doctor was brisk, efficient and totally disinterested. Vince didn't even remember whether he'd given his name. Later, Vince found out the doctor was on a retainer, a large one.

Before he left, just in passing, the doctor asked how it had happened.

"A pick-up basketball game at the Y," Vince said.

"They play rough there," the doctor said.

"It was for the pick-up championship of the world," Vince said.

"Of course," the doctor said, as if that explained it all.

Helen returned from seeing the doctor out.

Vince was buttoning his shirt. "You'd better call me a cab."

"You can stay in the spare bedroom," Helen said.

"If I stayed, it wouldn't be the spare bedroom."

"Then I'll stay in the spare bedroom and you can have mine."

"I'll take that cab." But even as he tried to tuck his shirttail into his pants he knew he wasn't going to make it. His knees seemed to be made out of Silly Putty. "On second thought, I'll take that spare bed."

When the bed was ready she called him; he went in and undressed down to his shorts. They weren't puce. They were a simple gray. He got into bed and pulled the covers up to his neck. A few minutes later she brought in a pitcher of water, a glass and the pills the doctor had left if his ribs started hurting him during the night. After she'd arranged these on the night table, he reached up, got her hand and drew her down to sit on the edge of the bed.

"I knew sooner or later that you would hire somebody to beat me up so I'd end up in your spare bedroom. I knew you were overcome with passion, how hard you'd fight against it, afraid to let me know how much you cared, afraid I'd treat you like dirt…"

"You knew all that?"

"And now you have me in your spare bedroom and I'm waiting patiently for you to make your next move."

"Patiently?" she asked with a mock raised eyebrow.

"Patiently going toward impatiently," he said.

"What would you say my best move is?"

"You've already ruined your reputation," he said. "You might as well enjoy it."

"You sound in pain," she said.

"What else but the pain of waiting patiently?"

She opened her hand and held out a capsule. "This is a sleeping pill."

"So you can overcome me while I'm drowsy?"

"Yes," she said, "yes."

He took the capsule and she sat on the edge of the bed until he dropped off. He didn't fight it. One moment his eyes were open and the next he'd dropped off.

Asleep, the long hard face didn't seem hard anymore. And she found herself smiling at the beginning of a light and irregular snore. That was something the girls at the office hadn't mentioned.

David Wardlaw returned from a special Junior League showing of the latest Atlanta Children's Theatre production around midnight. The showings took place two or three times a year. The invitees were the large contributors and political figures around the city who could help the Theatre. The show had been over by ten, and then there'd been a buffet and a bar set up in the lobby. David found himself being passed around from one attractive lady to another, and at the end he'd been released only when he'd assured them that he would repeat his gift of $1,000 for the coming year.

John met him at the door to the apartment.

"Is something wrong?"

"I tried to call you at the Alliance Theatre, but you'd left. Miss Frances is home."

"Here?"

"Yes, sir, she just arrived."

"Where is she?"

"In the kitchen, Mr. Wardlaw. I offered to fix her some dinner, but she said she'd make do with what she found in the refrigerator."

David handed his topcoat to John. "You might as well go to bed. I'll need breakfast at seven in the morning."

"Yes, sir."

David left him and went into his bedroom. He put his suit coat away and emptied his pockets. Then, puzzled and with some foreboding, he crossed the dining room and went into the kitchen.

Frances was seated at the small table off to one side of the large kitchen. It was the table where John usually had his meals. The remains of a large can of crab-meat, with a dab of mayonnaise and a sliced lemon, were on a plate in front of her. She waved a hand at him in which she held a bottle of Bass ale.

"Hi," she said.

"Hi, yourself." He got a bottle of ale from the refrigerator and opened it. He turned and looked at her. She was a large girl, dressed now in blue jeans and a man's shirt. She was like her mother in that, the large-boned body. Nothing could be done about that. No reducing salon or spa could promise to do anything with the frame she'd inherited. She'd just have to learn to live with it. Her dark hair was worn shoulder length, without curls or any of the high-fashion things girls her age did with their hair. Her face was long and boyish, pleasant but not what you'd call a pretty face.

"School out already?"

"For me it is," she said.

He edged a chair away from the table and sat down on her right. He took the fork from her and placed a chunk of crabmeat on a cracker. "You want to explain it to me?"

"Not especially," she said. "I might as well. You'll be hearing from the Dean of Women either by letter or phone in the next day or two."

"A problem?"

"Not for me. For them."

"What happened?" At the last moment, just before he put the cracker and crabmeat in his mouth, he picked out a piece of membrane.

"Somebody got the great idea of searching the rooms for drugs while we were in class. They found half an ounce of grass in my makeup kit."

"Yours?"

"Of course," she said. "On the flight down, I considered telling you that it really wasn't mine, that I was keeping it for another girl and didn't want to get her in trouble."

"Why didn't you?"

"I didn't feel like lying. It didn't seem to matter that much to me."

"Why, Frances?"

"Why wasn't I willing to lie?" She shook her head. "I know that wasn't what you meant. Why did I have the grass? Because I like it."

"Any other drugs?"

"No," she said. "No speed or anything like that. I'm afraid of LSD, too afraid to try it."

"So, they threw you out of school?"

"Not exactly. There was going to be a hearing. I decided that I wasn't interested in a hearing."

He lifted the bottle and drank from it. "Would it do any good if I called them in the morning?"

She pushed the crabmeat plate toward him. "I doubt it. It might save them a call, and now that you know about it it'll save them a long explanation."

"What do you want me to do?"

"Nothing, daddy. I'm not interested in college any more."

He shook his head slowly. "I thought you liked it up there."

"I changed my mind."

"Isn't this sudden?" he asked.

"If you want to call a couple of months 'sudden.' It seems a bit of a waste of time. What does French have to do with living, and what does Latin Literature have to do with anything? I guess I got bored."

"And boredom led to … the grass?"

"That's too easy. But you'd be surprised how much better a dull class is after you've had a couple of hits. Or how much better TV is if you're smoking a joint while you're watching it."

David looked at the bottle of ale and decided he didn't really want it. He carried it over to the sink and poured it out. "I don't know what to think about this, Frances. Maybe your mother would have an answer, but I don't."

"Mother wouldn't either," she said. "I think she'd cry for a day or two."

"That's probably true. What are your plans now?"

"I thought I'd find a job."

"What can you do?"

"Nothing," she admitted. "I think my education up to now has taken care of that."

He smiled. "No secretarial skills?"

She smiled back. "Not a one. Can't type, no shorthand and can't spell."

"I don't see any special demand on the labor market for your talents."

"I'll find something," she said.

"I'll find something for you at the office," he said.

She shook her head. "That's too easy. And besides I'm not pretty enough to be one of your receptionists … and you know it."

He put his hands on her shoulders and kissed her on the cheek. "We'll talk in the morning, or better yet at lunch. Is there anything you need?"

"Some patience from you," she said.

"You've got it." He released her and stepped away. "I'll call you from the office in the morning."

"Not before ten. Us dope addicts need our sleep."

"Not before ten then."

It took him a long time to fall asleep. Maybe he shouldn't have been surprised. She'd always been free-spirited, and perhaps a little too sure of herself. He'd promoted that part of her, knowing that she was never going to be a pretty woman in the way the world thought of pretty. He'd known that would make problems for her, and he'd wanted her to be strong enough to face the disappointments that might come to her.

A mistake, perhaps, and yet he knew that she was a basically sound person. The grass didn't mean anything. He'd read enough about that not to panic. It was just a matter of time and it would work out. And he would be as patient as he needed to be with her. But firm if he had to be.

And when he talked to the Dean of Women, he'd make sure the record was kept blank. He would make sure that nothing got back to Atlanta that would hurt her.

Edna decided that she'd fix an omelette for the Shooter. He sat at the kitchen table, eating cheese and crackers and drinking a can of beer, while she minced ham and green peppers and opened a can of sliced mushrooms. She broke the eggs in the bowl single-handedly.

Watching her as she moved about the kitchen, the Shooter decided he'd been hasty in his first judgment of her. Sure, she was tall for a woman and sure, she had a go-to-hell attitude. After some of the clinging types it was, to say the least, refreshing.

"I saw this movie once where the cook came over and sat on the butler's knee while the food was cooking."

"That cook wasn't doing an omelette. The timing's important and you don't have an omelette pan."

"I'll get one tomorrow."

"Anyway, I think Greta is more your type. The type for sitting on knees." She turned with the bowl in her hand, beating the eggs slowly with a long-handled wooden spoon. "Right?"

"Some people say I don't have a type."

"A great lover, huh?"

"That's what they say," the Shooter said.

"Secretaries and ushers who work at the Dome? What do they know?"

"You know better?"

"I know enough," she said, "not to be impressed by the packaging and the press releases."

"I was right. You do have a filthy mouth."

"Just because I'm not pre-sold? The problem is that sometimes the person being given the image by the PR men begin to believe all those lies are true."

"A lot of it's true."

She shrugged. She turned and poured part of the beaten eggs into the buttered pan. She sprinkled on ham and green peppers and mushrooms. Then, using a spatula and a fork, she folded the omelette. He watched the muscles in her legs and thighs as she struggled with the folding.

Nice, he thought, very nice.

The omelette done, she placed it in front of him with a fork and a napkin. "I'm going to make a small one for me."

"The cook has some privileges," he said.

He'd finished half of his omelette by the time she brought her smaller one to the table and sat down facing him. "How is it? They tell me you like good food. That is, the PR people tell me that."

"It's great," he said.

She took a small bite. "It's mediocre." She took a larger bite. "Perhaps I should have fixed you a hamburger instead."

She kept him off balance. He couldn't seem to get an edge on her. She always seemed to have the ready answer that undercut him, that sliced through the direct approach he'd used so well with other girls.

"When are we going to bed?"

"Not until I'm awfully sleepy," she said.

"You're going to bed with me, aren't you?"

"Not unless I have some kind of mental breakdown in the next half hour or so," she said.

"You'll like it."

"What did Maugham say? Something about the fact that one could have as much sex as one wanted, as long as one was willing to settle for corned beef and cabbage."

At one o'clock, she got her coat and her purse.

The Shooter yawned. "I'll call you a cab."

"You will not."

"What?"

"You'll drive me home, Eddie, just as if you were a gentleman."

"What's that supposed to mean?"

"An uncle of mine used to say that he opened doors for women, not because they were necessarily ladies but because he was a gentleman."

"I never said I was a gentleman." But the Shooter got his coat.

"Now you understand it," Edna said. "You'll drive me home, not because you're a gentleman but because I might be a lady."

They went out into the hallway. The Shooter pushed the down button. "Hell, you're the first one to complain."

"That confirms something I suspected about the kind of girls you attract. But I wasn't brought up to go home in a cab like a call-girl."

"Oh, shit."

Later, when they were driving through a winding road which was flanked by huge homes and massive lawns, he asked if she'd like to see the Saturday night game. "I can leave a ticket for you at the box office."

"Leave two tickets," she said.

"Why two?"

"I might bring my boyfriend."

Around two in the morning, there was a light rain and in no time at all, the rain changed to sleet. It wasn't a heavy sleet and it lasted only half an hour or so.

In the penthouse apartment of the Mitchell Towers, Wardlaw was in a deep, dreamless sleep. The temperature was 65 degrees exactly in his bedroom and he slept under a single blanket. Down the hall his daughter, Frances, remained awake reading *Cat's Cradle*. At two, she smoked her only joint and flushed the last few flakes and the paper down the toilet. In the sealed-off and soundproof apartment neither of them heard the sleet.

The sleeping pill might have lasted the whole night. It might have if during the sleet storm Vince hadn't turned on his side, his usual sleeping position. The pain from his ribs jarred him awake. He sat up and swung his legs over the side of the bed. He sat there, hunched over and sweating. His hand shook as he poured a glass of water and took two of the pills the doctor had left for the pain. He didn't sleep right away. He heard the sleet and it reminded him of awaking in a high-ceilinged room when he was five and six.

Only a door away, Helen Morris groaned in the heat of a sex dream. In it, both David Wardlaw and Vince Gorman were making love to her, taking turns mounting her. It would have been a disturbing dream if she'd remembered it in the morning. She wouldn't.

Harley Brisker was having the same dream, the one that had wracked him for years. In the dream, he'd talked Martin Luther King Jr. into letting him stay with him in Memphis. He was with Martin on the walkway of the Lorraine Motel; Martin said something, he leaned toward Martin to hear him better and he felt something hit him and throw him against Martin. Then Martin was cradling Harley on his knees and he was saying, "Harley, Harley, who would want to hurt you?" And Harley's dark blood smeared the front of Martin's shirt and soaked into the front of his trousers.

At the Madrid the Shooter was in a twilight sleep, still awake enough so that he could direct his dreams. He was sinking long jump shots from thirty feet out while Billy Cunningham and Joe Caldwell stood flat-footed and looked amazed.

CHAPTER EIGHT

Helen drank six ounces of unsweetened grapefruit juice and a cup of black coffee. Before she left the apartment, she looked into the spare bedroom one last time. Vince was still sleeping. The left side of his jaw was swollen and it looked like it might be turning blue from the bruise. That was going to be quite a five-o'clock shadow he was going to have for a week or two. He hadn't slept too well, she guessed, and she closed the door carefully behind her. On a last minute thought, she returned to the kitchen and left a note.

Saturday-morning traffic was slack and she made the drive to the office in a bit less than fifteen minutes. She parked in her usual spot at the garage across the street and, once in the Peachtree Investment Building, she signed the "in" ledger while the security guard watched.

The security guard wasn't the one who was usually there on weekdays, and she missed the nice words she got from Freddie Banks. He was an older man, in his fifties, who did a lot of gardening, and in the spring and summer he often surprised her by presenting her with bunches of flowers he'd picked from his yard just before he left for work.

"Is Mr. Wardlaw in yet?" she asked the guard.

"No, ma'am."

When she reached her floor, she found night lights burning. She walked through the still, empty offices, past the desks left neat for the long weekend. She left her coat and purse at her desk and used her key to unlock the door to the inner office.

Ten minutes later the water was boiling in the kettle, and she'd ground the correct measure of French-roasted coffee and placed it in the filter of the drip pot. She poured the water into the filter, got out a cup and saucer and placed them on the counter. At that moment she heard the elevator from the underground garage opening. With a quick look at the water level she hurried into the office and was waiting when Wardlaw entered.

He showed some surprise at finding her there. "You here, Helen?"

"I thought it might be a good idea," she said.

"Because of the Shooter?"

She nodded. She took his topcoat and put it in the closet.

"How's Vince?" he asked from behind his desk.

"He's not going to be pretty for a few days."

"I didn't know that he'd ever been," he said.

"Some of the girls in the office think so."

"That's odd." He turned in his chair and looked through the door that led into the kitchen. "Am I early this morning?"

She checked her watch. "I think we're both late, but the coffee'll be ready in a minute."

"Is there any reason why you can't have a cup with me this morning?"

"Office protocol," she said.

"To hell with that," he said with a smile.

In the kitchen she got down another cup and saucer and by then the water had settled through the grounds. She poured the coffee and carried the cups into the office. When she was seated across from him, she said, "I didn't have time to check the *Constitution* this morning. Did the fracas at the Ball Park make the front page or the sports page?"

"Neither so far." He sipped at his coffee. "I really can't see you at the Ball Park."

"I can't see myself there either," she said. "Never again."

"I didn't know you and Vince were a thing … is that how they say it now?"

"We're not. A drink after work became half a dozen or so and I lost count."

"Is that Vincent's technique?"

"I don't think he used any technique at all on me," she said. "It was a fun evening until the trouble with the Shooter."

"How bad was the Shooter … really?"

"A nasty little boy," Helen said. "He's got a thin layer of country boy charm over an ego that must weigh a hundred and ninety pounds."

"What should I do with him?"

She shook her head. "I wouldn't trust myself to say."

"He got you angry, huh?"

"Very angry."

"I'd like for you to be in the office when I talk to him. If you don't mind."

"I don't mind," she said.

The phone rang in the outer office, at her desk. "That's probably the Shooter now." She looked at the cups and hesitated.

"I'll put them away," he said.

It was the security guard from downstairs. Helen told him to send the Shooter up. He stepped out of the elevator, confident, smiling, ready to conquer the world. And then he saw Helen waiting for him and the smile left his face. He stammered a good morning, followed her through the maze of halls and stopped at the doorway to the inner office.

"Mr. Simpson to see you, Mr. Wardlaw."

"Come in, Eddie." He rounded the desk and put out his hand to the Shooter. After a brief handshake he turned to Helen. "Miss Morris, I'd like for you to stay and make notes of this meeting."

When she returned from her desk with a pencil and a note pad, they were seated. She took the other chair and flipped her pad open to a blank page.

"I don't think we need to make notes of the early part of our conversation," Wardlaw said. "I'll tell you when I want you to begin."

"Yes, sir."

Wardlaw turned to the Shooter. "Eddie, you seem to have a good many problems lately. Not on the basketball court but almost everywhere else."

"I don't think I hit that old man," the Shooter said, "no matter what Vince Gorman said. I could have hit a phone pole or a parked car."

Helen jerked her head up and looked at David. He met her gaze without blinking.

"It wasn't any of his business," the Shooter added.

"Is that why you started that trouble last night? Because you thought he'd come to me with the story about the hit-and-run?"

"You could say that," the Shooter said.

"You're wrong," Wardlaw said. "The story came from a watch captain at the Atlanta Police Department, a Noah French." Briefly, like a carpenter driving nails, Wardlaw recounted the circumstances that led to a suspicion that the Shooter was involved in the hit-and-run. At the end, he lifted the telephone receiver and asked, "Would you like for me to call Mr. French and have him confirm this?"

"No," the Shooter said. The bluster was gone. "Maybe I did it, but I don't remember doing it."

"That might be a defense. It might not be. I'd have to check it with a lawyer, but I think drunk driving and hit-and-run might carry with it some time in prison."

"You'd let that happen?"

"Being a basketball player doesn't give you the right to run over people and leave them in the road. Or the right to attack people in a restaurant."

"I'm sorry about what I did to Mr. Gorman," the Shooter said.

"That's between you and Mr. Gorman. If you have any apologies, you'd better make them directly to him. I'd guess that he might have enough witnesses to bring assault and battery charges ... and there might even be a damage suit for half a million or so."

"But he works for you," the Shooter said, "and he wouldn't ..."

"I have no control over people who work for me when it comes to their civil rights. Mr. Gorman will do what he wants to do."

It was far from warm in the office but the sweat was pouring from the Shooter's face. He dabbed at it with a handkerchief. Helen watched this and watched Wardlaw. As if he felt her eyes on him, he turned to her.

"Miss Morris, I think you can take a letter now."

"Yes, sir."

"Today's date and address it to Mr. Edward Simpson, ... his local address from the files."

"Yes, sir."

"Dear Eddie: This will inform you that as of this date you have been placed on probation. Your actions of the last two days have led me to question the value of your services. It may be that you are more of a liability to Wardlaw Properties than an asset. For the next year, the term of the probation, you will conduct yourself as a model citizen and a responsible person. Any questionable conduct will result in your suspension without pay under the terms of Article ..." He broke off and looked over at Helen. "Check Mr. Simpson's contract and find the proper Article, the morals one."

"Yes, sir."

"In that event the term of the suspension would be for one, two or five years depending upon the seriousness of the conduct." He looked at Helen. "The usual close. And I'd like three copies. One for Mr. Simpson, one for Coach Thorn and one for the file."

Wardlaw stood up and held out his hand. "It was nice of you to drop by, Eddie. Miss Morris will see you to the elevator."

The Shooter looked stunned. He mumbled a goodbye and started for the door.

"Eddie."

The Shooter turned.

"Ab Slaton will be put on waivers as soon as I can reach Coach Thorn."

⚜ ⚜ ⚜

Helen stopped by her desk long enough to lock the pad away and drop the pencil in the desk holder. She stopped in the doorway. "So that was what yesterday was about?"

Wardlaw nodded. "You're not satisfied?"

"Yesterday you asked me what a wino's life was worth? Does that mean that the wino? ..."

Wardlaw shook his head. "He's holding his own and he's getting the best available treatment."

"The Shooter's not worth it," she said.

"Vince didn't think so either. He won't deal with the Shooter anymore, even if he has to resign."

"Vince said that?"

"Of course, I didn't ask for his resignation."

She moved from the doorway, walking in until she was almost across the desk from him. "Since it's a Saturday and I'm not supposed to be here, maybe I can ask you a question. Why is the Shooter worth this?"

"He's not, but the timing is bad."

"The Convention Center?" she asked.

"Yes."

She waited, but when he didn't try to explain it further, she turned away from the desk. "You don't need the letter typed today, do you? Will Monday be soon enough?"

"Yes."

"Then I think I'll take the rest of the weekend off," she said.

He nodded, "Good-bye, Helen."

She said good-bye and went out, closing the door to the office behind her.

It was eight o'clock by his watch, tilted toward him on the night stand, when Vince awoke. He spent a minute listening, but there was no sound of movement in the apartment. That wasn't like her, not if he knew her at all. She'd be up and moving around if she was in the apartment. He pushed the covers aside and sat up slowly. The waves of pain stopped him a couple of times, but he knew he'd have to tough it out or spend the whole weekend in bed. He forced it, and the sweat popped out on his forehead and ran down his sides. On his feet, shaky and dizzy, he made his way to the hallway and listened with the door open. Still nothing. He worked his way down the hall to the other bedroom. The door was open. The bed was made and the faint scent of perfume and talcum remained in the air.

Gone. Had to be there to help out David Emmett Wardlaw. Couldn't take a Saturday off. Not her. Had to be there just in case the great man needed her.

Steadier now, he crossed the living room and entered the kitchen. Neat, very neat. A juice glass and a cup in the sink. And on the table in the breakfast nook, a note leaning against the sugar dish.

Vince—

Juice in the refrigerator. Instant coffee on the shelf to the left of the stove. Eggs and bacon if you can cook. Alka Seltzer in my bathroom if that's what you need. Should be back by noon.

Helen

He found the grapefruit juice and poured himself a large glass. After one sip he added sugar. Then he eased himself down into a chair in the breakfast nook and sipped the juice.

So much, he thought, for my morning-after with the virgin queen.

He was on a second cup of coffee and trying to decide if he wanted to try to cook the bacon and eggs when he heard the downstairs door open and close. This was followed by footsteps on the staircase.

Oh, shit, caught in my underwear.

He considered getting to his feet and trying to make a run for the bedroom. He was sensible enough to know that he wouldn't make it. And he was going to look pretty silly getting caught sprinting across the living room. Instead, he leaned back and raised his cup.

She must have looked into the bedroom first. It seemed some minutes passed before he heard her approaching the kitchen door. He waited until he saw the door pushed inward. Then he said, "Prepare to be shocked. I'm in my underwear."

"The puce ones?" The door stopped, cracked only a couple of inches.

"No," he said. "They're plain gray, puce without the blood this morning."

"I'll try to stomach it." She gave the door another shove and walked in.

"Don't mind if I don't stand up," he said.

"Are you shy?" Helen said. "That'll be a new one for the powder room."

"You won't tell," Vince said. "It'll ruin your reputation as the virgin queen."

"Have you had breakfast?"

"Not yet," he said. "The thought of my own cooking ..."

"Bacon and eggs?" At his nod, she placed a skillet on the stove and got out a carton of eggs and a package of bacon. As she laid the strips of bacon in the skillet, she asked, "Do they call me that?"

"The virgin queen? No, I call you that."

"It's colorful," Helen said, "but not too accurate. I was married once. Remember?"

"I was married once myself," Vince said.

"I didn't know that." Helen turned and looked at him.

"I don't put it on the employment forms. It's that long ago. When I was eighteen, I fell in love with the most beautiful rear end I'd ever seen. I met it on the beach ... Virginia Beach. I married it. After one year, I found out the rear end couldn't sing grand opera or discuss Russian novels."

"So, neither of us is," she said.

"You are. Some women grow the hymen back. How long's it been since the divorce?"

"None of your business," she said.

"That's long enough," he said. He eased back his chair. "I'm going to try to make it to the bedroom and put on my pants. Don't watch unless you really want to." He held onto the table and pulled himself out of the chair. The table creaked but held.

As he stepped away from the table, she turned and gave him a slow, long look. Then she smiled. "I don't see anything very frightening. Hairy legs and toenails that need clipping."

"You're not looking in the right place," he said. He made his slow, painful turn and stiff-armed the door. Before he released it she called him.

"How do you want your eggs?"

"Scrambled and running."

When he returned to the kitchen a few minutes later, he was sweating and shaking from the effort. He had on his trousers and his shirt and he'd managed his socks, but he'd had to let the buckles on his shoes go. He slumped into his chair and waited while she broke two eggs into a bowl and beat them slightly. For the second time in two days, he could feel the clammy underwear.

"This is two days in a row I've awakened in strange beds, without a fresh change of linen."

"You ought to carry a spare set with you." She tipped the bowl and poured the beaten eggs into the skillet. "I know whose bed you awoke in this morning. Whose bed was it yesterday?"

"A traveling lady salesman," he said.

"Really?" She laughed. Then, after stirring the eggs around in the skillet for a few seconds, she scooped them into a plate with bacon and brought the plate to the table. "Is it true what they say about traveling salesladies?"

"Every bit of it."

She brought a pot of water to the table and made a refill for him and a cup for herself. She sat down across the table from him. Grinning, she reached over to the plate and picked a slice of bacon from it. "Did you like her?"

"I don't think so. In the bar that night she looked a lot better than she did in bed." He took a sip of coffee. "But, of course, every man is expected to do his duty."

"That's an awful thought."

"Isn't it, though?" he said.

"Do men think that way?"

"Some," he said.

"I couldn't stand it if any man felt that way about me, as though I were some disagreeable job like taking the garbage out."

"There's a difference," he said. "You wouldn't be."

"I can't believe anything you say."

"That's a beginning. If I stay here and let you nurse me, you'll fall in love with me—for all my bad qualities and my one or two good ones."

"I know some of your bad qualities," she said. "What are the good ones?"

"Things a virgin might not be interested in."

"Oh, those. I've heard about those."

"And you're not intrigued at all?" he asked.

"Not a bit," she said, smiling.

"You're lying in your teeth."

The smile remained, but it was shaky. "I'm not."

He finished the scrambled eggs. He picked up the last slice of bacon and ate it slowly. "I think I'd better leave. I've got things to do, but I thought I'd ruin your day before I leave. You're a beautiful woman and you're going to waste. And you damn well know it. If Wardlaw loved you, he'd build a building on you or a shopping mall. Me? I don't build buildings, so I'd be satisfied to curl your toenails and give you a strawberry rash all over."

"Don't talk to me that way," she said.

"It's a waste."

"Worry about your own waste," she said, angrily.

"I am and you're part of it." He gripped the table edge and pulled himself up. "Don't save all that goody for David. He's dead and full of old ashes."

He reached the door before she stopped him. "I was at the office this morning when he had his meeting with the Shooter."

"And?" He caught the door frame and turned.

"You didn't tell me about the old wino out on Peachtree Road."

"Nobody knows what an old wino was doing in that part of town. It's like the riddle at the top of the Hemingway story. What was the leopard doing on the top of that mountain?"

"You were helping David cover for the Shooter."

"I like the way you say *were*. It was my job. Did you think I spent my time taking school kids around on tours?"

"No."

"I have a certain talent, and David was the only one to recognize it. I'm ruthless and sly and sneaky and dishonest. And David tells me to do things but not to tell him how I did it."

"But you said you'd quit before you'd do anymore covering for the Shooter?"

"It came on me suddenly yesterday. I was squatting and running a steam hose under the Shooter's XKE to wash away any blood or tissue that might be under there and it came on me that this wasn't the way I'd planned to spend my life."

She went pale and took a choking swallow or two. "You did that?"

"It's no worse than a mother cleaning a baby's bottom." He stepped through the doorway and let it close behind him. Back in the bedroom he put on his tie and struggled to notch the buckles on his shoes. Going back toward the living room he put on his suit coat and got his topcoat from the closet. He dropped the topcoat over the back of a chair and dialed a cab. When he looked up, she was standing nearby.

"Where are you off to now?"

"To look for new sewers to play in," he said.

"Damn you, Vince."

"What does that mean?"

"You turn it all back on yourself," she said.

"Don't you know false modesty when you hear it?" he said. He put his topcoat over his arm and started down the stairs.

"I liked part of the evening," she called after him.

"Of course, you did," he said. He went outside and looked at the cold February morning street. A few minutes later the cab came for him.

Vince paid off the cab and walked over to the entrance to the garage.

Mason looked up from his morning paper, the sports page, and pushed back his chair. "Morning," he said, dropping the newspaper on the desk and standing up.

"Is it done?"

Mason nodded. "Had a man who worked half the night. Now it looks like nothing ever happened to it."

"I appreciate the service," Vince said.

"We like your business," Mason said. "It's back here."

Vince followed him through the office and back into the open work area. It smelled of oil and grease and metal filings and paint. Mason stopped at one of the stalls. "There she is."

Vince took his time looking the blue XKE over. It was good work. The fender looked as good as new, and the headlight had been set in well. "What's the damage?" He reached into his pocket and brought out his fold of cash.

"Odd thing," Mason said. "Usually I just read the sports page. Yesterday, I bought myself an afternoon paper and read the front section."

"I'm in a bit of a hurry," Vince said.

"I happened on one thing. Seems a wino got hurt in a hit-and-run out on Peachtree."

"Winos ought to drink less wine," Vince said. He looked into Mason's fish eyes and peeled off four fifties. He handed them to Mason and Mason fanned them out and shook his head.

"I was thinking more about five hundred," Mason said.

"It won't hurt you to think anything you like," Vince said.

"I'm not joking," Mason said.

"Neither am I."

"The police might be interested."

"That cuts both ways," Vince said. "You ever wonder why I picked you out to do this kind of work?"

"I do good work," Mason said.

"So do a lot of other people. No, I checked you out. Maybe you'd like a copy of that report sometime. It seems you also work over hot cars, give them new identities and ship them north."

"I don't believe you've got any such—"

"I can send you a copy by messenger within the hour," Vince said.

Mason looked down at the four fifties. He pushed the bills together and handed them to Vincent. "I guess it's a standoff then."

Vince handed the bills back to Mason. "I pay slightly dishonest wages, but I don't pay blackmail."

Mason stood beside the ramp and watched Vince drive the XKE out into the street. Vince nodded and waved, but Mason didn't wave back.

Vince dropped the keys, along with a five, into the doorman's hand. "I don't feel like making the trip. Bring back my car keys."

Five minutes later, Vince drove his Ford away from the Madrid Apartments parking lot. There was a scent of perfume in it.

That boy's been turning my car into a whorehouse, he said to himself. Then he drove to the underground parking lot and rode the elevator up to David Wardlaw's office.

CHAPTER NINE

Ethel Ann wasn't in bed with him when he awoke and Harley thought, Oh, God, not again, please don't be out at another one of those shopping centers selling cakes and cookies. If the hospitals and the kindergartens got her attention during the week, the cakes and cookies sold for some good cause always seemed to ruin his Saturdays.

But the noise that he'd thought was the wind in the trees outside the bedroom or an early morning rain wasn't either. It was the sound of the shower running in the bathroom. He rolled out of bed quickly, threw his pajama top across the bed and stepped out of the bottoms. He opened the door to the bathroom quietly and eased in. The air was fogged with steam and he could smell the lemon soap she used. He had the shower stall door open and was in the shower with her before she had any warning.

"What are you doing in here?"

"It ought to be obvious," he said, locking his arms around her waist and pulling her against him.

She looked down at him. "It is obvious."

He took the cake of soap from her hand. "And I need a shower too."

It was a brief shower for Harley and they didn't take a long time drying off. There were still drops and damp spots on both of them when they fell across the bed, laughing and clutching at each other.

"What brought this on?" she asked.

"You know," he said, "I think I smell as good as a lemon."

"What brought this on?" she insisted.

"This?" He looked down where she was holding him.

"No, all this passion."

"If this isn't passion, I don't know what it is." He nuzzled at her, feeling the damp places where the shower cap hadn't completely covered her hair. "I guess it was seeing my chance to catch you on a Saturday when you weren't out selling Girl Scout cookies." He laughed. "Next time wear your Girl Scout uniform. It turns me on."

"That bothers you, all the social work?"

"Talk later," he said. "This just ain't the time."

Harley finished his breakfast and was considering a third cup of coffee when the door bell rang.

"Who would that be?" Ethel Ann asked.

"Somebody who doesn't like us." He stood up and pulled his robe closed. "I'd better answer it. You're too naked."

"I'll dress." They went into the living room together and he waited until she was up the stairs and out of sight before he opened the front door.

Hap Seaver stood in the doorway. "Can I come in, Harley?"

"What's wrong? Did you forget to pay your phone bill this month?" He motioned Hap inside and closed the door after him.

Hap looked around. "Is Ethel Ann here?"

"Where the hell else would she be this time of day?" He choked off the rest of what he wanted to say. "She's upstairs dressing."

"We need to talk in private."

Harley nodded in the direction of the kitchen. "Help yourself to a cup of coffee. I'll put on some slacks and a shirt." He saw Hap through the door into the kitchen and went up to the bedroom.

"It's Hap," he told Ethel Ann. "He wants to talk in private."
He dressed in a pair of tan cotton pants and a t-shirt.

"I'll do the grocery shopping then."

"Need any cash?"

"I'll cash a check. It's amazing how they even cash checks for blacks when the husband is vice president of a bank."

"Isn't it, though?" He slipped his bare feet into a pair of loafers. "See you when you get back."

Down in the kitchen, he poured himself half a cup of coffee and sat down across the table from Hap. "All right, it's private now. Ethel Ann's going off to shop."

"You threw shit in the soup last night."

"It wasn't my soup."

"You made me look bad."

"That might have been what I had in mind," Harley said.

"At least you could have waited until I got there."

Harley shook his head. "I might have if that flock of whores hadn't shown up."

"I told them not to do that."

"I didn't like the way they were thinking. He's black and we know he'd just love to put his black thing in some of that white meat."

"It was a mistake," Hap said, "and they know it now."

"The whole damned thing was a mistake."

"It could still work."

"Not anymore. What I don't understand is how you had brass enough to involve me. What gave you the right to pick me as somebody who'd sell out?"

"I thought you could use the ..." Hap broke off and shook his head. "The people who get the Convention Center are going to have a lot of clout around this town. And the members of the committee who make it possible are going to have some strong friends."

"And some enemies," Harley said.

"No matter how you vote, you're going to have enemies, so it's a damn sight better to pick the strongest friends you can find."

"I'll stay where I am," Harley said.

"It won't surprise you then to find out you're the only vote the Boulevard site has left."

"Not a bit."

Hap pushed back his chair and stood up. "You surprise me, Harley. I came over here thinking I'd have to duck punches and, instead, you're as calm as can be."

"This might hurt your feelings, Hap, but I never really expected much of you. It was just a matter of time."

"No hard feelings?" Hap held out his hand.

"Lots of hard feelings." But he stood up and gave Hap's hand a brief squeeze.

At the front door Hap said, "See you," and went out.

"This afternoon." Harley closed the door behind him.

A few minutes later, Harley was scraping the dishes and stacking them in the dishwasher when the phone rang. He took the call at the kitchen phone.

"Mr. Brisker, this is David Wardlaw."

Harley looked for a towel, and when he couldn't find one close by, he dried his hands on his pants. "I'm glad you called. Hap Seaver just dropped by. It was a last minute move to see if I'd go with the group."

"I thought they might."

"I'm the only vote left for the Boulevard site."

"I can't think of anybody I'd rather have with me," Wardlaw said. "But it's not over. We're going to shake the tree and see if we can't find an apple or two that'll fall. That's why I called. I want you to leave this to me. Don't contact anyone. Be evasive if they contact you."

"Fine with me," Harley said.

Before he closed out the call, Wardlaw gave him a private unlisted number where he could be reached. Harley wrote it down on the memo pad Ethel Ann kept by the phone.

He finished with the dishes and then, to escape the noise of the dishwasher, he went back upstairs and stretched out on the bed. It smelled of lemon soap.

The Shooter had breakfast at a café on Ponce de Leon after he'd taken the XKE out for a test run. It was a light breakfast—one egg, dry toast and hot tea. When he finished, he walked a few blocks to settle the breakfast. The walk lasted about ten minutes. It was cold and windy out on the street so he wasn't bothered or recognized.

At the end of the walk, he drove down Ponce de Leon and turned right onto Boulevard. He followed Boulevard until he reached the Dome. He parked in the player parking lot and the guard at the entrance waved him in. After he dressed in his workout clothes, he stretched out on the trainer's table for ten minutes or so. He was the first to arrive for the morning workout. Not even the equipment man or the trainer had arrived yet.

At 10:30, he left the locker room and followed the tunnel out to the court. The basketball caddy was on the floor, and he scooped out a ball and began walking the circle, from baseline to baseline, shooting from about twenty feet out. The shots were falling, either way he threw them up—either the high, soft jumpers or the low, flat shots with a clothesline trajectory. When he completed one circle, he moved out another ten feet and moved from baseline to baseline once more. Here, at thirty feet or so, the shots weren't falling as well, but he was still hitting better than seven out of ten. At the end of this circle of shots, he moved to the other end of the court and played around with a hook shot he never used in a game and never would. It wasn't falling, and he was about to give it up, when the first of the Cracker players came in. They were bitching like they usually did about the morning workout on the day of a game. The morning workout was something Bill Sharman had started with the Lakers, and now other teams were trying it. Sharman believed that the workouts got the players thinking basketball and sharpened their edge. Coach Thorn was willing to try anything. It had worked with the Lakers and it might work with the Crackers.

The Shooter didn't mind the morning workouts. If they hadn't been scheduled, he'd have had to find a backboard and a hoop on his own. After the Friday layoff, he needed the shooting to steady his hand and keep his eyes sharp.

At the other end of the court, it was all grab-ass and horseplay. Big Ed Brewster was in the center of it, dribbling around and clowning. He was jabbering away, and now and then the Shooter could hear his name used but he couldn't hear enough to know what was being said. Big Ed was as black as the ace of spades and he'd been the team leader and the high scorer on the team before it moved to Atlanta. With the arrival of the Shooter, the offensive set-up had changed, from one built around the center and the forwards to one centered around the guards. With this change, Big Ed had become sullen and bad-tempered with the Shooter. With the old members of the team he was loose and easy, joking and laughing. With the Shooter around, he looked like he'd just eaten something that hadn't agreed with him.

One of the reserves, a six-seven white forward from St. Josephs, loped down the court and joined the Shooter.

"Want me to front you?" Ernie Turner asked.

"Sure." For the next few minutes Ernie Turner tried to guard the Shooter. Turner was slow and awkward and the Shooter worked him over pretty well, faking him, dribbling around him and putting his shots up.

"Shooter," Ernie huffed at him, "you're too much."

When Ernie begged off and walked down the court to look for a towel, the Shooter turned and found Ab Slaton standing at mid-court, dribbling a basketball while standing in one spot. Ab grinned at him and dribbled over to him, lofting a high shot that missed the backboard and all.

"How'd it go, Shooter?"

The Shooter didn't know how to tell him. It wasn't going to be easy whatever way he handled it. "I'm on probation for a year. Any trouble and I'm out."

"He say anything about me?"

"I tried my best for you," the Shooter said.

"What does that mean?"

"He's mad at me and he's mad at you too."

"All I did was try to help you," Ab said.

"I did my best." The Shooter knew how lame that sounded.

"What'd he say?"

"He said he was putting you on waivers."

Ab was holding a basketball. Now he whirled around and drop-kicked it into the stands. "Thanks a lot, Shooter."

"Ab … I did …"

"Sure, you did." Ab turned and walked slowly to the other end of the court.

The Shooter remained alone at the basket. No one joined him, and the few times he looked at the other end of the court, Ab Slaton was sitting at the players bench, stretched out, his head back.

When Coach Thorn came out of the tunnel, over the thunk of basketballs, the Shooter heard him call Ab Slaton over to him. The Shooter watched Ab walk over to the coach. Before they turned to go back up the tunnel, Ab looked down the court toward the Shooter. All the Shooter could do was shake his head.

Forty minutes later, when the Shooter left the court and went into the locker room, he passed Ab Slaton's locker. The locker was empty except for a damp towel and a pair of dirty white socks.

❧ ❧ ❧

Jim Sims came to the door of room 21 and looked out at Vince with red, bleary eyes. He was dressed in jockey shorts and a wrinkled shirt he'd probably picked up on the way to the door. "What you want?"

"To talk to you. I'm Vince Gorman. I'm from David Wardlaw."

"Oh." He took a deep breath and struggled to focus his eyes. "From Mr. Wardlaw, huh?"

"That's right."

"Could you? ..." Sims turned and looked past the living room toward the bedroom. "Could you go somewhere and have a cup of coffee and come back in fifteen minutes? I need to get ... cleaned up."

"Sure." Vince backed away and Sims closed the door.

Vince went down to his car and drove it into a parking space near the stairs that led down from the second-floor landing. Five minutes passed, and then the door to room 21 opened and a blonde with a beehive hairdo came out and walked down the stairs toward him. Vince waited until she was a step or two away, just about to pass. He rolled down the window and said, "Hey, honey."

She stopped and then came over and looked into the car. "I don't know you, do I?"

Up close he could smell her morning breath. It was a combination of whiskey and God-knows-what-else she'd put in it the night before Sims hadn't even given her time to borrow his mouthwash before he threw her out.

"You're supposed to," he said. "I was invited to the party last night. At the last minute I couldn't make it."

Her face registered the bruised and swollen jaw. "You got hurt, huh?"

He nodded. "And seeing you I'm sorry as hell."

"That's nice."

"I'd like a rematch sometime," he said.

"It could be arranged."

He leaned away from her and punched open the glove compartment. He got out a pad and handed it to her, along with a pen from his shirt pocket. "Name, address and phone number."

She hesitated. "You sure you were invited?"

"Sure. I was just up to see Jim Sims. He got shy about you, so I'm giving him a few minutes before I go up to talk the business we were supposed to talk last night."

That convinced her. She wrote for a few moments on the pad and handed the pad and pen to him. *Angela Marshall, room 5,* and a phone number.

"You live here in the motel?"

"Sure. And the number there is the switchboard."

"I might come by and visit you in a while," he said.

"Don't I ever get any sleep?" But it wasn't really a protest.

"With Sims and Johnson around last night you got some sleep."

"An hour or two," she said. She frowned. "You look like you've been in a fight."

"My cat scratched me," Vince said.

She laughed. "We haven't talked about money. I'm expensive."

"I figured that."

"We're talking about five-oh," she said.

"Reasonable at any price."

"Give me time for a bath."

"I've always thought water was sexy. How about you?"

She winked and walked away. He turned and watched her through the rear window as she crossed the U-shaped parking area. Her room was on the ground level, and he made a mental note of the location. Then he tore off the top sheet from the pad and placed the sheet in his pocket. He waited another ten minutes by his watch and when he knocked at room 21. This time Jim Sims opened the door dressed in slacks and a clean tie and shirt.

Sims waved him into the room. "All I've got is instant."

"Fine with me." Vince dropped his topcoat over the back of a chair and sat down on the sofa. He lit a cigarette and looked around. Sims had used part of his fifteen minutes to straighten up the room.

"Odd you'd come by this morning." Sims placed a plastic cup of coffee on the table in front of Vince. "I guess Harley Brisker got in touch with you."

"Not with me, but we heard from him."

"Of course," Sims said, "Harley left so early I'm not even certain he understood what we were talking about."

"I think he understood enough."

"I don't think so. I had the feeling Harley thought we were setting up some kind of combine that could guarantee the Convention Center site to the highest bidder."

"I've got plenty of time," Vince said. "You can explain it to me and I'll explain it to Harley."

"It wasn't like that at all. It was more a matter of making sure the committee did make a choice. With all these factions pulling against each other there's a chance we might not make any decision at all this year."

"And you don't want that?"

"Of course not. And neither does the Governor. You know how much income the city and the state are missing out on because they don't have a building that can hold a really large convention? Millions. Why, with the Convention Center built, we could probably make a bid for the Democratic and Republican conventions in 1980. They would put the city and the state on the map."

"All this Chamber of Commerce shit aside," Vince said, "how were you going to decide which site to vote for?"

"I don't know."

"It's getting late. The meeting's hours away."

"There's still time," Jim Sims said.

"I'm going to be blunt. What do you want?"

"The three of us? ..."

"No," Vince said. "What do you want?"

"I'm not sure I want anything."

"It's wonderful meeting a public servant like you." Vince drained off the coffee and slammed the plastic cup down on the coffee table. "I think I made the trip for nothing."

"I don't understand why you came to see me."

Vince stood up and looked over at his topcoat. "I came to ask what you wanted. I guess I'll take your word you don't want anything."

"I can't bargain with you without talking to Senator Johnson and ..." Sims stopped.

"Hap Seaver?"

Sims lowered his eyelids and nodded.

"We won't deal with Seaver. He's out. And all Senator Johnson wants is money. That's easy." Vince fixed him with a hard, appraising eye. "I thought you had more imagination than that."

"Such as."

"I'm not in the business of making guesses."

"The way you talk, I think you've already made a guess."

Vince let the impatience flare out for an instant. "Come on, Sims, you act like you've still got your cherry. I might be wasting your time, but you're sure as hell wasting mine."

"Is Lester going to run?"

Vince put his head back and laughed. He sat down again. "That's more like it. I think Lester will run again, but the word is he's lost ground. So, the primary might be a dog-and-cat fight. The man who gets an early start and has the money and the organization behind him is going to stand a good chance of taking a four-year lease on the Governor's mansion."

"I'm not well enough known."

"Look at Sam Nunn. He had an ice cube's chance in hell, but now he's Senator Sam Nunn and he's up in Washington. Money and organization, that's all it takes."

"Will Wardlaw make me a promise?"

Vince nodded. "Of course, when he gets the Convention Center on the Boulevard site, he'll have to stay in the background. He wouldn't want anybody to think his support was a bribe. After you win the primary, the support will be open. Like any good Democrat, he'll back the party's choice."

"Is his word good?"

"Like a mother's love," Vince said.

"I'll have to think about it."

Vince got up and struggled into his topcoat. The ribs hurt when he moved his arms. "I'll call you at noon."

"I'd rather speak to Mr. Wardlaw."

"That can be arranged."

"Are you going to talk to Senator Johnson?"

"I'm not sure." Vince buttoned his topcoat. "Not if I can help it."

"What am I going to tell Johnson?"

Vince cracked the door and felt the cold wind after the oppressive heat in the room. "You'll think of something."

"You weren't kidding, were you?" Angela had taken the beehive wig off and he could see that her real hair was cut short and a kind of dirty blonde. She had on a white terrycloth robe that ran down to just an inch or so below her crotch. Behind her, in the bathroom, he could hear water running. "Come on in."

"Thanks." He followed her in and saw that the bed was still made from the day before.

"I'm going to take my bath now."

"Go ahead."

"It's a big bathtub," she said.

"I'll watch. I just had a bath."

She gave him a hard look. "You're not strange, are you?"

"Straight," he said. "No kinks in me at all."

"I've had a hard night. I don't think I could stand a kinky one right now."

"Nothing to worry about with me," he said. He dropped his topcoat on the bed and followed her into the bathroom. He stood in the doorway and watched as she made an exaggerated, dancer-like bend to turn off the water. It was a clean shot up her crotch. She straightened up and winked at him. The robe fell from her shoulders and she slipped it off and tossed it to him. He got his good look at her then. Her pubic hair had been cut and shaped into the design of a heart.

"Like it?" she asked.

"I've never seen anything like it."

"I read somewhere... it might have been in some women's magazine... that the jet set girls were wearing it like this."

"The rest of it's pretty remarkable too," he said.

"I think so too, but I get a kick out of hearing men say it." She lifted her hands and pressed the hard, apple-sized breasts until the nipples firmed up and pointed at him. "I think I'm getting to you."

"I think you are too."

"Now I can take my bath." She turned away from him and stepped into the tub.

Vince walked over and sat down on the john seat.

"I'll make it a fast bath," she said.

"Take your time. Get loose."

"Loose?" She laughed.

"Maybe I should have said relaxed." He laughed with her. "That must have been some party I missed last night."

Angela twisted her mouth. "It was downright godawful."

"What was the problem? Sims seems ordinary enough."

"It wasn't Sims," she said.

"It must have been Johnson then."

"A big fat guy from the country?"

"That's the one," Vince said.

"All he wanted all night was head."

"I thought girls didn't mind that."

"They don't, unless the john gets rough," Angela said.

"And Johnson did?"

"He'd liked to have choked Mary Beth to death. And that's not all. He bit her titty so hard the teeth marks show."

"That must have hurt," he said.

"It's not just that. Mary Beth's going to be out of work for a few days. Until the marks go away. Nobody wants to pay five-oh for somebody who looks chewed on."

"I can see that." He shook out a cigarette and lit it. "Was there a black guy there?"

He could sense that she didn't want to answer him. It was still the South, even though Atlanta was often spoken of as a part of the New South. "One was there when we first went in, but he looked afraid and he left before the party started."

Vince smiled. "I think that was Harley. He's so straight, he still loves his wife."

"Another black guy came later, but I didn't have anything to do with him. I think his name was Happy or something like that."

"Hap," Vince said.

"That's it."

"He enjoy the party?"

"Not much," she said. "He couldn't keep it up."

"Poor old Hap." The easy part was over. Now it was time to shift ground. "They talk any business while you were around?"

"I'm beginning to wonder about you."

"What about me?"

"You're asking a lot of questions," she said.

"I'm in the middle of this thing with them. I want to make sure they're not trying to double-cross me."

"They talked about some conventions or something like that. It didn't make much sense to me."

"They mention any special part of town? Boulevard? Whitehall? The Civic Center?"

She shook her head. "You've got to realize the girls and I weren't there to talk politics or anything like that."

"Can I use your phone?"

"It's by the bed," she said.

He sat on the edge of the bed and dialed David Wardlaw's private office number. Briefly he covered his conversation with Jim Sims. "I think the hook's in him."

"I thought it might work that way," Wardlaw said. "What now?"

"I think I'd better buy us a Senator."

"Johnson?"

"I'll see what his hide's worth."

When he returned to the bathroom, Angela was out of the tub, toweling off. As soon as he crossed the doorway, he began shaking his head sadly. "The mistake I made was checking in with my boss. Business just came up." He reached in his pocket and peeled off a couple of twenties. "How about a rain check?"

She took the twenties and put them on the john seat. "I was just getting to like you."

"Hold the thought. I'll be back as soon as I can get free."

"Call first, huh?"

Senator Johnson was the only member of the General Assembly Vince knew of who lived in a boarding house. It was a four-story wood-frame house far out Ponce de Leon. Parked out front, looking up at the wide porch with the dozen or so rockers, Vince decided that Senator Johnson was probably the only member of the General Assembly who was saving money on his *per diem*.

There was an old man, bundled up and with clouds of condensation billowing around his head, seated in one of the rockers.

He was smoking a twisted, lumpy roll-your-own he'd made from Prince Albert or Bugler. The grains of spilled tobacco peppered his coat front, and there were dark specks of burn marks on the coat that went back through the months if not the years.

"Senator Johnson in?" Vince asked.

"Might be," the old man said, "but he didn't come down to breakfast. Missed a good breakfast too."

"Which room is his?"

"The second floor, last room at the back on the right."

Vince thanked him and went inside. It was eighty or so inside the house, and to make it worse Vince could smell what they'd had for supper the night before. The scent of fried fish and boiled cabbage seemed to be layered on the walls with a paint brush.

He found the door and knocked.

"I don't want breakfast," Johnson grumbled at him from beyond the door.

"This isn't about breakfast."

"Who are you?"

"I don't like talking business in hallways," Vince said.

"Just a minute."

After a wait of a minute or so, the bolt snicked and the door opened a few inches. Senator Johnson looked out at him. Vince could see he was wearing the bottom half of a pair of long underwear and the top of a ragged blue pajama suit. "Who are you?"

"I'm from Mr. Wardlaw."

Johnson swung the door open. "Come on in."

Vince stepped in and Johnson closed the door behind him. It was a dark old room, drafty, with a high ceiling. An iron bedstead, painted dark green, filled most of the room. To the right there was a dresser with a cracked mirror and to the left a window with an iron steam radiator below it. The one chair in the room was piled high with clothing. Johnson moved ahead of Vince and scooped up the wads of clothing and tossed them on the bed.

"Sit down, Mr.? ..."

"Gorman," Vince said.

"I don't think I've heard of you."

"You know anybody else who works for David Wardlaw?"

"I guess not."

"Then there's no reason you should have heard of me."

Johnson turned and got a pair of pants from the clothing he'd just tossed onto the bed. "You want to see me for any reason?"

"Harley Brisker had a few words with us."

"I knew we couldn't trust that nigger. I told Sims, but he wouldn't listen to me."

"We trust him," Vince said.

"You do?" He brushed some lint from one leg of the pants. "I guess you paid enough for his black ass then."

"We haven't paid him anything."

"That's what you say." Johnson stood up and stepped into the pants and pulled them up over the long john bottoms. He closed the zipper and sat down on the edge of the bed. "I never knew one you couldn't buy for a few dollars."

"Times change."

"You come all the way over here to talk about Harley Brisker?"

"Partly," Vince said.

"We've talked that nigger down to the nub. You got anything else to talk about?"

"The Convention Center site?"

"You wouldn't be about to work your way around to offering me a bribe, would you?" Johnson asked.

"That's your word for it," Vince said.

"Fuck all this being careful with words. Say what you want to say."

"What's your price?" Vince asked.

"What's your offer?"

"That's not the way I bargain."

"You always get your own way?"

"Either that," Vince said, "or I go home and cry all day."

Senator Johnson reached under the bed and brought out a pair of scuffed black shoes. He dug out black ankle-length socks from the shoes and put them on, wheezing with the effort. "All right, we'll try it your way." He looked around the room. "This place is like living in a chicken yard. Your company owns some apartments, don't it?"

"Some," Vince said.

"I'd like one of those when I'm in town for Assembly session."

"That might be arranged."

"Rent-free," Johnson said.

"Of course."

"And I want fifty thousand dollars."

"Almost everybody I know would like to have fifty thousand dollars," Vince said.

"You think that's high?"

"A bit."

"I got a lot of expenses."

Vince looked around the room. "I can see you do."

"I mean, up home. I'm buying myself the whole side of a mountain."

"Buying that mountain is your problem, not ours."

"You got a figure in mind you think is fair?"

"Ten thousand," Vince said.

"You must think I come cheap."

Vince shook his head. "There's no assurance you can deliver for our site."

"I swing some weight," Johnson said. "Might be somebody'll cross over when they see how I vote."

"*Might* is nothing we pay hard cash for."

"Twenty thousand," Johnson said. "It won't buy as much of the mountain, but I'm not greedy."

"Twelve," Vince said.

"Fifteen."

"Twelve."

"When would I get it?" Johnson asked.

Vince stood up. "This evening if the vote goes the right way."

"Seven o'clock here?"

"Eight," Vince said.

The old man, it seemed, had given up because of the cold. As he went down the steps, Vince looked back and found the chair rocking by itself in the wind.

CHAPTER TEN

A few minutes after ten, Frances Wardlaw awoke in the unfamiliar atmosphere of her bedroom in the penthouse of the Mitchell Towers. It wasn't home, and it never would feel like home to her. In her own way, she understood why her father had sold the house on Paces Ferry and moved to this concrete and glass and steel tower. But, even with sympathetic understanding, she never awoke in this room, furnished as it was with taste and care, without feeling that she'd stayed overnight at a motel.

At breakfast, she horrified John by insisting that she'd eat in the kitchen so that she could talk to him while he did his morning chores. It was awkward at first, and she guessed that it was because her father kept his distance and John wasn't sure how to deal with someone who didn't. It was, in the beginning, as if he expected Wardlaw to storm into the kitchen and question the way her breakfast was served.

"Mr. Wardlaw called at ten," John said.

"To see if I was awake yet?"

"Yes, ma'am." He brought the coffee pot to the small table and refilled her cup. "He wanted me to ask you if you'd mind having lunch here today instead of eating out."

"Here's fine with me."

"He said, if you didn't mind, perhaps you'd like to plan the lunch."

"That's easy," Frances said. "Shrimp curry the way you made it last time."

"I'm not sure Mr. Wardlaw..."

"Of course he liked it," Frances said. "It was new to him, but one more time and I'm sure he'll love it as much as I do."

"If you're sure ..."

"I've been dreaming about it for more than a month."

When breakfast was finished, and he'd cleared away the table except for her coffee cup and the morning paper, he got his jacket from a hanger next to the pantry. "Miss Frances, I've got to go out for an hour or so."

"I hope it isn't because I chose the shrimp curry. If it's that ..."

"It's no trouble at all." He came to the table. "You see, the secret is that you've got to use the freshest shrimp you can find, and I need two coconuts and a mango if I can find one."

She wanted to apologize for putting him to all that trouble. It might have been better just to tell him to fix whatever he liked. Perhaps John understood her hesitation.

"To tell the truth," he said, smiling at her, "I like the curry myself. But if you fix it right, it's too much bother to fix it for myself." He winked. "It's much better to prepare it for three."

After he left, she carried the newspaper into the living room and drank a final cup of coffee and read the paper from cover to cover. Most of the names in the political and social news didn't mean anything to her. Atlanta was her home, she supposed, but it seemed so large, so unfriendly, so hard to envision all at once in her mind. She didn't have a home, and sometimes it seemed she didn't have a hometown either.

The last few minutes, Frances stood behind John and watched him prepare the sauce. The refrigerator was already filled with small dishes, each containing about half a cup of a fresh chutney, made from the freshest fruits and vegetables he could find. Her favorite was there, dates and thin slices of coconut with green ginger and lemon juice and a number of spices. But there were others she didn't know and she wasn't sure, even after she'd tasted them, whether she could say what each contained. She felt a special warmth for John, seeing how many chutneys he'd made. The last time there'd only been two fresh chutneys and one bottled one. This time she counted six. The bottled chutney was for her father, because he hadn't liked the fresh ones.

At quarter to one, while John was setting up the chafing dish in the dining room, she left him and went back to her room. She changed into a dress and high-heeled shoes. She knew her father wouldn't say anything if he'd found her in flared jeans and sweater. Not a word, but somewhere in the back of his mind, he'd probably make a mark against her, like jeans and a sweater weren't quite proper.

Her father was waiting for her in the living room. He got to his feet, smiled at her and put an arm around her. "I think you and John are conspiring against me."

"Why would you think that?"

He nodded toward the chafing dish with its blue flame burning under it. "I peeked."

"Are you sorry you let me plan lunch?"

His arm tightened around her. "Of course not." He led her toward the end of the table where the chafing dish was and the two places set. "But I have one question. What does one drink with curry?"

"Water," she said, "but I think we can break the rules and have a beer."

Oh, that first taste. That blend of beautiful and strange spices. The strange color and texture of the sauce. The odd admixture of fruits and vegetables in the chutneys. The taste buds seemed to be dancing on her tongue.

Across from her, serious and trying very hard, her father ate a large serving and followed it with a smaller second helping. As she'd predicted, he had only a forkful of each of the fresh chutneys. And, because the sauce was spicy, he drank two beers while she drank one. When they had finished, he went into the living room to wait for his coffee. She ducked into the kitchen to tell John how great it was, how wonderful, how even her father had eaten two helpings.

His wrinkled face warmed to the compliment, but he leaned toward her and said, "I think we might have it again soon, maybe once a month, on an evening when Mr. Wardlaw is having dinner out."

"I'd like that."

"We might do clams in the shell next time."

"Let's do," she said.

Seated next to her father a minute later, she saw a thin film of perspiration on his forehead. "Oh, daddy, I hope you didn't mind."

"It was ... an experience."

"Daddy, I think I'm going to give up trying to change you."

"No, don't," he said. "I know I'm probably not handling it well, but I like the fact that you believe I'm worth changing."

"Poor old pussycat," she said, leaning over and kissing him on the cheek.

"How was your morning?"

"I just loafed. I've been trying to decide if I'd make a good shop girl."

"And what do you think?"

"I'd be bored to death."

"Helen Morris might have an idea. Would you mind if I asked her?"

"Of course not," Frances said. "I like Helen."

He drained his coffee cup and stood up. "Is there anything you need?"

"I need some money. I have that wad of credit cards, but ..."

He took out his money clip. "How much?"

"Oh, thirty dollars."

He gave her two twenties. "If this will hold you until Monday, I'll have some money transferred to your checking account."

"Thank you." She kissed him good-bye and said she'd see him later. As soon as he left the apartment, she went to her bedroom and changed from the dress into flared jeans and a sweater. By

2:30, she was down on the Strip, down in the Tenth Street area. It was hippie territory, where all the street people hung out. It was obviously the place to buy an ounce of grass. And, she'd decided, no matter what her father thought or what her former college thought, she was going to buy an ounce and smoke it whenever she wanted to. It was, she decided, her right.

Even in February, the line of street people snaked from Seventh Street to Tenth and back. It was a thin line because of the cold and the wind, but the hardy ones still did the three-block walk, the walk that had built into a kind of statement, "I'm in a hurry, I'm going here, I'm going there, and I've got business."

But within minutes the ones who'd been hurrying toward Tenth Street could be seen hurrying back toward Seventh, again with the energetic, purposeful stride.

Frances left the No. 10 bus on the corner of Eighth and Peachtree and put herself into the flow. For the first circuit, she got some nods and a black or two wanted to know if she'd been well-fucked the night before and did she need it now. But no one offered her dope. On her second lap, after she'd turned around at Tenth and started back, two boys in their late teens stepped away from a phone booth next to a gift shop.

"You looking for something, chickie?"

"I might be." At his nod she followed him until they were in the shelter of the phone booth, using the booth as a windbreak. "I want an ounce of grass."

"I would too," the tall one said. He had long, fair hair and he was handsome in a gawky way.

The other boy had red hair and was missing a couple of teeth in front. A droopy mustache covered it until he smiled. "Everybody would. Right, Ringo?"

"I don't mean to waste your time," Frances said.

The tall one, Ringo, said, "You got a driver's license?"

"Yes." She reached into her purse and fished out her wallet. She flipped over the card file and held the license toward him.

"Even narcs have driver's licenses," the other one said.

"I know that," Ringo said, "but I like to look at pictures." He stared at the photo. "It's not a good likeness."

"I let my hair grow longer," she said.

"You got twenty dollars?" Ringo asked.

"Yes."

"Well, the price is twenty-five."

Frances shook her head and dropped the wallet back into her purse. "I'll look around."

On the corner of Eighth, another boy caught up with her. He was struggling to walk, one leg swinging out wide to the side. "I saw you talking to Ringo and Sundance. You want to make a buy?"

"Yes." She turned around and looked back at the phone booth. Ringo was inside making a call and Sundance was at the booth door, his head pushed inside. "Those are silly names. Do they take them seriously?"

"About as serious as they are about staying out of jail. Everybody on the Strip has two or three names."

"What's yours?"

Up close, now that she faced him, she could see that his hair looked bleached almost red, but his beard and eyebrows were coal black. "They call me Devil."

"How'd you hurt your leg?"

He shook his head. "You sure are innocent." He shook his head again. "You got a car?"

"No." She thought she'd better check the price. "How much?"

"Twenty." He nodded in the direction of Ringo or Sundance. "They try to rip you off for more?"

"Yes."

"Ringo's greedy," Devil said. "I'm not sure he's going to make it on the Strip." He took her arm. "I'm parked behind the Follies."

They walked through the parking lot. He pointed toward a mustard-colored '70 Mustang. "That's mine there."

"How far is it?"

"Not far." He unlocked the door on the driver's side and then, painfully, slowly, he got in behind the wheel and reached out to unlock the door on the passenger side. "Get in. It's five or six blocks."

After she was in, he turned the Mustang and left the parking lot at the exit next to the Radio Shack. He cut into the traffic heading out Peachtree toward Tenth. When they passed the phone booth Sundance stepped away from the phone booth and gave them the high finger.

"A bad loser," Devil said.

At the corner of Tenth, he took a right and worked his way over into the left lane. He took a left onto Piedmont and followed it to Fourteenth. After a quick left onto Fourteenth, he was heading back toward Peachtree. He slowed and Frances saw him looking up into his rear-view mirror. Satisfied, she guessed, he made a right onto a small wooden street. Frances didn't get the street name from the sign. About four houses in, he turned up a driveway next to a small wooden frame house.

"This is the place," he said. "Come on in."

She stood in the driveway and waited while he worked his way out of the seat and crabbed his way up the steps to the porch. She followed him, and when he unlocked the door and waved her in she stepped past him into the living room. It was, surprisingly, a neat and well-kept house. The walls were a deep olive color and there was a light green sofa, a coffee table and a couple of wicker easy chairs.

"It used to be you didn't have to lock your doors down here on the Strip. Now everybody is ripping off everybody else—TVs, stereos and anything else that has a resale value." He nodded toward the sofa. "Have a seat."

When he returned a couple of minutes later, he carried a tightly wrapped plastic bag in one hand and some cigarette papers and a jar with some cleaned grass in the other. He put the wrapped bag on the table in front of Frances and sat on the edge of the coffee table. "Now for a taste of the sixteenth ounce."

"What?"

"You want to try it, don't you?"

"Sure." She watched while he put a magazine on his lap and rolled a tight, hard smoke with grass from the jar. He put the joint aside and poured the flakes that had fallen on the magazine back in the jar. He tossed the magazine aside, handed her the smoke and lit it for her. She did it the right way, getting her puff and holding it down in her lungs. He took it from her, made tight-lipped sucking noises and got his hit.

When he could breathe again Devil said, "You're a big horse woman. I don't think I've seen you on the Strip before."

"I don't live down here," she said.

"You don't look like you do." He passed the joint back to her and waited while she had a hit. "You dress too well."

Frances looked around the living room. "You live here by yourself?"

"I'm between old ladies right now," he said.

The first toke hit her. It was the strongest grass she'd ever smoked. It almost knocked her backwards.

"Wicked stuff, huh?" he asked.

"Wheeeew."

"Have another."

"I pass."

"Go ahead." He held it to her mouth. She took a short hit and choked. "Don't waste it." He held the joint to her mouth again and she took another hit and held it down this time.

By the time they finished the joint she felt stunned, like she'd been knocked down and had her brain scrambled. Devil limped over to the radio and turned on some loud rock and when he came back, he was talking to her, but it didn't make much sense.

The next thing she knew he was seated on the sofa next to her and his hand was stroking her face.

"Big horse woman," he seemed to be saying over and over.

After Helen replaced the bed linen in the spare bedroom, she cleaned the bathroom and the kitchen. As a final chore, she put all the trash and garbage into a plastic trash bag and carried it down the back steps to the nook formed below the steps. She moved as quietly as she could, on her tiptoes, but as she turned and started back up the steps the back door on the ground floor swung open.

"Come in here, you wicked woman, and tell me what you've been up to." Amy Starret was in the doorway, grinning at her. She wore a bathrobe and had curlers in her hair.

"Now, Amy…"

"If you think you can run a cathouse right over me and not make me curious…"

Helen laughed. "You always did have a dirty mind."

"A cup of coffee?"

"I've had too many."

"Tea then?"

She followed Amy into the kitchen. She didn't want the cup of tea, but it might save a lot of trouble later. Once Amy got curious, she wouldn't give up until she knew what she wanted to know. It wasn't as if she was prying. Amy and her husband, Reg, were her best friends in Atlanta. In the year she'd lived in the apartment above them, Amy had tried to match her up with her old boyfriends and Reg had introduced her to several architects at the firm where he worked. Nothing had come of the dinners and the theatre dates, but Amy and Reg didn't seem discouraged.

"Tell me all the sexy details." Amy put the kettle on and came to sit across the breakfast nook from Helen.

Helen told her a carefully edited version of the previous evening's happenings. She left out names and places. "And I brought him to my apartment to clean him up some and try to find a doctor who'd make a house call."

"Ah," Amy said, "the good nurse make-out."

"That's what he thought," Helen said, and then she realized that she hadn't intended to reveal that much. She found herself blushing.

"If he thought that, you certainly couldn't let it happen. No matter what you intended when you brought him here."

"I didn't intend anything," Helen said. "I'm not even sure I like him."

"What's his problem?"

"He's been running through the typists and receptionists like English flu."

"You mean he's not a virgin anymore?"

Helen looked at Amy's purposely blank face and laughed, and Amy's face cracked and she joined in. "It does sound silly, doesn't it?" Helen asked.

"I don't see why a woman would want a man unless he's got the stamp of approval from some other women. Now you take Reg..."

"I don't want him," Helen said.

The kettle whistle sounded and Amy left the breakfast nook to pour a cup of water and add a teabag. Seated again, she said, "Now you take Reg. He was wearing himself down to nothing when I first saw him. He was so thin he'd hardly cast a shadow. I was working down the hall from Basteen, Kutcher and Williams and I saw that poor man dragging in every morning and then leaving at five with some girl for drinks and god-knows-what and I said to myself, that man must have some special talent."

"You sound like you were horny," Helen said.

"Oh, I was," Amy said, "but I wouldn't let him know."

Helen let the teabag take its time. And now that the direction of the conversation had changed, she felt much more comfortable. Of course, because it was the way conversations usually went with Amy, she knew that she would remember her original curiosity sooner or later. "So you set out to meet him?"

"Did I ever? You see, all morning, until lunch he'd be crossing the hall to the water fountain. He must have been drinking gin. Well, I'd pick my times, and about three times a day, I'd see him heading for the water fountains, so I'd run out and get there first. I'd bend over and have a delicate drink while he got a good look at my ass." She reached down and gave her hip a hard slap. "Oh, it was a beautiful ass in those days."

"What was it Keats said about his girlfriend, Fanny? That she looked better from the back than she did from the front?"

"You've been reading again," Amy said. "Anyway, after about two weeks, he couldn't think of anything but me."

"So he arranged an introduction?"

"Not him. One day, when he reached around me and held the water button for me, I got a close look at that red hair and those blue eyes and I came close to having an orgasm on the spot."

"Got a faceful of water, huh?"

"I couldn't swallow," Amy said. "I saw him outside."

"Reg?"

"No, the man who stayed in your apartment all night."

"Oh." Helen realized that Amy had made the leap and now she'd come back to Vince and the doctor. "When was that?"

"When he left. When he was waiting for the cab."

"What do you think?"

"He looked...pretty battered. Once he looked up at your window, and I thought he looked like a predator."

"You're kidding, Amy."

"No, from the way he looked I expected him to charge back up the stairs and tear all your clothes off."

"That's your imagination again."

"Is he interested in you?"

"It's hard to say."

"He wants to screw you and you won't let him?"

"I don't want to be an anonymous chunk of meat," Helen said.

"Because of all those other girls?"

"Yes."

"You don't have much faith in yourself, do you?" Amy shook out a cigarette and lit it. "Back to my story. I knew if I ever got Reg into my bed, he'd never want to leave it."

"You hadn't been married before, had you?"

"No." Amy considered that for a moment. "I guess you mean if I'd had one bad marriage, I wouldn't have been so sure of myself."

"Something like that."

"Oh, honey," Amy said, "I guess I'm not helping much, am I?"

"I didn't realize I needed help."

"All of us do."

"I'm happy enough."

"*Enough* is the weak word there," Amy said.

The tea had cooled. Helen drank the last half cup in a gulp and stood up. "Thanks for the tea."

Amy followed her to the back door. "I have a feeling this one, the one I saw outside, just might be the right one."

"Amy, you're an incurable something-or-other."

Behind her, as she started up the flight of back steps, Amy called, "You want to go shopping, call me."

"Not today. Yesterday was a bit more than I planned."

"You didn't tell me about that."

"Some other time."

On the way out of the Dome after the morning workout, the Shooter got almost to the parking lot before he remembered Edna and the tickets. His first temptation was to forget it altogether.

All those girls out there had a crotch, and it was a waste of time hanging around with a girl who didn't want to use hers. But he had to admit to himself that he was intrigued. If nothing else, he wanted to see if she wouldn't, after all the crap of the night before, turn into a cunt after all.

At the business office, after the long walk around one side of the Dome, the Shooter asked to see Art Jansen. The girl at the window knew him, and she preened as she opened the door and asked him in.

"What can I do for you?" Art asked.

"I need two tickets for tonight's game left at the ticket window."

"Sure thing, Shooter." Art went over to the Ticketron and punched some keys. After a couple of readouts, he punched a few more keys and the tickets came out. Coming back toward the desk where the Shooter was, he stuffed the tickets in an envelope. "What name, Shooter?"

"Edna."

"What last name?"

"Just Edna."

Art wrote on the envelope and turned it so that the Shooter could see what he'd written. Her name and compliments of the Shooter. "They'll be waiting for her."

Later, on the way across the lot he realized how silly he'd looked. Leaving two tickets for some girl and not even knowing her last name. Hell, back in the business office they were probably having a big laugh on him. The Shooter woke up this morning and didn't remember the girl's last name. Maybe a wink or two. That Shooter gets a lot. And some of the girls acting like they didn't know what they were talking about.

But they did, and that was what eased his embarrassment. So, what if he didn't remember the girl's last name? Instead of looking bad, maybe it was cool. The Shooter gets a lot and he doesn't even remember their names and the girls don't get insulted.

And all the talk about getting a lot made him uncomfortable, especially after the way Edna had acted the night before. Like it was sewed up. Now that friend of hers, that girl Greta, she wouldn't leave a man with blue balls.

Shit, the thought of it was bothering him. And because he couldn't think of anything else to do, he drove out toward Buckhead and The Little Old Wine Shoppe.

When the Crackers season began back in October, he'd been getting a lot of ink, not only in the sports pages but in other sections as well. The most absurd of them all was an interview with the lady who wrote food columns for the Thursday morning food section in the *Constitution*. The arrangement for the interview was made by the publicity people, and the Shooter didn't know anything was expected of him until the lady writer and the photographer showed up that afternoon at his apartment with Johnny Edmunds from the publicity office.

The Shooter offered drinks around. The lady writer sipped her scotch, got out her pad and asked, "Mr. Simpson, what do you cook?"

"Nothing."

"Nothing?" The lady writer raised an eyebrow at Johnny Edmunds.

"Sure, you cook some things, don't you?" Johnny Edmunds moved over until he stood next to the Shooter. He looked one step away from a panic.

"Sometimes I cook myself a hamburger."

"Well, that's a beginning," the lady writer said. "How do you go about it?"

"I take this ground meat and I pat it out and I put it in the skillet and that's all."

"Is it ground beef or ground chuck or ground round?"

"Just ground meat," the Shooter said.

She still hadn't made a note on the pad. "All right, what do you do to the ground meat before you cook it?"

"Nothing."

"Don't you add anything to it?"

"No."

"This is absurd." The lady writer tossed back the rest of her drink. She and Johnny Edmunds went shopping while the Shooter and the photographer had a couple of drinks. The photographer, who said he took better pictures when he was oiled, said, "Shooter, you're okay. God, I get tired of those fags who say they toss in two tablespoons of dried cat meat and a dollop of day-old whale sperm." And he'd toasted that with another drink.

The food reporter and Johnny Edmunds returned an hour later with a huge bag of groceries. Johnny helped her unload the bag and then mixed her another drink while she arranged the first picture. She dumped a pound of ground round into a mixing bowl and arranged the other ingredients on the counter so they'd show in the shot. One item she'd bought was a can of jalapeno peppers. For the first picture, the Shooter stood over the mixing bowl with one of the peppers in his hand, sniffing it. He made the mistake of getting too close to it, and the strong burn of it almost blinded him.

After the photographer had that shot, and a couple more for insurance, the Shooter stepped aside and the food reporter concocted the burgers. When they were in the skillet and cooking, they posed the next picture, the one of the Shooter turning the burgers. The final picture used in the article was one of the Shooter seated at the kitchen table having his first bite of the burger. He only took one bite of it, and the photographer got his usable shot then. His second shot, the one he sent the Shooter later, was of the Shooter's face when the jalapenos began to burn the roof of his mouth.

The lady writer had one taste of the burgers and said, "They're godawful."

The article was on the first page of the food section the following Thursday. The photographer had been right. He did work well while oiled. And the article made much of the bachelor cook, in this case Eddie "the Shooter" Simpson, who liked Mexican foods so much that he'd concocted his own version of a hamburger which drew upon the mainstays of Mexican food for its originality.

The Shooter kept the recipe around, just for a joke, until he had it memorized.

Shooter's Jalapeno Burgers
1 pound ground round
1 egg
2 tablespoons grated onion
1 tablespoon chili powder
2 medium jalapeno peppers, diced Salt and pepper to taste
Combine ingredients in mixing bowl. Fry in butter over low heat. Place on bun with grated cheddar cheese and sauteed strips of green peppers.

After the article, he got a lot of ragging from the other Cracker players. They told him he could always get a job as a short-order cook if he couldn't make it as a ball player. And they kidded him about whether he was going to play while wearing his chef's hat.

The main thing that came out of the experience with the food reporter was an embarrassment that led the Shooter to pay more attention to what he ate and drank. He wanted to be thought of as someone who knew about good food and drink. The food part was easy. He started eating in good restaurants and, in time, he moved past steak and roast beef.

Wine was harder. That was how he came to spend so much time and money at the Little Old Wine Shoppe. He bought a fifty-bottle wine rack and had it fitted into an area at the rear of the pantry. And now, when he didn't know anything else to do, he'd stop by and pick up a couple of bottles to put aside.

On this day he bought a '68 Medoc, a '70 Grave, and a '69 Pommard. The owner, flitting around him, assured him the wines would double and triple in value in the next few years. Not that the Shooter bought them for that reason. At first, he bought wine just to fill up the rack. It was show and nothing else. But then he'd started drinking some of the wines, when he didn't want to leave the apartment or when he was trying to impress some cunt or other. He found he was training his tongue, and he thought with horror of the pop wines he'd drunk back in college.

Back at the apartment, he put his purchases away, white wine to the right and red wines to the left of the rack. He placed them according to year, the older wine to the top of the rack and the younger wines below.

He undressed in the bedroom. Usually he took a short nap after a morning workout. He'd just settled back into his pillow when the phone rang.

"Do you know who this is?" It was a woman's voice.

"No."

"You've forgotten me already?"

Shit, another one of those. "When did I meet you?"

"Last night."

"Oh, Greta."

"Ouch," the woman said, "that hurt."

"Hello, Edna."

"I guess that's what I get for being coy," Edna said.

"You said it. I didn't." He doubled his pillow behind his head. "I left the tickets for you. They're under your first name. I don't know your last name."

"I've made a good thing of not telling you."

"I looked silly," the Shooter said, "reserving the tickets for you."

"Poor thing," she said, as if talking to a baby. "Can mama kiss it and make it well?"

"Watch your language. I'm undressed and in bed."

"This late in the day?"

"I'm resting after a workout. Come join me."

"No."

"It's a big bed."

"I've seen it," she said. "But I have some doubts that it's big enough for you and me and all those other girls."

"Send Greta over then."

"You forget," Edna said, "she's a working girl."

"Too bad." He paused for a moment. "You bringing a boyfriend with you tonight?"

"I was. Maybe I ought to bring Greta. You seem pretty interested in her."

"I suspect she swings," he said.

"I don't talk behind a friend's back."

"You don't have to. It's written on her forehead."

"And what's written on mine?" she asked.

"Question marks."

"That's witty."

"Am I going to see you after the game?" the Shooter asked.

"Do you want to?"

"Yes. That is, I think I do."

"I'll think about it between now and then," Edna said.

"You can't be any more exact than that?"

"No."

"Let me know what you decide." Angered a little, he said good-bye and hung up before she could say any more. Usually, he didn't have any trouble getting to sleep after a workout. Not that he felt tired, but it was a long season and the main thing a nap did was give his legs some rest. It didn't do much good. He'd feel rested during the first quarter; then his legs would go, and the rest of the game he'd be playing on reflex and guts.

Today he couldn't sleep. It was that goddamn girl bugging him. Screw her, he hissed to himself. Oddly, it didn't have any force behind it this time.

❧　❧　❧

Harley Brisker didn't leave the house all morning. When Ethel Ann returned from her shopping, he went out to the driveway and brought in the grocery bags for her. It seemed enough food to feed an army for more than a week, but he didn't say that to her. He knew she was a careful shopper. It was an attitude that went back to the early days of their marriage. The quality and the cuts of meat might be better now, but she still searched the paper for weekend specials and saved the stamps the stores gave.

After the grocery bags were empty and the meats stored away, Ethel Ann came into the living room. "What did Hap want?"

"He wanted to slip out of a corner he'd backed himself into."

"I thought you and Hap were friends."

"Barely," Harley said. "He tried to suck me into a shady deal."

"The Convention Center?"

"Yes."

"I wish you'd never gotten involved with that," she said.

"I am, so there's no good wishing I wasn't."

She sat down on the sofa next to him. "You seem low today."

"I'm not." And then, because they hardly ever lied to each other, he corrected himself. "Yes, I am."

"Why?"

"I feel somebody's made me their nigger."

"That's silly, Harley. You're your own man, and you've been as long as I've known you."

"I'm wondering now. Isn't that how they make you their nigger ... by letting you do what you believe in when it goes along with what they want?"

"And if you didn't believe in what they wanted?"

"That hasn't happened yet."

"Would they lay the law down to you?" she asked.

"Probably not. It would be a bit more subtle. Some way of letting me know my other work wasn't going too well. Some way of letting me know that the Board of Directors wasn't altogether pleased with me. Something like that."

"What would you do then?"

He shook his head. "I don't know. I really don't know."

She leaned toward him, and he put up an arm and caught her. He could smell the subtle scent of her, the perfume that was so much lighter and more expensive than the one she'd been wearing when he first met her. "I thought you were much happier now than when you were teaching school."

"I am except when the blues get me and I start picking and pulling at things. It's like I can't turn it loose until I've looked at it from all sides."

"And you'd rather be blind in one eye?"

"No," he said.

"You'd rather be Hap Seaver and know you're dishonest?"

"No."

He could feel the beginning rumble of her laugh. "Then what's wrong with you, Harley?"

"Lord knows." He let his arm slide down behind her and pinched her behind.

She jerked away from him. "Harley, stop that."

"On your behind it won't show," he said.

"Now that you've given me a blue mark to go with my black, are you feeling better?"

"Some," he said.

"Then let me go so I can start lunch."

At five of two, Harley was in the hallway outside of the committee meeting room. He was the only member there, and he had the strange feeling that he'd overslept the meeting by a day and missed it altogether. Of course, there was another possible explanation: that the House and Senate members supporting the other two sites might be having last-minute meetings. For nose-counting and backbone-stiffening, he decided.

At exactly 2:00, by his watch he heard the elevator doors open and close. It was about time. More than time. The way it was going the meeting wouldn't be underway until 2:15 or later.

He turned and looked down the hall. He was surprised to find that the two men approaching him were uniformed security men.

"You Mr. Brisker?" one asked.

"Yes."

"They tried to reach you at home but you'd left. Senator Mast wants you to call him at home."

"What's wrong?"

"The meeting's postponed until tonight, I think."

Harley left them and rode the elevator down to the first floor where there was a bank of pay phones. He fished out two dimes from the change in his pocket and made his first call.

CHAPTER ELEVEN

Before he stepped into the shower, Vince sat on the edge of his bed and dialed David Wardlaw's private number. After he listened to Vince's accounts of his meetings with Jim Sims and Senator Johnson, David said, "It sounds like it might come to something."

"Don't count on it," Vince said.

"Why not?"

"They shift once, they might shift again."

"Let's hope not," David said.

"You need me for the next hour or so? It's something personal."

"If I need you, I can find you."

"I doubt it," Vince said, "but you can try."

After he finished his shower, Vince stood in the steamy bathroom, staring down at a bottle of lime cologne he'd taken from the back of the medicine cabinet. After a moment or two he said, "Oh, what the hell," and splashed some of it on his chest and a liberal palmful on his face. He wrinkled his nose, waiting for himself to become accustomed to the scent, and walked into the bedroom where he dressed in clean underwear, dark slacks and a gray tweed jacket.

His first stop after he left the house was Children International, a huge toy shop in Lennox Square. He was in the shop for ten minutes, and at the end of that time he walked out with a three-foot-high stuffed dog. The dog was black with white spots and had a chain on the top of its head. When you pulled the chain, the dog gave a pleasant, not at all frightening bark. It was a happy, friendly yap rather than an angry bark, and Vince had listened to it several times before he nodded at the saleslady and offered her his Master Charge card.

Heading back toward town, he got onto Piedmont and remained on it until he reached Monroe. He turned right on Monroe and followed it until he passed the Grady High Stadium. He made his right onto Eighth. After he crossed Charles Allen, it was a changing street. He noticed a couple of new apartment buildings and that several houses had been renovated. The odd thing was that the renovated houses all had either brick or wood partial walls at the edge of the sidewalks. Vince didn't know why the walls were there, but they looked like Watts architecture.

Near Eighth and Argonne, he pulled into a driveway of a small two-story brick house and parked behind a two-year-old black Dart. The Dart had a dented left rear fender he hadn't seen before. So much for that. She'd always had trouble getting in and out of parking spaces at the supermarkets.

The trim on the house had been painted back in the summer, and he knew what the painting had cost because he had paid for it. The elm beside the driveway had been pruned and some dead limbs cut away. He knew what half-a-day's wages for a tree service was. He knew, as well, what the city taxes were and what the mortgage payments for a $29,000 house were by the month. If he didn't know by the penny, it was just a matter of consulting his check book.

The front door opened as soon as he reached the porch. She'd been watching for him. He said, "Hello, Joyce," opened the screen door and stepped inside. As it was each time, he visited the house, the overpowering scent of a room freshener assaulted him and he braced himself not to flinch. From the look of the living room and the dining room beyond, he knew she'd spent all day Friday and part of the morning today cleaning and dusting and waxing. The house and the furniture were all very correct and all very exact, but it didn't look like anybody lived there. It had the warmth and personality of a showroom in a big furniture discount store.

"I wasn't sure you were coming," Joyce said.

"I said I would."

He passed her and put the stuffed dog on the sofa. When he turned back to her, he saw that she expected it and he put out his arms and held her. That was all he wanted to do. But she lifted her face toward him and he could see her eyes closing and he leaned down and kissed her.

Joyce Akerman was thirty-one and she looked every year of it. Her hair was red, shoulder length and waveless. Against the bright red, her skin seemed especially pale, but up close the skin across her cheeks and the bridge of her nose was coarse, damaged by a mild case of acne back in her teens.

Holding her he could feel the tight, unyielding foundation garments, and he knew that she hadn't been dieting as she'd told him she had. She had a tendency toward overweight, and it was getting away from her. In another year or two, if she wasn't careful, she'd begin to develop a waddle.

"Take off your coat and stay a while," she said.

"Might as well." He took off his topcoat and dropped it over the back of a chair.

"You want to see Timmy now?" she asked.

"Timothy," he said.

"All right, Timothy," she said.

He got the stuffed dog from the sofa. "I'm ready. I hope he'll like this."

"He will." She put out a hand and stroked the fur of the dog. "He likes soft things."

He followed her down the short hallway to the bedrooms. The bedroom to the right was hers, a frilly, colorful room with a large double bed in it. The door was fully open. Directly opposite was Timothy's room. The door was cracked slightly. At the door, hand on the knob, she stopped. "Let me make sure he's not...wet."

He waited in the hallway while she went inside and closed the door behind her. He could hear a gurgling and the faint soft words as she talked to Timothy. Just before she opened the door for him, he heard the opening and closing of a diaper pail.

"He's fine now," she said.

I won't let it show, I won't let it show, he told himself as he crossed the room. It wasn't a crib. It was more like a hospital bed with the rails you could raise on both sides. And there in the center of the bed was Timothy. It was his fourth birthday and he was still like a baby. The hand up in the air, almost covering Timothy's face, had a crooked and claw-like finger, and the face beyond the hand was flat and almost featureless, with hooded eyes and badly curved teeth.

Vince leaned over the bed and placed the stuffed dog on the bed.

"Happy birthday, Timothy."

Timothy began to coo and gurgle, and behind him, close to him, Joyce said, "See? He knows you."

And this time, as each time before, he fought back the urge to tell her that Timothy didn't know him at all, that he only recognized the smell of the lime cologne and that was why he wore it.

It had been a casual affair, one that started over a few drinks at a bar. It had been a bad time for Vince. The job at the law firm wasn't going well and he knew that there was a better than fifty-fifty chance that he wouldn't last. And Joyce, while not very bright and not the best company in the world, had seemed to care for him. The lovemaking had seemed good at the time and the affair had lasted longer than most of his involvements. Perhaps the affair lasted as long as it did because she always seemed to be waiting for his call, at any hour of the night, and her apartment became a refuge from all the bars and all the petty things going on at the office.

In the fourth month, when she told him she was pregnant the surprise sobered him for several days. He withstood the tears and the hysterics and stuck by his original statement that he didn't want to get married again but that he would accept the responsibility. He would take care of Joyce while she had the baby and he would support the baby after that.

It was supposed to have been a mistake. He wasn't sure that it was. She was wearing an IUD, and each time they made love he'd watched while she inserted the foam. Later, looking back on it, he had the feeling that she'd probably had the IUD removed, certain that if she became pregnant he would marry her.

The affair ended that week. He borrowed enough from his father in Wilmington to cover her expenses after she quit her job and enough to pay hospital expenses when Timothy was born that February four years ago. He was at the hospital that night. The young doctor who attended the birth came into the waiting room and asked for Mr. Akerman. At first Vince didn't react. He caught himself when the doctor asked again. He went over to the doorway.

"Mr. Akerman?"

"No," Vince said, "but I'm the father."

The doctor led him out of the doorway and down the hall. "There's one problem. It's early to say and I don't mean to frighten you. I'd need a specialist to be sure, but I think your son has Down's Anomaly." The doctor looked into Vince's puzzled face. "It's what you call Mongolism."

"Look at him," Joyce said now. Timothy hugged the stuffed dog to his chest and Vince reached out and pulled the chain. At the happy barking, Timothy tightened his arms around the dog, like he was squeezing the life out of it. "He loves it already. I've never seen him like this."

"Let me know if he learns to pull the chain," Vince said.

"I'll teach him."

"I hope he learns before he tears it up."

"That's not his fault," Joyce said stiffly. "He likes to…hold things too tightly."

"I know it's not his fault." Leaning over he ran his hands over Timothy's hair, smoothing it. The hair was damp and his forehead was clammy. "He can tear up as many stuffed dogs as he likes."

"He knows you. He really knows you."

"Why not?" He forced the smile. "He ought to know his father."

In the hallway outside of the partly closed door to Timothy's room, he knew it was going to happen, as it did each time he made his visit to the house. It haunted him, no matter how he tried to prepare himself for it. Nothing worked, not even trying to wash it out of his mind. It was one of the reasons why he'd cut down visits to Timothy.

Joyce looked into her bedroom. "We can…if you want to."

It was her pride, her damaged pride, that made her phrase her offer as if it was something that had nothing to do with her need, only his. It was, he guessed, defensive. If he refused her it wouldn't hurt her as much. It would all be on him, the need or the lack of it.

"Let's do."

Dark in the room, the shades down and the drapes drawn, and he was trying to remember how it had been five years ago, how the passion had been so that it would happen again. And this time, as it usually was, somehow it was there and they made slow, passionless love, hearing the wind in the tree outside the window, hearing the stuffed dog bark once in Timothy's room.

"You love Timothy, don't you?"

Their breath was slow and easy, minutes after the lovemaking was over.

"Yes," he said.

"I couldn't stand it if you didn't. It's not his fault."

"I'm going to love him all of my life and all his life," he said.

"I'm sorry." Her hand touched his face. "I'm here alone so much and I think about it too much and when I don't see you for a long time, I think it's because you don't love Timmy."

It was there, the hurt, the ache in his chest so that he couldn't swallow and couldn't breathe. Yes, she meant that, but she also meant the old hurts, the knowledge that he didn't love her, never had and never would.

"I'll come once-a-week from now on," he said.

"He's getting better. Really, he is. You might not notice it. Seeing him every day like I do you'd notice it."

"I'm sure he is. I can tell."

Taking her hand from his face and holding it flat against his chest he drowsed for half-an-hour. At the end of that time, he dressed and looked into Timothy's room once more before he left. Timothy had already torn off one of the stuffed dog's ears.

Harley Brisker's call reached David Wardlaw just as he arrived back at his office after lunch with Frances.

"Yes, Harley?" He shifted the telephone as he worked his arms out of the topcoat.

"Something's going on. The meeting's postponed until eight tonight."

"Any reason given?" He dropped the topcoat over the back of a chair.

"That's the funny part," Harley said. "Sims says he's too sick to make the afternoon meeting, but he thinks he'll be all right by tonight; and Johnson said he had to fly home for a couple of hours because of a sickness in the family." Harley paused. "Does this make any sense to you, Mr. Wardlaw?"

"I think they needed a few more hours for their dealing."

"It's bad then," Harley said.

"They didn't stay bought."

"Bought?"

"We convinced Sims and Johnson to support the Boulevard site. At least I thought we had."

"You said *bought*," Harley said.

"*Convinced* might be the better word."

"Mr. Wardlaw, I don't want to be involved in anything like bribes."

"You won't."

"I mean it, Mr. Wardlaw."

"You have my promise. Nothing will be done to compromise you."

"I'll depend on that," Harley said. "And I'll be at home if you need to reach me."

As soon as Harley was off the line, David got out a list of numbers that Vince had given him a few months back. It was an assortment of bars and girls' apartments. It took twenty minutes to work his way through the list. No luck. No one had seen him, and a couple of the girls had been abrupt and unpleasant. He put the list away and sat looking at the receiver for a long time before he dialed Helen Morris's number.

"Helen, this is David. Is Vince with you?"

"I haven't seen him since early this morning," she said.

"If he calls you, have him get in touch with me."

"Yes, Mr. Wardlaw."

"I liked David better." He was about to end the conversation. On impulse alone he added: "Are you going to the Cracker-Squire game tonight?"

"I thought I might."

"Perhaps I'll see you there."

"Perhaps," she said.

⚜ ⚜ ⚜

Vince arrived while David was in the kitchen making himself a cup of hot tea. Vince leaned against the door frame and asked, "How are things?"

"Going to hell," David said.

Vince followed him back into the office. He heard David's account of the phone call from Harley Brisker in silence, nodding a time or two. At the end, he reached across the desk and got a cigarette from David's pack.

"I think you're going to have to find Sims and Johnson again," David said.

"We won't have to," Vince said. "They'll find us." He lit the cigarette and waved it at David. "Look at it this way. They've got our offer and now they're trying to see if anybody will better it. By meeting time this afternoon, nobody had. Otherwise they'd have gone on with the meeting. And they'd have sold us out."

"What if they make a better deal between now and the eight-o'clock meeting?"

"Then we'll hear from them again to see if we'll raise the ante."

"And if they don't get a better offer?" David asked.

"We'll hear from them anyway...to reaffirm the deal with us."

David lifted the teabag from the cup and winced as he squeezed the tea from it. "You sure?"

"Eighty percent," Vince said. "They're greedy, so they'll be back one way or the other."

"I'd rather talk to them right now."

"It wouldn't do any good. They're out selling their ass, and they can't sell it to more than one person at a time."

"When will they call?"

"Between now and eight."

David leaned back in his chair and lifted the cup of tea. He looked at Vince over the rim. "That's a long afternoon."

Devil said, "Have another hit and then we'll talk about fucking."

"I've got to go." But Frances was still stunned by the strength of the grass. It got her to thinking about the way some grass users talked now and then, as if grass was sometimes boosted by the addition of another drug. She'd talked to a boy about that once and he'd laughed at the whole idea. "It would make it too expensive," he'd said. And he'd gone on to talk about grass the way some people discuss wine, how climate and soil make a big difference in the strength and quality of the stuff.

"You'll like it," Devil said. "Come on, uptown girl."

"I'm expected home."

"We'll make it a short one then," Devil said. "A half-hour fuck."

She giggled. It was such a silly brag. Devil misunderstood the giggle and reached down and rubbed the crotch of his jeans. "You're going to like this."

"I'm really going. All I want is the grass and nothing else."

"You'll get the grass," he said. "But first let's get down to the skin. You give good head?"

Her knees didn't want to work, but when he leaned toward her, she gave him a shove and pushed away from the sofa. Dizziness got her and he grabbed her arm as she hesitated. He held on and pulled at her. He was too strong for her and she fell onto the sofa again. It was time to scream if she was going to scream. She wasn't sure why she didn't, unless it was because she wasn't sure anyone would hear her.

"Come on, bitch, before I really get mad."

His free hand slid up her stomach and clawed at her breasts. His nails dug in and hurt her. She cried out and swung at him.

He ducked under the swing and pushed her back. He fell on top of her, and the top of his head struck her on the point of her chin. She fell back, more than stunned now, and opened her mouth wide to scream. Devil must have felt her deep intake of breath. He reached up a hand and clapped a hand over her mouth, shutting the scream off.

It was time to try something else. She remembered the stories girls had told her and she tried to knee him in the groin. He slipped the knee and took its impact on his thigh.

"Don't fight it, bitch. You're going to love every bit of it."

Panic was hurting her. She couldn't breathe with the hand over her mouth and she was having trouble adjusting to breathing through her nose. She shook her head, no, no, please no. But he couldn't hear her and he didn't want to hear her.

She knew she was weakening. It was just a matter of time, and she began to think that it might be better to give in, to let him have his way. If she didn't, she was afraid he'd begin to beat her.

The words were forming in her mind. All right, I'll do it. And as soon as the surrender settled upon her, she began her nod, the nod that meant she would go along with him. At that moment there was a loud noise at the door and it flew open. Part of the lock broke off and skidded across the floor toward the sofa. Two men were in the doorway. One was young, a tall broad-shouldered man with fair hair and blue eyes. The other man was older, going toward fat. Both of them wore suits.

"That's a lousy door you've got there," the older man said. He moved out of the doorway, one hand deep in his suit coat pocket. "Narcotics," he said, taking out a leather I.D. case and flipping it open.

Devil dropped his hand from her mouth and she put her hands on his chest and pushed him away.

The young man looked down into the ash tray where the butts were lined up. He picked up the jar of clean grass and smelled it.

When he replaced the jar on the table he looked over at Devil. "Stuff that thing back in your pants, you freak."

Frances looked down and saw his thing hanging out of his fly, red-tipped and erect, and she let her head fall back and closed her eyes.

"Hope we didn't interrupt anything important," the older detective said. And then he laughed.

The call came in at 3:30. Wardlaw passed the phone across the desk to Vince. "You answer it. You've done all the talking to them so far."

The caller wasn't either Sims or Johnson. It was John, Wardlaw's cook. "Mr. Gorman, is Mr. Wardlaw there?"

"Yes, do you want to? ..."

"No," John said quickly. "I don't know whether to talk to him or not. You see, Miss Frances is in trouble. I want to help her, but I don't know what to say to Mr. Wardlaw."

"Where are you?"

"I'm at the police station. I was going to put up a bond, but I thought maybe ..."

"I'll be there in ten minutes. Don't do anything until I get there."

"Yes, Mr. Gorman."

Vince put the receiver down and turned to David. "I've got to go out for an hour or so. It might be more. It might be less."

"Vince, dammit, you know they might call any minute."

"It's important. A girl I know is in jail."

"Let the pig wait."

"Not a chance." Vince got his topcoat from the back of the other chair at the front of the desk. "And I don't think you've got any reason to call her a pig."

David took a deep breath and let it out slowly. He shook his head slowly. "I think this waiting is getting me on edge."

"I'll call as soon as I can. If they call you, get a number where I can reach them. That is, if you still want me to handle it."

David nodded. "I'm sorry for what I said. You need cash for her bond?"

"I think they'll take my check." He stopped in the entrance-way that led to the elevator. "It *is* important, David."

David turned in his chair and watched the elevator close behind him. He put his head back and closed his eyes.

Damn Vince and his harem of girls.

After Vince introduced the bail bondsman to John, he took John aside and told him to take Frances to the coffee shop down the street and wait for him. From the policeman behind the cage, he found out the names of the arresting officers. Ransome and Kendall.

"Where'll you be?" John asked as he started out.

"Don't ask," Vince said.

Ransome and Kendall were pointed out to him down a long hallway near a coffee machine. The heavy, older detective was leaning against the machine, looking down into a cup and frowning. The young one was seated on a bench. He'd finished his coffee and was using the cup as an ash tray.

"You the two who arrested the guy and the girl on drug charges? Ransome and Kendall?"

"I'm Ransome." The heavy policeman pushed away from the machine. "You their lawyer?"

"I'm a lawyer," Vince said, "but I'm not representing either of them." He took a card out of his wallet and passed it to Ransome.

Ransome read it and handed it to the young detective.

"I'm Kendall," the young one said. "So, she's *that* Wardlaw?"

Vince nodded. "How about telling me about it?"

He listened them out, nodding a few times. At the end of it, he got up and fished a dime out of his pocket and bought himself a cup of coffee. "What are you charging her with?"

"Possession to sell," Ransome said.

"You ask the guy whose stuff it was?"

"He says he didn't even know the stash was in the closet and he just can't figure how it got there." He curled his lip. "He thinks the previous tenant left it there."

"You ask him about the girl?" Vince asked.

"He says he picked up the girl on the Strip and they went over to his place to ball. *Ball* was the way he said it."

"He's probably protecting her," Kendall, said.

"The girl got into town last night ... late ... from Northampton, Massachusetts. She hasn't been in town since the first of January. I can prove that."

"Well, she makes friends fast," Ransome said. "You should have seen them. All over each other. His meat hanging out of his pants."

"How was she dressed?"

"Well, she was..." Ransome looked over at Kendall. "Well, her clothes were pulled around and ..."

Kendall shook his head. "She had all her clothes on. Even her shoes. She told us she went to the house to buy some grass, but when she got there the guy started trying to force her to go to bed with him." He closed his eyes tightly. When he opened them again, he said, "I keep seeing it in my head, the way it was when we kicked the door down. His hand was over her mouth, like he was keeping her from yelling for help."

Vince sipped his coffee. "I'd like to keep the girl out of this."

Ransome shook his head. "Everybody wants to keep somebody out of it."

"The guy could clear her. All he'd have to do is admit the dope is his and she was just trying to make a buy."

"Little chance of that. He's foxy, this one."

"Maybe he's smart enough to know the difference between a charge of possessing to sell and a charge of attempted rape," Vince said.

"You're kidding," Ransome said.

"I'm heading now down to the coffee shop to talk to Frances. I can bet money I can be back at the station in no more than half an hour to file the charges."

"You think she'll go along with that?" Kendall stood up and tossed his cup in a trash barrel. "Rape charges can be messy things."

"So is a charge of possessing to sell," Vince said.

"You know this girl long?" Ransome asked.

"Five or six years."

"What the hell was she doing down on the Strip?"

"Trying to buy herself some grass, I guess."

"That doesn't make her a model citizen," Ransome said.

"It doesn't make her a criminal either." Vince held his hands out in front of him. "Arrest me too. I've smoked a bit of grass. Arrest about seventy percent of the kids out there. Arrest about thirty or forty percent of the law-abiding middle class too."

Kendall looked over at his older partner. "It might be worth a try. Faced with the attempted rape, he might break and admit possession."

"You think she'll make the charge?" Ransome asked. "It's no good unless she's willing to back up the threat."

"I'd bet on it."

"Let's try it out on him," Ransome said.

"You try it," Kendall said. "I'd like to go along with the lawyer here and get the rest of her story." He gave Vince a questioning look. "If it's all right with you."

"Fine with me."

"Why?" Ransome asked.

"When we talked to her before, we assumed it was all a lie. Now this slick dude here comes in and tells a different story. I want to be sure which way it really was."

"If you think so," Ransome said.

"I think so." Kendall turned to Vince. "You can get mad if you want to, but I spend about half my time getting pissed about how money makes things move. Just once I'd like to think the person was worth it."

On the walk from the police station to the coffee shop, the young cop asked, "You her boyfriend?"

"Huh?"

"You go with her?"

"You got to be kidding," Vince said. "I'm an uncle figure."

"I just wondered."

"Besides being an uncle type, she's not the kind that interests me."

"She's damned attractive," Kendall said. "That was what got me so mad when I saw that freak pawing at her."

"What's your full name?"

"Pete Kendall."

"I always thought Frances was a little on the large size."

"Hell," Pete Kendall said, "who'd want a woman who was just a bag of bones?"

"You might be right," Vince said. And he turned and gave the young man a searching look.

Vince left Pete Kendall at the booth with John and Frances. At the pay phone in the rear of the coffee shop, he called Wardlaw's private number. When David answered he told him his business was almost over and he thought he'd be back in the office in thirty or forty-five minutes.

"No hurry," David said, "and it looks like my guess about a long afternoon was an understatement."

When he reached the booth, John was seated across the table from Frances and Pete Kendall. He had a glass of beer in front of him. On his wrinkled face there was a puzzled expression. Vince understood his confusion. When he and Pete had first entered, he'd seen Frances' first look at Kendall—and her recognition had been followed by the deepest blush he'd ever seen. Now that blush was gone, and as Vince sat next to John and listened to Frances, he realized that she'd just about finished her account of the time she'd spent at Devil's place.

"That freak bastard," Kendall said, and then he broke off in confusion and blushed. "Excuse me."

"Just so you believe me," Frances said.

"I believe you," Kendall said. He slid out of the booth and stood up. "It's kind of early, but I'll call Ransome and see if there's any word yet." He walked toward the pay phone.

"He seems like a nice guy," Vince said.

"The way he acted when they kicked the door in, I didn't think so. Now, I do."

"You act right," Vince said, "and I'll get you a date with him."

She blushed. "He's probably married."

"It's easy enough to find out."

"Vince, don't you dare."

Kendall returned to the booth. "He's still talking to the guy."

"You think Frances ought to go back with you and file charges?" Vince asked.

Kendall shook his head. "I hope that won't be necessary. Let us try the threat on him first."

"Thank you," Frances said.

"I guess we'd better head out then," Vince said. And when he saw the reluctance on both Frances' face and Kendall's, he decided to see how he'd function as a matchmaker. "Pete, if you won't think this is a bribe, I'd like to leave a couple of tickets for you at the box office for the Cracker-Squire game."

"I'd like that," Pete Kendall said.

"Of course, if you want to bring your kids, I can leave an extra ticket or two."

Kendall looked at Frances. "I don't have a wife or kids."

"Your girlfriend then," Vince said.

"That's tonight's game, isn't it? It's kind of late to call anybody." His eyes were still on Frances. "Will you be there?"

"In the same box," Vince said. He turned to Frances. "He might as well join us in the Wardlaw private box."

"It's not really a box," Frances said. "It's a room."

"You'll be there?" Kendall said.

"Yes."

"See you then. You'll remember my name?"

"Pete Kendall," Frances said.

Kendall left and Vince turned and winked at John. "He seems like a fairly nice guy. Too bad he's so ugly."

"I'd say rugged-looking."

"Oh … you … you … I know what you're doing, and I'm going to pay you back somehow."

"You don't have to go to the game," Vince said.

"I said I was going and I will."

Vince laughed. "John, take this young lady somewhere to have her hair done, and when she gets back to the apartment make sure she puts on a dress. I have a feeling young Kendall doesn't care for women who wear blue jeans."

He left them on the street and got his car from the lot and drove back to Wardlaw's office.

CHAPTER TWELVE

"Nothing yet," David Wardlaw said.

Vince nodded and carried his topcoat over and put it in the closet. On his way back to the desk, he stopped and looked out the wide window that overlooked the downtown business section. Dark clouds were gathering in the west, and as he watched there was a sprinkling of rain on the window. He looked down at the model of the Boulevard development. The Convention Center block looked especially "iffy" in the light of the last two days.

"They'll call, unless somebody's locked them away from a phone."

David shrugged. "You get things settled at the police station?"

"It wasn't hard."

"One of your girl friends?"

"Just a girl I know," Vince said.

"You seem to know a lot of girls."

"I'm a boy," Vince said. "I'm supposed to know girls."

"I could use a drink," Wardlaw said. "There's a new bottle of good scotch in the kitchen."

Vince moved toward the kitchen. "Rocks?"

"Rocks."

Vince returned with two glasses filled with ice cubes and a bottle of Glenlivet. "Getting fancy," he said as he broke the seal and poured two large shots.

"I thought I'd try a single malt."

"Tastes like scotch," Vince said, grinning at him.

"Is Helen one of your girls?"

Vince looked at Wardlaw for a long moment. "Which Helen is that?"

"Helen Morris."

"That's an odd question coming from you. It takes a lot of balls to ask it."

"Just making conversation," Wardlaw said.

"The hell you are."

"Just curious."

"The hell you are."

"Maybe it's not a good question." He lifted his glass and looked at Vince over the rim.

"It might be a good question for you. There's just nothing that says I have to answer it. Or even like the question."

"I thought it was a fairly innocent question."

Vince nodded. "But there are some other questions hiding behind that one."

"Forget I asked it then."

"If I can."

"I guess it looks like prying," Wardlaw said.

"It is prying."

"Helen had a hard time with that husband of hers."

"She's a strong woman," Vince said. "I don't think she ever cared beans about him. Substitutes don't last long. People find out that substitutes are worse than nothing at all."

A puzzled look crossed Wardlaw's face. "Who was he a substitute for?"

The phone rang. It caught them both by surprise. Wardlaw reached for the receiver, but Vince got there first.

Wardlaw nodded and leaned away.

"Vince Gorman here."

"Jim Sims."

"I thought it might be," Vince said. "You over your monthly or whatever it was?"

"I'm getting better by the minute."

"I figured as much."

"Expenses have gone up," Sims said.

"It's been that way all year." Vince looked at Wardlaw and nodded. "Where can I meet you and Johnson?"

"That's just it. I'm not sure we want to talk to you at all."

"What does that mean?" Vince asked.

"We want to talk to Wardlaw. Just Wardlaw."

"That might be worked out. Hold on a minute." Vince put his hand over the mouthpiece. "He wants to talk to you."

"I'll have to do it," Wardlaw said.

Vince uncovered the mouthpiece. "He'll talk to you. Where?"

"My motel room," Sims said.

"You've got to be kidding. Mr. Wardlaw doesn't like talking into tape recorders and he doesn't like whores suddenly appearing out of nowhere."

"You're not very trusting, you and your boss."

"Not very."

"Where?" Sims asked.

"How about our offices here at Peachtree Investment?"

"Now you're the one with the balls," Sims said.

"A bar then." Vince thought for a few seconds. "There's a bar on Peachtree Road near Garden Hills. It's called The Haven."

"I can find it," Sims said.

"Forty-five minutes?"

"I'll be there."

"What about Johnson?"

"I'll be alone," Sims said. "Johnson will go along with what I agree to."

"Agreed."

Sims hung up and Vince replaced the phone in its cradle. "You got any idea how to play this, David?"

"Just bargaining."

"Not exactly. I wouldn't put it past Sims to try to record the whole conversation. He's not the kind of person you can trust, so he doesn't trust anybody either."

Wardlaw lifted the phone and dialed the one-digit number that connected him with his driver in the underground garage. "I'll be leaving in five minutes," he said.

"Some things you can do. Sit close to the jukebox and feed it a lot of quarters. Don't talk unless you're covered by music. If he gets there first, don't sit at any table or booth he picks out."

"What do I agree to?"

"That's up to you. You're the one who knows what it's worth to you."

"You're not much help," David said.

"Not that much has changed. Johnson still wants money, but now he wants more of it. Maybe he wants a dancing girl who comes with the apartment. Sims still wants to be governor. Could be he just wants you to spell out the kind of support you'll give him."

"That sounds easy enough."

"It won't be. The main thing is that you don't blow your cool. Think of the transaction as buying a pound of liver at a supermarket."

"Why?"

"Because this is a nasty little man. Remember how he tried to trap Harley. The moment you let it float up. the moment you take a long look at him and assess the kind of person he is, you're in trouble."

"I think I can handle it," David said.

Vince went to the closet and got out both topcoats. He tossed Wardlaw's to him and got into his. "I hope you can."

"Where'll you be?"

"Out," Vince said.

"Can I reach you?"

"I'll reach you, either at home or the office."

"I might need you," Wardlaw said.

Vince shook his head. "I'm already on overtime."

Wardlaw's driver stood behind the passenger door, holding it open. Vince saw Wardlaw into the Continental, gave him a little wave and walked over to his Ford. He followed the Continental out of the underground garage, and when Wardlaw's driver turned right and began the box-step route that would put him on Peachtree Street, Vince took a left. In some ways they were going in the same direction, but Vince didn't want to follow Wardlaw even those few blocks.

Vince parked at the curb in front of the Tudor style house and looked up at the second floor where Helen's apartment was. She wasn't expecting him and she might not be there and even if she was, she might not want to see him. He was trying to decide what to do when the door on the ground floor opened and the woman came out. She made a production of checking for mail, and then she stood on the tiled porch and looked down at the lawn. Whatever else she seemed to be doing, he knew that she was trying to get a closer look at him. It was time either to drive away or get out of the car. He didn't want to be thought a prowler, so he got out and walked up the stone path. The woman lifted her head and looked at him.

"Hi," she said. "You were here last night, weren't you?"

"Guilty," he said.

"Helen didn't tell me your name."

Vince grinned at her. "Maybe she didn't want you to know it."

"You don't look too battered to me."

"I recover fast." That meant Helen had talked to the woman about him. He could understand that. Helen didn't want the woman to misunderstand why he'd stayed at the apartment the night before. Or, maybe Helen and this woman were friends and the talking had been for some other reason.

"I heard the water running a few minutes ago. I think she was drawing a bath."

"You think she needs somebody to scrub her back?"

The woman looked him up and down and smiled. "I always did."

Vince crossed the porch and put a hand on the knob of the screen door. As he opened it she followed him and stopped just a couple of feet behind him. "You going to call the police and report a prowler?"

"Lord, no," the woman said, "I'm going to sit in my living room and lead the cheers."

"Bless you." He opened the screen door and tried the inner door. It was unlocked. He stepped in and started to close the door behind him. Just before the door was fully shut, she leaned in and winked at him.

On the way up the stairs he almost decided that he was going to the wrong apartment.

Helen didn't hear him mount the stairs or enter the living room. The stereo receiver was on one of the classical-music stations and it sounded like they were playing a Bartok string quartet. He didn't know which one. He took off his topcoat and dropped it on the sofa. He stopped in front of the stereo receiver and twisted the dial until he found a rock station.

The change of stations frightened her. He could hear the fear in her voice. "Who's in there? Who is it?"

Vince turned the volume down. "A friendly rapist. The same one who was here last night."

"Vince?"

"Yes." He turned the volume up again. He left the living room and went into the kitchen. He found the bottle of J&B and some ice cubes in the refrigerator. He fixed himself a scotch on the rocks and walked back through the living room and down the hall to the bedroom. He entered her bedroom and found the door to the bathroom was open, the full-length mirror on the door fogged over.

"Anybody home?"

"Don't you dare come in here," she said.

"Just to the doorway."

"Vince, don't…"

"You can try to beat me to the door, but you might not make it." He reached the doorway and leaned against the door frame. "At least now I know you're a clean girl." He looked down into his glass, still not looking toward her.

"This isn't going to do you any good. If anything…"

"I wasn't doing any good anyway," Vince said. "And if you're thinking of yelling rape, don't. I met the lady downstairs and she knows I stayed here all night. It can't be pleasure one night and rape the next afternoon."

He lifted his head and looked at her. She'd scooted down into the tub. Only her head and her knees showed above the clouded, soapy water. Her mouth was tight and hard. She wasn't, he saw, very amused.

"On second thought, I'll wait for you in the living room."

"You'd better leave," Helen said.

"Not after I've seen your knees." He backed out of the doorway and went through the bedroom. He pulled the bedroom door closed behind him and returned to the living room. He played with the stereo dial until he found the Bartok string quartet again. He sat down on the sofa and sipped his drink. He hadn't known exactly what he was going to do when he entered the apartment, and he still didn't. It was odd, a crazy thing, the kind of escapade he was more likely to indulge in when he was drunk. And, except for the one drink with David Wardlaw and the one drink he now held in his hand, he was cold sober.

Ought to do something about that. He finished his drink and went back into the kitchen and fixed another. He made that one last, and there was still part of it left when he heard the bedroom door open about fifteen minutes later. He stood up when she entered the living room. She was wearing a dark wool pants suit and kid-leather boots. Her face looked as if she'd made it up hurriedly, and she was brushing her hair as she crossed the room.

"Let me fix you a drink, Helen."

"I don't know what you think you've accomplished by this."

"I finally saw your knees," he said. "How about that drink?"

"I'm going out."

"Really? I thought we'd spend the evening in front of the fireplace, talking and kissing and acting like teenagers."

"Is being a Peeping Tom a teenaged trait?"

"Is that what you call that? That little peek at your kneecaps? Lord, lady, I don't know what I'm going to do with you."

"You're not going to do anything with me," Helen said. "The one thing you can do is leave."

"I've got it now. I've been trying to figure out why I came blundering up here. You ready for a shock?"

"If it's really a shock."

"Mr. David Wardlaw asked me, right out of the blue, if you were one of my girls. I think the fact I stayed here last night, even as banged up as I was, confused him. You see, old David is so straight, all he knows how to screw with is money. Just that, nothing else. Doesn't know the first thing about screwing with women. So naturally he figured if I stayed in the same apartment with you, we must have made the beast with two backs all night." He laughed. "I think I could sell what he saw in his mind to one of those skin and screw movie houses on Houston Street."

"What did you tell him?"

"About what?"

"About whether I was your girl … or one of your girls."

"I told him you had skin as smooth and cool as ice cream, that you have breasts like puppies with warm noses, that there wasn't a stretch mark or a wrinkle on you."

The hairbrush in her hand slowed and then stopped altogether. "I don't think you told David that."

"And that wasn't all I told him. I told him you wore blue underwear with "Try it, you'll like it" written across the front in old English script." He remembered the whore at the Executive Motor Hotel. "And I winked at him and told him your pubic hair was cut in the shape of a heart, just like the jet-set ladies wear theirs."

"What did you really tell him, Vince?"

"That we were deeply in love and that I'd given up all those other girls."

The brush moved again. "Did he believe you?"

"He always believes me," Vince said. "I never lie to him."

"The truth, Vince."

He shrugged. "I don't remember the exact words, but I think I told him I didn't think it was a hell of a lot of his business."

"That sounds like the truth. For the first time." As the brush whipped through her hair, her eyes were closed so that he couldn't see her eyes. "But David asked? He really asked?"

"I think I heard your little heart skip three or four beats. The great man asked. The great man noticed."

"You're silly, Vince," she said. But her face was still and intent.

He drained down the last of the drink. "Where are you going?"

"Like you said: none of your business."

"Let's see, let's see." He put the empty glass on the coffee table and stood up. "It's Saturday night. For drinks and dinner, I don't think you'd wear the pants suit. It's nice, but I don't quite see you in that in one of the better places." He walked around the table and looked her up and down. "Boots. That makes dinner out even more unlikely. So it's pub hopping ... or sports. Bedroom sports or otherwise. With you I'll strike the bedroom sports. So, it has to be"—he snapped his fingers—"The Cracker-Squires game."

"That's some charade," Helen said. "You knew the whole time."

"I guessed. I knew you were one of the Shooter's most rabid fans."

"Don't you know most women go to basketball games to see the men's legs?"

"The Shooter's legs are bowed."

"But he's cute," Helen said.

"I'll go to the game with you."

Helen shook her head. "No. Thanks anyway."

"I'll see you there."

"Perhaps. The Dome seats sixteen thousand. All you have to do is buy a ticket."

"Me buy a ticket? I'll be in the Wardlaw box."

"Lucky you."

Vince saw it wasn't going anywhere. It was going round and round. It had lost its energy. "You win a few, you lose twice that many."

"Last night I liked you," Helen said.

"I thought you did too. Except for the fight—if we can call it that—it was a great evening. Warm and real and just a little bit absurd."

"I think you broke it just now."

"No," he said, "not by anything I did today. Maybe by what I said. That David showed some interest."

"No, Vince."

"Oh, yes." Vince got his topcoat from the sofa. "I don't think anything I did here changed anything. I didn't rape you. I didn't stare at you like you were a blue movie. And I didn't put my hands on you."

"Thank you." But the tone was wry.

"I'm sorry, Helen, I really am."

She didn't answer him, and he nodded once and went down the steps without looking back. He got into the Ford and drove straight to the Executive Motor Hotel. He parked as close as he could to room 5. Angela answered the first knock. She was dressed in cut-off blue jeans and a white t-shirt without a bra.

She recognized him and blinked. "It's you after all."

"I came to see your valentine," he said.

David Wardlaw had never met Jim Sims, but he'd seen his picture in the newspaper now and then. He remembered the face, the crew-cut hair. At the same time, he assumed that Sims must know him from the same kind of circumstances. Otherwise it was going to be a strange game of blindman's buff. Or an encounter of spies who didn't know the recognition sign.

He didn't see Sims. Early, he guessed. He saw an empty table in the back of the bar near the jukebox. He seated himself there and when the waitress passed, he ordered a scotch on the rocks and, paying ahead of time, asked her to bring him a couple of dollars in quarters.

It wasn't a very nice bar, and he wondered if this wasn't Vince's idea of a joke. Perhaps ten years ago The Haven owners had started with high hopes. They'd spent quite a bit of money trying to reconstruct their idea of what an old-time tavern might have been. They'd collected artifacts of the period, the brass spittoons, the ornate tap handles, the beer barrels, the bung starters and some of the old signs. At the end of the bar nearest him there was a "Free Lunch" sign, though the food there was the usual snack things around a chafing dish that had been picked clean of everything but the sweet-and-sour sauce. The bar itself was a beautiful reconstruction. It had a fitted marble top over what seemed to be a heavy oak body. And there was a brass foot-rail that went the length of the bar.

Looking at the barroom now, David thought he detected the sign of neglect, the open acknowledgment that The Haven would never be anything but a neighborhood bar. It showed in the scarred tabletops and the chairs that needed repair, in an overall feeling that the room hadn't been really cleaned or dusted for some time.

His drink came. He didn't touch it right away. He didn't know how long the bargaining session might last, and he wanted to be sure that he'd approach it with a clear head.

Sims came in a few minutes later. He looked like he'd dressed carefully for the occasion. He wore a dark blazer with silver buttons, gray flared slacks and a tie about as wide as a baby's bib. He nodded at David and walked quickly toward the table. David held the handful of quarters, ready to rise and go to the jukebox. At the last moment, he stopped himself and stacked the quarters on the table in front of him. It seemed silly, this spy's concern about security. Maybe that was the way Vince would handle it, but David didn't feel that it was his way.

Jim Sims sat down across the table from him, his face burnished by the cold wind outside, his brush-cut hair looking stiff and electric. David looked him over as the waitress appeared at Sims's elbow and Sims ordered a bourbon with a water chaser. The wide tie was gray with a sailing-boat design and was held in place by a large tie tack in the shape of crossed tennis racquets. All very sporting, David thought, but he'd heard that of Sims—that Sims considered himself quite an athlete, that he somehow saw it as an extension of his wartime role as a fighter pilot.

At the table there were none of the courtesies, the handshaking or small talk. It was business and nothing but hard business. And, from the wary way Sims looked around, David realized that it wasn't going to be a long meeting. He understood then that the selection of The Haven by Vince hadn't been a joke. It had, instead, been the result of careful calculation. It wouldn't do for it to be known that Sims and Wardlaw had met a couple of hours before the decision was to be made. Such an account of a meeting in the *Constitution* or the *Journal* would ruin both of them.

The waitress brought Sims's drink, and David waited until she walked away. "I thought all this had been settled this morning."

"It wasn't." Sims sipped his drink. "That was just the first step in the negotiations. I'd assumed that Mr. Gorman would understand that."

David shook that off. It wasn't worth wasting time on. "You've talked to the others since then?"

"I'd rather not say which ones I've talked to or haven't talked to. Or what we've been talking about."

"That's your business," David said, "but I'd like to know how I'm supposed to know that you talked to anyone at all, that you aren't just jacking up the price artificially?"

"You'll have to trust me."

David didn't say anything or change the expression on his face.

"I can only say that your original offer has been bettered. It seemed good at the time, but it doesn't anymore."

David sipped his scotch. It was watery. He pushed it aside. "What do you think would be a reasonable offer?"

"Senator Johnson isn't happy with the offer made him this morning. He thinks it isn't realistic in terms of the long-range benefits the Boulevard site would bring to you."

"How much?"

"Twenty-five thousand."

David nodded.

Jim Sims's eyes narrowed and he leaned across the table. "Does your nod mean yes?"

David shook his head. "It means I understood what Johnson wants. That's all."

"I see."

"I'd like to know what you want," David said.

"I want the same things I outlined to your man this morning, only this time I want it spelled out a lot clearer."

"For example," David said.

"That vague offer wasn't enough. I want it spelled out. I want a primary fund of two hundred thousand." He held up his hand as if to shut off protest, although David had not moved or opened his mouth. "Of course, I wouldn't expect you to put up the whole amount. There must be other wealthy men who'd donate to the fund if you asked them."

"They might."

"I'm certain they would. You have a reputation as a man who isn't wrong often. I understand why you wouldn't want to support me openly during the primary. It might hurt both of us. So, I'll settle for a two-hundred-thousand-dollar primary fund. After I've won the primary, I would expect open support from you. And with a campaign chest of some size, I think I'd stand a better-than-average chance of winning."

"You don't seem very sure of yourself."

"Let's say I'm being modest," Sims said. "You know as well as I do that if I win the Democratic primary, there's not a Republican in the state who could beat me."

"That might be true. On the other hand, the primary fund might be money down the drain."

"That's my fee whatever happens," Sims said.

That was odd, David thought.

While he'd been talking to Sims, David had been looking away from his face, afraid that Sims might read what he was really thinking. At first, he'd fastened on the tie, and then as the talk went on he'd found himself staring at the tie tack, the one in the shape of crossed tennis racquets. The intricate detail of the racquets astounded him. He thought he could see the separate strings of the racquet, the crossed strings like a kind of grill work. And below that he noticed that the top two buttons of his blazer were still closed. That was odd also.

"It's a fee that might be met," David said. "One major problem is that, even for the two hundred and twenty-five thousand dollars, you can't promise anything more than a stand-off. You can't really deliver the five votes."

"That's true. On the other hand, with four votes and with the four of us holding the line I think we'll find that someone will cross over and join us."

"When you say four votes, I assume you mean that Hap Seaver will be with you?"

"I think Hap will go along with us," Sims said. "Otherwise, he's going to be very lonely out there by himself."

"But even with Hap, there's no guarantee?"

"It's a negative guarantee," Jim Sims said. "If the Boulevard site isn't selected, then no other one will either."

"And that's the best we can hope for?"

Jim Sims nodded. "And, when the meeting tonight runs toward midnight, someone will crack and move over to us."

David looked up and saw the waitress standing at the end of the table. "Another drink?" she asked.

Sims nodded. David shook his head.

"What's all the change for?" Sims asked.

David looked down at the stack of quarters, and when he looked up again, he found himself focusing upon the tie tack. "I thought about playing some music."

"Thought I might be late, huh?"

"Or that I was early," David said.

The waitress placed the shot of bourbon in front of Sims and refilled the water glass from a pitcher she carried. As she backed away from the table Sims said, "Just as well you didn't. It's hard to talk over all that loud noise."

"Perhaps," David said. He lifted his eyes and looked at Sims. "That's an interesting tie tack you've got there."

"You think so?" Sims lifted his hand as if to touch the tie tack. Inches away, the hand stopped short.

"You mind if I look at it?"

"Well… it's kind of hard to take off," Sims said.

"That's all right. You don't have to take it off." David leaned across the table and when his hand was close to the tie tack, he dipped lower suddenly, caught the tie and flipped it up. That was it. Wires ran from the back of the tie—from the tie tack—down to the belt and around to the side.

The movement caught Jim Sims by surprise. When he saw what David had done, he pushed his chair back a foot or so and smoothed the tie back into place. "What are you doing?"

"You know."

"I don't know."

"Unclip it and pass it to me," David said.

"What?"

"The tape recorder."

"I don't have any," Sims said.

"I'm not going to put myself into a position where I can be blackmailed."

"It's not for the purpose of blackmail," Sims said. "I want to be sure you keep the bargain."

David put his hand palm up on the table in front of Sims. "The tape recorder."

It was a hard moment. It may have been seconds, but it seemed like hours before Jim Sims dropped his eyes and unbuttoned the dark blazer. He reached under the blazer, the hand moving back to the left hip. He hesitated for a long-caught breath, and then he unclipped a small tape recorder that fitted into his palm and brought it out. When it was in front of him, he unplugged the wires that ran to it.

"Here." He dropped it into David's hand.

"I'll be back in a moment." David pushed back his chair. He took a second to look around the bar, and when he located the men's room he headed in that direction. He waited until a man at the urinal left and then he placed the tape recorder on the ledge of the closed window and found the rewind button. He rewound the tape back part way and stopped it. He touched the play button.

"...wouldn't expect you to put up the whole amount. There must be..."

David stopped the tape. The sound quality was good, the voice coming in clear and distinct. It was obviously Sims's voice, and he knew, without listening, that the recorder had probably picked up what he'd said as well. He didn't need to listen. He touched the rewind button and held it down until the tape was all on one spool. He took the spool with the tape on it off the recorder and placed it in his pocket.

He returned to the barroom and sat down across from Sims. He put the recorder on the center of the table. Sims pulled it toward him and looked down at it.

"Now you could blackmail me," Sims said.

"You have my word I'll burn it as soon as I reach my apartment."

"And your word that you won't blackmail me is supposed to be better than my word that I won't blackmail you?"

"Yes," David said.

Sims lifted the recorder and placed it in his blazer side pocket. "I guess I'll have to."

"Unless we want to fight over it."

Sims forced himself to laugh. "It's not worth all that."

"I don't think so either."

Sims let out a deep breath and grinned at him. "Well, we still have a deal, don't we? Hell, I tried it and you caught me at it. That's no reason to scrub the deal."

That was the hard one. Since he'd left the bathroom, David knew that it would probably come down to that sooner or later, and he hadn't been sure how he'd react. Ten years of planning and work were involved. It wasn't an easy thing to put his back to it and know that all that time and effort would come to nothing.

"I think you'd better take your next best offer … if you have one."

"You've got to be kidding."

"No." David said.

"You're giving up fifty or sixty million dollars. Why?"

"You don't give up what you don't already have," David said. "Maybe the rest of it is that the view down here, this close up, isn't one that I like very much."

"Look, you're grown up, Wardlaw." Sims leaned across the table, his voice pushing with urgency. "You know as well as I do that it doesn't matter who you have to work with. It's the final result that matters."

"You know," Wardlaw said, "I still believe that, but this time I pass."

"That's your last word on it?"

"Take your best offer."

Jim Sims pushed back his chair and got up. He hadn't moved many steps from the table before he turned and came back. "I can't leave that tape with you."

David waved a hand at the waitress. When she reached the table David asked, "Got a pair of scissors?"

She said there was a pair behind the bar, and while she went to get them David found a clean ash tray at a nearby table. For the next ten minutes, while Jim Sims sat across the table and watched, David cut the tape into a thousand bits and pieces. He pushed the spool across the table toward Sims and then after stirring the scraps of tape around he lifted the ash tray and poured about half the contents into Sims's hand.

After Jim Sims left, David carried the ash tray into the bathroom and flushed his half of the tape bits down the toilet. A few minutes later, seated in the back of the Continental, he knew that giving in to his anger and disgust had been a costly luxury. But he felt, oddly enough, alive and vibrant, as if he'd been through some kind of emotional steam bath and cold shower that left him tingling all over.

CHAPTER THIRTEEN

At 5:30 the Shooter left his apartment and drove to The Steak Plank, a new restaurant that had just opened in the shadow of the Dome. He ate a small rare steak and drank a cup of hot tea. It was 6:20 when he left the restaurant and drove into the players parking lot. The guard at the locker-room entrance waved him in. He undressed at his locker and put on his uniform. Then, carrying his shoes and socks, he walked barefoot to the trainer's office. He stretched out on the training table and dozed until he heard some of the other players enter. The sound of the horse-play and laughter seemed far away from him. It was as if he were shrinking, moving away from them. And he felt himself getting smaller and smaller.

Ben Bob Turner found him sleeping on the training able and woke him by tapping him on the shoulder. "You must be in a hurry to get taped," he said.

"Some," the Shooter said.

After Ben Bob took off his jacket and rolled up his sleeves, he taped the Shooter's ankles. Finished, he straightened up and taped the Shooter on the hip. "How do they feel?"

The Shooter stood up and walked across the narrow room. He squatted and flexed his ankles. "Fine," he said.

Back in the locker room, he put on his socks and his basketball shoes without bothering with the laces. Taking special care not to trip over the laces, the Shooter left the locker room and went down the tunnel to Coach Thorn's office. Thorn was behind the desk reading the *Journal* sports page. He didn't hear the Shooter enter. The coach went back to another era of basketball, the time when a guard could be five-ten and get by. Now, the Shooter knew, he'd have trouble getting a scholarship to a good basketball college.

"Coach?"

Coach Thorn folded the paper and dropped it on the desk. "Everything all right, Shooter?"

"I guess so."

"Have a seat. You got a problem?"

"It's not that," the Shooter said. "I was wondering about Ab."

Coach Thorn looked down at his desk and shook his head. "I can't do anything about it."

"You think somebody'll pick him up?"

Thorn nodded. "The Carolina Cougars need a guard and so do the Tams."

"It's my fault he's in trouble. I hope he catches on somewhere."

Thorn gave him a hard look. "You really mean that?"

"It's my fault."

"I'll tell you what I'll do. I'll put in a call to Larry Brown up at Carolina right now."

"I'd appreciate it," the Shooter said.

"It's done then." Thorn lifted the phone and placed it on top of the newspaper. "Thanks for stopping by."

Coach Thorn was dialing when the Shooter left the office. He returned to the locker room. It was loud and noisy, and Big Ed Brewster was in the center of it, clowning and farting around. The Shooter sat down on the bench that faced his locker and tied his shoelaces.

"You feeling sad, Shooter?"

The Shooter looked up and realized that all the sounds of the locker room had stilled. Big Ed was standing at the far end of the locker room, one foot up on the bench.

"No, Ed. Why should I?"

"Lost your asshole buddy, that's why," Big Ed said.

The Shooter shrugged. "It don't matter. I can play ball with midgets."

"You hear that? Big Ed put his head back and hooted. "You listening to the Shooter, Bert?"

Bert, the second-year black guard who'd be replacing Ab Slaton, pulled the red uniform top down over his head and grinned at Big Ed. "I hear him. And, man, that's something I'd like to see. The Shooter out there with four three-foot midgets, doing it all himself."

"You know I didn't mean it that way," the Shooter said.

"Of course, you didn't," Bert said. Wry, harsh, unfriendly.

"It would be a sight, though, wouldn't it?" Big Ed said. The laugh that followed had anger and ridicule in it.

The Shooter stretched out on the bench and closed his eyes. There was still fifteen minutes before the warm-ups began at 7:30. Eyes closed, the talk droning on and on, he began to wonder if he could pick out Edna in the crowd. He wasn't sure where the seats were and, for just a second, he had some trouble remembering exactly what she looked like.

When Ethel Ann came out of the kitchen, Harley was rubbing his eyes and blinking at the television set.

"Ready for supper, Harley?"

"As soon as I'm awake," he said.

It had been a long afternoon after his return from downtown. The abrupt cancellation of the committee meeting was one more absurd move in an already overburdened process. At first, he was angry and then he was driven past anger into a brooding thoughtfulness.

Ethel Ann watched him without saying much. It was her way, something they'd developed in their relationship over the years of marriage. There was a simmering period when Harley appeared to be cooking some problem down to its essence and preparing to deal with it. When he was ready, he'd let her know and they'd talk about it.

So she sat on the sofa next to him and knitted while be watched the televised S.E.C. basketball game of the week: the game was between L.S.U. and Auburn. She knew, just from his face, that it wasn't a game where he was pulling for either team. It was a distant disinterest, and she knew the simmering was going on. From time-to-time, she had to leave him to check on a chuck roast in the kitchen. And several times, she refilled his coffee cup. At half time she left him staring at a gymnastics team performing at center court and went upstairs to the bedroom. She did some cleaning in the bathroom and, remembering their morning lovemaking, changed the bed linen. Passing through the living room a few minutes later, she found Harley stretched out on the sofa. He was snoring lightly. She left the TV on, went into the kitchen and added the parboiled vegetables to the roasting pan. And a half hour later, when supper was ready, she looked into the living room and found that Harley had finished his nap.

"It smells good all the way in here," Harley said.

"It's supposed to," she said. "That's part of the secret."

While he washed up, she set the table in the dining room with her best china and her wedding silver. As an afterthought, she got out two bottles of Michelob and poured them into the long-stem glasses.

Harley stopped at the end of the table and looked at her. "You sure I need a beer?"

"After an afternoon of coffee?"

"Let's hope I don't get too tipsy to vote tonight."

"Not you." The fact that he'd mentioned the committee meeting meant he was getting close to the edge. It wouldn't be long. But she didn't want to force it, and she talked of other things during the meal, waiting for him to find his own time. It wasn't during the meal and after he'd gone upstairs to dress, she remained behind long enough to clear the table and put the dishes in soak in the sink. On her way through the dining room, on her way up to the bedroom, the phone rang.

"Mrs. Brisker?"

"Yes."

"This is David Wardlaw. I'd like to speak to Harley."

"Hold the line, please."

Harley was seated on the edge of the bed, tying his shoestrings. "It's Mr. Wardlaw on the phone."

He nodded and picked up the receiver. "Yes, Mr. Wardlaw." He listened for a minute or so and she could see his brow wrinkling. He nodded to himself, as he might have nodded to Wardlaw if they'd been facing each other. At the end of that minute or so he said, "I guess that tears it."

His mouth got hard as he listened once more. "I don't think you know me very well, Mr. Wardlaw. If I wanted to shift my vote, I had better than an average chance yesterday. And the reason I don't hang up on you is that I believe your offer to free me is a sincere one. The only problem is that I am already free." He nodded and the hard line left his mouth. "Of course, I accept your apology."

He pivoted slightly and looked at Ethel Ann. "I'd like that too, Mr. Wardlaw. Please call me when you'd like to have that talk." He said his good-night and put the phone down. He went to the closet and got out a white shirt.

"It fell apart," he said.

"The Boulevard site?"

"Yes."

"How?" She moved close to him and began helping him with his buttons.

"I don't know exactly. He didn't say. But I have a feeling that he might be a bit more honest than I gave him credit for being. I think some part of the under-the-table bargaining bothered him and he backed away."

"Where does that leave you?"

"All alone in left field," he said.

She stepped past him and selected a tie for him. "Something's been bothering you all day."

"Money and power. Power and money. I guess I'm an innocent, but I always thought decisions got made on a give-and-take process, a small compromise here and there. The last couple of days, I've been seeing it another way, and I haven't liked it one damned bit." He took the tie from Ethel Ann and, without looking at it, threaded it under the collar. "Like Wardlaw there. Money and power up to here." He touched his nose. "But he might be better than I thought. He's got a lot tied up in the Boulevard site. He wants it until he can taste it. Years of work and planning are involved. But he backed away. I feel a little cleaner now."

After the knot was in the tie, she reached out to pull down and adjust his collar. "I thought we were going to have a long, soul-searching talk."

"I thought so too."

"Come home as soon as you can," she said. "Don't go off drinking with the boys."

"There aren't any boys over there I want to go drinking with." He slipped into his suit coat and put his topcoat over his arm. Side-by-side they walked down the stairs and to the front door. "I don't think I'll be long."

"I'll wait up."

He winked at her. "I thought you would. You're a lusty woman."

"I didn't mean *that*," she protested.

"I did," he said.

David Wardlaw replaced the telephone receiver and walked down the hall to Frances' room. The door was open, but he knocked and she came out of the bathroom, brushing her hair.

"Hi," she said.

"How was your day?"

"Not too good. How was yours?"

"The same as yours, I think." He sat on the edge of the bed. "You going out tonight?"

"Just to the Dome."

"That's the second dress I've seen on you in one day. That has to be a record."

"I've got a date ... sort of." She blushed and looked away.

"What does that mean?"

"He doesn't know it's a date," she said.

"Anyone I know?"

"I just met him today."

"That's fast," he said.

Frances placed the brush on the dresser top and turned to face him. "It was rather hard for him to miss me, Daddy. You see, I met him when he was arresting me."

In the few minutes it took her to tell him about her afternoon down on the Strip, and at the police station, he sat very still, hearing the words but paying more attention to her face, reading the truth of what she said there. At the end of it, when she told him about John's part in it and how Vince had applied pressure, he let out a long, low breath.

"Someday," he said, "I'm going to have to smoke some grass just to see what there is about it that's worth all this trouble."

"That would be fun," she said, grinning at him. "Just as soon as I get some."

"That's not a promise," he said quickly.

"We'll see."

"And this young policeman ... he seemed interested in you?"

"I think so. And that's why I thought I'd better tell you about the arrest. I don't want him reassuring you all evening when you don't know what he's talking about."

"Is that the only reason?"

"It was one of the stronger reasons," she said.

"And you like this young policeman?"

"I don't really know. I think so." Her face became very serious. "And, Daddy, please don't try to buy him for me. I know you think I'm an ugly duckling, but I'm really not a bad girl under all this." She made a motion that encompassed her large-boned body.

"I never thought that," he said. "You're like your mother, and that's the nicest thing I can say about you."

"That is nice," she said. "That's the nicest thing you've said to me in a long time."

He stood up and looked around her room. "Is he picking you up here?"

"Of course not. He doesn't know it's a date."

"Ride over with me then."

"I'd like that."

"Stay a bit longer," Angela said.

Vince had just returned from her bathroom where he'd showered. Now he stood at the end of the bed, toweling off. She saw that he was looking at her so she flopped her knees apart and did a little one-two-three hump at him.

"I can't." Once again, he marveled at the heart-shaped pubic hair.

"That's what *you* say." She nodded at his groin. "The other part of you seems interested."

"I've got to talk to him," Vince said. He put his back to her and dug his boxer shorts from the pile of clothing on the chair beside the bed.

"That's not fair," she said.

"Sorry." He dressed quickly. When he was seated on the chair notching the buckles of his shoes, he watched her roll across the bed and go into the bathroom. She came out wearing the short terrycloth robe. "I hope you take Master Charge," he said.

While she was laughing, he took out a roll of money and peeled off three twenties. "Enough?"

"Enough," she said, "and it's been fun."

"Ditto," he said.

"You come back, you hear?"

"Bet your ass on it," he said.

At his apartment in Ansley Park, Vince took a few minutes to run an electric razor over his face. He could no longer smell the lime cologne, but deep in his inner nose he could still smell Angela's perfume and the healthy sweat of the afternoon. To counter that, he slapped on an English after-shave that had the scent of wild spices. He dressed in a red blazer and gray pants, and drove to the Dome.

The security guard at the entrance to the executive parking area waved him in. At the executive entrance he showed his pass to the new guard there, who didn't know him, entered the elevator and rode it to the third level. On that level, just outside the elevator, was The Redneck Lounge, which was open to box and suite holders. On all the plans, and even after the Dome was completed, the lounge was not named. The first inclination had been to call it The Cracker Lounge. But a bad joke, made at a nearby table one night, playing upon the fact that "cracker" really meant "redneck" had led Vince to suggest that they call the third-level bar The Redneck Lounge. Wardlaw had balked at first, but he had the name tried out and found that most of the box and suite holders liked the name. There was something a little "precious" about drinking in a bar called The Redneck while wearing a $400 suit and escorting a wife or girlfriend who was more accustomed to drinking in places with much more chic names.

Vince looked in The Redneck on the way by. Most of the tables were taken, and, as he watched, the appetizer carts moved from table to table and the waitresses scurried to the bar and back. The lounge more than paid for itself. Drinks were expensive, the appetizers were free and no money passed hands. Checks were signed at the table, and bills were sent off at the end of each month. The bill included ten percent for service. There was no tipping.

Vince reached the Wardlaw suite. He was the first to arrive, though the bartender, Al, was already in place behind the bar, and chafing dishes and sandwich trays had been arranged about the room.

The suite had been planned after the ones at the Astrodome and Texas Stadium where the Cowboys played their games. There was a wide though narrow window that overlooked the center area of the basketball court. Flush against the window there was a low bar counter with a row of ten high-backed bar stools covered with red leather. All around the room were Dufy sports prints, sailing and racing scenes, and all of the furniture was covered with soft red leather. It was, as a writer in *Sports Illustrated* had tagged it, "Atlanta safari" decor.

Each time, entering the suite before a game, Vince smelled the good heady scent of the leather. As time passed, he lost that smell in the smoke and alcohol and in the process of getting used to it.

"A drink, Mr. Gorman?"

"Vodka martini." He went to a table with two phones in the left corner of the suite and sat in a low leather camp stool. He dialed the in-the-building number of the business office. He identified himself and said, "I need to get in touch with Mr. Wardlaw's secretary. Could you check the season ticket list and find where she's seated?"

Al brought him the martini while he waited. He sipped at it and listened to the shuffling of pages at the other end of the line.

Then the girl was back on the phone. "Miss Morris has seats in section M. The seats are on row E, numbers 1 and 2."

Vince thanked her and hung up. He dialed the number for the house manager and asked that an usher be sent up to Mr. Wardlaw's suite. Leaving the phone table, waiting for the usher, he remembered that he hadn't eaten dinner. He crossed to the bar and lifted the cover from one of the chafing dishes. "You know what this is, Al?"

"Sweet and sour shrimp, I think."

"You cook it, Al?"

"You got to be kidding, Mr. Gorman."

Vince dipped out a dozen or so of the large shrimp, careful to bypass the chunks of pineapple and other fruits and vegetables, and carried his dish to the bar counter that overlooked the court. He ate the shrimp while he looked down at the seats below. He couldn't figure where Section M was, but he assumed that Wardlaw had probably given Helen good seats near mid-court.

Al opened the door to the usher's knock. Vince gave the usher Helen's seat numbers and asked him to wait there for Miss Morris and have her join Mr. Wardlaw and Mr. Gorman in Mr. Wardlaw's suite.

He finished the shrimp and carried the dish over to the bar. Al swept the dish from the bar with hardly a wasted motion. Vince looked at the finger-shaped sandwiches on the trays. "What kind are these?"

"Most of them are cucumber and cream cheese." Al wrinkled his nose.

"What?"

"It was a last-minute order from Mr. Wardlaw. I'll tell you, the catering service had a time finding cucumbers this time of day with the supermarkets closed."

"Why would? ..."

"Must be some reason," Al said.

Vince lifted one of the sandwiches and downed it in two bites. "Not bad," he said.

As he walked back to his martini, Al picked up one of the sandwiches and sniffed at it. "Try it," Vince said.

He stood at the window and looked down at the floor. The Cracker team was coming out on the floor. The Shooter was in the lead, dribbling a basketball. He turned toward the basket to the right and drove in for a lay-up. The file of other players peeled off behind him, the player behind him taking the rebound and wheeling to fire it to a player charging toward him. The first phase of the warm-ups was on.

Vince turned to Al. "How was it?"

"It's all right, but I wouldn't want them in my lunch bucket."

On the court, breathing easily now, feeling the first sweat break, the Shooter went through the lay-up drill. He knew the fans were watching him and he started showboating a bit. His final time down the lane he took the ball, took his step and a half, and as he went into the air turned his back and did a two-handed backwards stuff. The crowd roar went up.

Not long after that, one of the ball boys wheeled the ball caddy onto the floor and started tossing the balls to the players. The Shooter took a ball and dribbled away from the basket. While the others were trying their jump shots he dribbled out to mid-court and just stood there, getting the feel of the ball. He didn't need his eyes on the ball. He was looking up at the stands, trying to find Edna. He knew roughly the area where the business office usually set aside tickets for the players and he searched it well. He'd about given it up and was turning away when he saw Edna following an usher down the aisle. She was looking at him, and he was lifting his hand to wave when a young man moved around her, no longer blocked by her, and took her arm. He was a good-looking guy, tanned and with the shoulders of a swimmer.

The Shooter said, "Shit," and dropped the ball. He turned and dribbled about three or four steps and threw it up from about fifty feet out. It was a still moment at the hoop, no balls bouncing off it, and the Shooter's shot went in without hitting iron, only net.

The roar again, which meant they were still watching him. A second-line forward took the rebound, gawked at him, and then tossed the ball back. The Shooter took the ball, put it on the floor for a tap or two, and then jumped to his right and let it go. It fell in from about forty feet out. The crowd roared once more, even louder this time.

Big Ed Brewster took his rebound and whipped it back out to him. It burned against his hands, but he didn't hesitate. He took the ball high, made his one step and jumped it up. The shot was long. It glanced off the backboard, hooked to the left, touched iron and fell through. Thirty-five feet.

"Screw her," the Shooter said to himself. "At least the ball is falling through."

For his next shot, from twenty-five feet out, he made a break for the left corner. He took a pass and threw it up on a clothes-line. The ball brushed iron on both sides and fell through. Big Ed Brewster took the flat fall of the ball and dribbled out toward the Shooter. About twelve feet out Big Ed pivoted, stretched out his full height and released the ball with a looping arc. He didn't wait to see if the ball fell through. He trotted over to the Shooter.

"You going to shoot like that all night...from out around Cain Street and Peachtree...I'm going to pull myself a muscle and sit this one out."

The Shooter shook his head. "Showing off for this cunt."

Big Ed understood that. "Now, Shooter, if it doesn't queer your plans for the evening, you let me have the ball a few times and I might make myself some trim points."

"How many points you want?"

"One hundred," Big Ed said and the hard roar of his laugh carried all the way up to the second level of the Dome.

It was a quarter of eight when Wardlaw and Frances arrived at the suite. Frances was rosy-faced from the cold, and Wardlaw looked happy, as if the pressures of the day hadn't bothered him. Again, as he did each time, Vince marveled at how much Frances looked like her mother. Especially now when she was wearing a dress.

Frances waved and stopped at the bar to speak to Al. Wardlaw brought her coat and his over to the closet. Vince followed him over and waited until he closed the closet.

"It's just as well you didn't call me," Wardlaw said. "It was a disaster. I blew it."

Vince heard his brief account of the meeting. "The bastard got tricky," he said at the end.

"You'd have handled it better," Wardlaw said. "You wouldn't have blown up."

"I'm not so sure about that." He looked at his watch. "If you've got second thoughts, I can still try to patch it up."

David shook his head. "I won't do business with them. I'll clear that thirty acres and plant it in field peas and corn."

"And invite everybody in town to come over and pick a bucket?" Vince laughed. "It's a hell of a good PR idea."

"Remind me of it in the spring."

They turned as Frances walked toward them.

"A dress." Vince said, "It must be an occasion."

Frances blushed. "Now both of you have made fun of me."

"That's not fun. That's envy for whatever young dude you're wearing it for."

The blush deepened. "I'm not wearing it …" She broke off and angled back toward the bar.

"I owe you an apology for this afternoon," Wardlaw said as he watched her move away. "I want to thank you for what you did for her."

"I'd have helped her even if you weren't her father," Vince said. "Aside from a few minor faults, I like the way she's grown up."

"Daddy!" It was a delighted shriek from Frances. "You remembered."

That explained the cucumber and cream cheese sandwiches.

"And it looks like hundreds of them," she said, holding up one of the finger sandwiches.

A phone rang. Vince got it. It was the security guard downstairs. "There's a Peter Kendall down here says he was invited to the Wardlaw suite tonight."

Vince covered the mouthpiece so the guard wouldn't hear him. "Anybody up here know somebody named Peter Kendall?"

"It's him," Frances said. She dropped her eyes. "You know."

"Send him up," Vince said.

Moving toward Frances, he grinned, but then he saw the excitement and the fear in her face. He decided it wouldn't do to tease her anymore. But there was one thing he could do. He leaned over Frances and began telling her a long-involved story about a spring vacation from Duke, one he'd spent in a cheap hotel in New York. At first, she seemed puzzled, and then she got involved in the story and was laughing that beautiful, natural laugh when the door opened and Peter Kendall came in.

It was the effect Vince wanted and it hit young Peter Kendall squarely between the eyes. Next to Vince, Wardlaw had been puzzled by the burst of storytelling. During the introductions, seeing the stunned look on Kendall's face, he decided that, whatever the reason, it had certainly worked to the benefit of Frances.

"A drink, Mr. Kendall?" Wardlaw asked.

"I'd feel better if you called me Pete."

Looking him over, Vince decided that Kendall had spent part of his afternoon getting buffed and polished. The blue double-knit jacket wasn't especially expensive, but it had been tailored to a degree so that it fit his wide shoulders and narrow waist. The dark gray slacks looked almost new and the black chukka boots had a shine you could see a reflection in.

"Pete then." Wardlaw said.

"I drink mainly beer," Pete said. "I'll take a beer if you have one." He eyed the impressive row of bottles behind the bar. "If not, I'll…"

Al had been listening. He reached into the beer cooler beneath the bar and brought up a bottle of Bass Ale. "This all right?"

"Fine," Pete said. He took the glass of ale and, turning from the bar, he smiled at Frances. During the introduction, Pete had looked as though he were confused and in shock, and this was the first real communication between them.

Vince, to the side and looking at them over the edge of an empty martini glass, read the intimate shock that ran between them, and he made a mental check mark that everything was fine, that they were on their way to whatever beginning point young people went with their romances these days. He decided he and Wardlaw were in the way. He touched Wardlaw on the shoulder and drew him over to the bar counter over next to the window.

"I sent word down for Helen to join us when she arrives." He looked at Wardlaw. "You mind?"

"I'm glad you did."

"I thought you might be," Vince said.

"And I'm confused."

"I knew you'd be."

To avoid Wardlaw's searching glance, he looked at Frances and Pete. Even crusty, tough Al had read the young people correctly and he'd put his back to them, giving them a kind of privacy. Now Frances was encouraging Pete to try one of the cucumber and cream cheese sandwiches and, watching Pete's face, Vince knew that Pete was going to like those sandwiches even if they made him break out in hives.

"Introduction of players," Wardlaw said.

Vince reached for the sound knob below the window that let the game noises into the suite.

"I had trouble finding a parking space," Helen said. She stood with a hand on the back of one of the high-backed bar stools. "That poor usher looked like he might cry when I showed up. I think he was getting ready to enjoy the game."

Pete and Frances were seated at the left of the window, on the last two stools. Vince and Wardlaw were seated in the center. Now Wardlaw got up and moved over to his right to give Helen a seat between him and Vince.

"Game's just started," Vince said.

Helen nodded at him, a nod of recognition, but there was a distance and restraint in her face as she looked at him. Vince saw this and understood it, and a strong regret moved in him. He turned away from her and looked down at the floor of the Dome. Al, the bartender, hovered behind Helen. Vince heard her order a Bloody Mary.

On the other side of Vince, Pete couldn't hold back a shout. "Look at that mother go!" he yelled as Julius Erving took the fast-break pass just beyond the foul circle. He took his one and a half steps and went into the air. He still seemed to be rising as he made his one-handed flying dunk. The crowd roared to its feet. Down at the Cracker bench, Coach Thorn got to his feet and made the "T" sign with his fingers. On the court, as soon as the ball was in play, the Shooter turned to the nearest official and called a time-out.

The score was 10 to 4 in favor of the Squires.

Al placed a Bloody Mary in front of Helen and backed away, warmed by her smile of thanks.

"Shit," Coach Thorn said. The starters were seated on the bench, and the reserves were standing behind him. Thorn was a towel-twister and the Shooter stared at his hands as they turned red and the cords stood out on the backs. "Shooter, where's your head tonight? Bert's expecting a pick and you're cutting to the corner."

"Right," the Shooter said.

"Erving's last two points to you," Thorn said.

"Right," the Shooter said.

"If you've got problems, the court's not the place for them. Out there you're supposed to be setting picks, making some high percentage shots and ... goddammit ... playing some defense."

The Shooter nodded. Thorn gave him a hard look and passed on to Big Ed. "You got to be helping out on Erving. Frank can't handle him alone. Nobody can. As soon as he makes his move from the corner you've got to ..."

The Shooter turned Coach Thorn off. It was like turning the sound off in a car at the drive-in-movie. The faces were there and the mouths were moving, but he didn't want to hear any more of it.

When the buzzer sounded to end the time-out, the Shooter moved to mid-court and took the ball from the official. He flipped it in to Bert and got it back. Big Ed was free for a split second, moving in and out of the three-second lane, but the Squire center moved in and covered him. The Shooter dribbled across the thirty-foot mark, the line that circled the end of the court. Beyond this line, any shot that went in counted three points. Still dribbling, the Shooter backed over the thirty-foot line and stopped. When the Squire guard moved out to pick him up, he moved forward one step and put the shot up. The ball danced on the rim and went in. The crowd roared to its feet. The score was now 10 to 7.

"Three-point shot by the Shooter," the public-address announcer said.

He heard this as he turned and sprinted back down the court, looking back over his shoulder to locate this man. And he wondered if Edna was yelling along with the rest of the crowd. And as soon as he asked it, he told himself that it didn't matter. "Screw her and her fancy boyfriend. Fuck her."

His man had the ball and was moving to his left. The Shooter stepped out and challenged him, hands up, eyes on the other guard's feet. He was watching the feet for the sudden cut and move, for the stop that would mean that the guard was going to put the ball up.

"Try your luck," the Shooter shouted at his man.

The guard said, "Fuck off, Shooter."

The Shooter moved in and hit him with a hip and made a reach for the ball. He heard the first note of the whistle and knew the foul was being called on him. He let his right hand, the one reaching for the ball, swing upwards. The hand clobbered the guard on the ear.

"Sorry," he said.

He'd turned away and was heading toward midcourt to take up his defensive position when the guard jumped him from behind and landed two blows to the back of his head. The Shooter spun away and put up his hands, clenching them into fists. Before he could swing the officials jumped in and pulled the Squire guard away from him.

The crowd roar changed to hissing and booing as the officials walked the guard over to the Squire bench. The guard was twisted around, screaming something back at the Shooter. The Shooter couldn't hear exactly what he was saying because of the crowd noises. The Shooter shrugged and spread his hands as if he didn't know exactly what the whole thing was about.

The roars and the boos got worse, and the official whistled for a time-out. The Shooter grinned to himself as he walked off the court and sat down on the bench. Big Ed sat down next to him and let out a big blow of breath.

"That boy's got a bad temper," Big Ed said.

The Shooter shook his head. "I hardly touched that dude."

"Neither does Joe Fraser," Big Ed said. "The wind when he misses knocks them down."

At the half-time break, the score was 48 to 45 in favor of the Squires. Julius Erving was having a great night. Neither Frank alone or in combination with Big Ed could hold him down.

The Shooter had fifteen points. He was well on his way to his game average.

Harley Brisker sat alone at one corner of the overlarge table in the committee meeting room. The meeting had been called for eight, but the members didn't seem in any hurry to arrive on time. At eight on the dot, only two members of the committee were in place: Harley and the presiding officer, Senator Robert Mast.

Three other members drifted in by quarter after eight. The final three arrived at 8:25. They were laughing as they came down the hall. When they reached the doorway Jim Sims, Senator Johnson and Hap Seaver choked the laughter back and walked into the room with the dignity and purpose of better men than they were.

Senator Robert Mast waited until these three were seated before he called the meeting to order. "I have here a letter from the Governor." He held up a sheet of paper. "It's dated today. It was delivered by messenger this morning." He folded the letter and put it on the table. "I don't see any reason to read this letter. It's exactly like the ones he's been sending us for the last two weeks." He lifted his head and looked down the length of the table. "In fact, it might be a Xerox copy of the one he sent us last Thursday."

He grinned and shook his head at the laughter. "Still, it goes without much more saying, that the Governor is pushing us. If we don't make some kind of decision tonight and send it on to the General Assembly on Monday, I think we can assume that the Convention Center will have to wait until the next meeting of the Assembly. It's something the Governor doesn't want, it's something I don't want, and, I might be taking too much on myself, but I don't think any of you want that either."

He looked down the table, waiting.

A chair rasped back and Hap Seaver stood up. "I'd like about two minutes of the committee's time."

"Go ahead, Hap," Senator Mast said.

"As you know, throughout these deliberations, I've been a strong supporter of the Boulevard site."

Someone down the table, behind a hand, mumbled, "Oh, God, not another speech."

"No," Hap said, "not another speech. I'm going to spare all of you that." He spread his hands, as if calming a larger crowd. "As I've said, I've always been behind the Boulevard site. What I'm going to say now might be misunderstood." His eyes flicked toward Harley and past him. "While I'm still behind the Boulevard site and its selection, I think I'm realistic enough to know it doesn't stand a chance."

Harley looked away from Hap. His eyes moved over the other members and he caught their quickening interest.

"For that reason, with some real regret, I'm going to vote for a site that has some chance of getting enough votes to carry. In this same spirit, I'm going to ask that others of you consider similar shifts in the interest of getting this Convention Center funded and construction underway as soon as possible." He smiled a broad, toothy smile. "I'd like to think we can get this selection over in time to have a few drinks on this Saturday night. Without rushing those drinks."

Hap sat down and nodded to Senator Mast. Senator Mast nodded back and looked down the table. "Any other comments?"

Jim Sims rapped the table top with his knuckles.

"Yes, Jim?"

Sims didn't stand up. He leaned forward on his elbows. "I think we owe Hap a real vote of gratitude. In the past, I think he has spoken very eloquently when he's tried to win support for the Boulevard location. And I, for one, know how he must feel now, having to give up on something he's wanted so long."

So the ducks are all in a row, Harley thought.

Jim Sims lifted his elbows from the table and leaned back. "I believe we can make some progress now, thanks to Hap."

"Mr. Chairman." Across the table from Sims, Senator Johnson struggled to push his chair back and get to his feet.

All according to a script, Harley thought. Cues and entrances and speeches all planned out.

"Go right ahead," Senator Robert Mast said.

Senator Johnson grinned at them. It was a foolish clown's grin. "I've been thinking on what Hap there said about a drink. Besides appreciating what Hap said about putting aside our own wants just to get this thing underway, I like that idea of getting this over so we can take the cap off the bottle." He eased his bulk back into his chair. "I think we ought to vote."

"Any objections?" Senator Mast asked.

There weren't any.

After he voted, Harley watched Senator Mast. He could see how the vote was going. At first Mast met his eyes, but then, as the votes edged toward the Whitehall location, the one Mast supported, Mast's eyes dropped and he became especially interested in the tabulations he was doing. So he'd known the script as well, Harley thought. And because he was a fair man, Harley couldn't feel any anger toward him. Until a couple of hours before, it had been very likely that Sims, Johnson and Seaver would have been voting with Harley. Perhaps then his would have been the eyes that looked away.

The vote was over in a matter of minutes. The Whitehall site received six votes and the Boulevard and the Civic Center site one vote each.

Jim Sims wanted the committee to declare the selection unanimous, but neither Harley nor "Bunk" Hamilton, who'd voted for the Civic Center site, would change their votes. "Bunk" Hamilton hadn't said much, but Harley could see that he was looking at Jim Sims like he wanted to fight. Harley didn't think it would happen, but he understood how Hamilton felt.

After the rush to finish the vote, it seemed odd that no one appeared in a special hurry to leave. They stood around in clusters of twos and threes as if they expected something to happen. Harley got into his topcoat and pushed in his chair. Across the table from him, "Bunk" Hamilton did the same.

Senator Robert Mast stopped beside Harley. "That's the way it happens, Harley."

Harley nodded. "That's true."

"You mad?"

"It's over. No reason to be mad."

"I'll see you, Harley."

"Sure," Harley said.

Harley reached the hall before Hap Seaver rushed out and caught up with him. "You got a second?"

Harley turned. He made an effort to keep his voice level and neutral. "Sure, Hap."

"Look, this doesn't change anything, does it? We're still friends, aren't we?"

"As much as we ever were," Harley said.

He walked away from Hap. He reached the elevator and touched the down button. The doors opened and he stepped inside and closed the doors behind him.

That was one Saturday shot to hell.

CHAPTER FOURTEEN

The trainer, Ben Bob, slipped the Shooter a note when he came back on the floor just before the start of the third quarter. Ben Bob did it on the sly because Coach Thorn didn't approve of that kind of thing on the bench during a game. But at the moment the note was passed, Coach Thorn was huddled with the official scorekeeper going over the foul count on the players for both teams.

> *Eddie,*
>
>   *Would you like to meet me and my cousin, Fred, for a drink after the game? He's not my boyfriend. We'll wait for you at Entrance A.*
>
> *Edna*

The Shooter folded the note and tucked it into the sock on his right leg. He turned and looked up at the crowd until he found her. When their eyes met, he nodded. She waved and he waved back. As soon as he turned, he saw Coach Thorn standing behind him, scowling.

"My cousin's up there," he said.

"And so's my Great-aunt Charlene," Coach Thorn growled at him. But the scowl didn't last. Thorn was pleased to be only three points behind the Squires at half time. "Keep your mind on the game. Your cousin'll keep 'til afterwards."

"Right, Coach."

Thorn turned away and then turned back. "Ab Slaton... I think the Carolina Cougars will pick him up."

"Thanks."

The buzzer sounded at mid-court. The third quarter was about to begin.

While Frances and Helen were in the ladies' room, Pete Kendall slipped into the chair next to Vince. "Maybe I should have called you earlier. The freak decided to tell a straight story. Frances is out of it. Just like she'd never been there."

Vince saw it in his face and heard a hint of it in the tone of his voice. "And you're not entirely happy about it?"

"It's mixed," Pete admitted. "Oh, hell, I know Frances isn't the kind of girl who belongs in this kind of situation. The better I know her, the more sure I am of that."

"So what's choking you?"

"I don't like money and power erasing things."

"I offer you any money?" Vince asked. "I lean any power on you?"

Pete shook his head. "No, but it's there."

"To be used if I wanted to use them—is that what you're saying?"

"Yes."

"I'll make a deal with you, Pete." Vince looked across the room as Helen and Frances entered. "You spend the rest of the evening with Frances. You find out what kind of person she is. You do that and then you can call me the first thing Monday morning. If you think there's any reason why she ought to go to court and get muddied up in the process, I'll be glad to bring her right over to the police station and turn her in."

"You play rough," Pete said.

"And while you're at it you'd better decide what the charge against her is going to be."

Pete shook his head. "I don't know of any charge I'd bring."

"Then how about having a few more of those goddamn cucumber sandwiches? The girl looks just fine to me."

"Doesn't she though?" Pete stood up. "I guess I'm just being an ass."

"Or," Vince said, "you wanted me to know you were an honest cop."

"Rough, very rough." Pete left him and joined Frances.

Frances had been talking to Helen, and Vince's guess was that they'd been talking about Pete. Now, as Pete approached them, Frances turned and Vince saw her face. It was like a flower opening up.

But at the same moment Helen turned away from Pete and Frances and saw that Vince was looking at her. The look she gave him was like a flower closing.

That hurt. Maybe it shouldn't have, but it did.

Down on the court, the center jump signaled the beginning of the third quarter.

"Do some of that slick shit to me, Shooter."

This was from a new Squire guard. The Shooter had been beating the replacement guard up and down the court, the one who'd replaced the hothead who'd jumped the Shooter in the first quarter. Now the Squire coach had gone to a third guard. The new one was named Franklin Cort. He usually didn't play much. He was slower and heavier and hard-muscled. He had a profile like the side of a claw hammer.

"Play ball," the Shooter said.

Cort slowed his dribble and danced back, just out of the Shooter's reach. "Show me how mean you are, Shooter."

"Play the game," the Shooter said.

Cort dribbled suddenly to the left a couple of steps and cut for the basket. The move surprised the Shooter, and when he moved to block the lane, Cort rammed into him, knees, elbows and feet striking out at the Shooter. The whistle blew as the Shooter went down hard.

The Shooter looked up into the face of the ref. "Blocking," the official said.

The Shooter got up slowly. He'd been hit so many times by Cort that he didn't remember the one that mashed his lip, but he could feel it fattening up. As he moved away, he heard Cort say, in a whisper that only he could hear, "Let's do that four or five more times."

"Fuck off," the Shooter hissed back at him.

It looked like it was going to be a long third and fourth quarter. On the next three times down, the Shooter put up the ball and scored each time. But when the Squires had the ball, true to what he'd said, Cort was driving on him. One was called a charge and the other a block. And each time he and Cort went down. The elbows and knees were out. Cort's shoulder was down like he was delivering a block.

The Shooter could feel the lumps and the knots coming up. The puffed lip was bleeding a little on the inside of his mouth, and his jaw ached as if a tooth might be loose.

At the next time-out, Coach Thorn took a look at the Shooter's lip and asked if he wanted to sit out the rest of the quarter. The Shooter shook his head, and, as the coach looked away, he took the towel from around his neck and spat blood into it. He looked up at the clock to see there were still eight minutes left in the third quarter.

The Shooter knew he shouldn't have been in there, not under the basket where the heavy rebounding was going on. He wouldn't have been if he hadn't been following Cort, who had made his cut under the basket just as the other Squire guard put the ball up. The shot didn't fall through. As it hit the rim and went straight up, a little less than a ton of muscle and bone went after it. The Shooter was caught in the middle and had a good angle on it. With everybody leaning in toward him he found some spring in his legs and went up after the ball. It was on the tip of his right hand and he was bringing over his left hand when something struck him across the shins and flipped him. He fell forward, the ball forgotten, and he just had time to put out his hands to cushion his fall so he wouldn't take the force of the fall on his face. His hands did soften the fall, but he felt a numbness all the way up his shoulders. He took part of the fall on his right hip, and he knew he'd be lucky not to get a hip pointer out of that.

He was trying to get to his feet when he felt an arm go around his waist and lift him. The help was coming from Frank Oates, the forward who was having trouble guarding Julius Erving. It was the first time Frank had ever done anything friendly; he was opening his mouth to thank him when he saw Franklin Cort.

Cort was grinning at him. It was time to fight, he knew that. The grin meant Cort had cut his legs from under him. But when he raised his hands and tried to pull the fingers in to make fists, he found that his hands were still numb.

Big Ed Brewster made his move then. He'd come down with the ball and was holding it now that the whistle had blown. Now, he stepped forward and whipped the ball into Cort's stomach. As Cort bent over, the breath knocked out of him, Big Ed leaned in and hit Cort in the face three times as fast as the Shooter had ever seen anybody hit. Cort went down, his face blank and stunned.

Frank Oates leaned in toward the Shooter. "You stand up all right?" When the Shooter said he could, Frank withdrew his arm and made a run to back up Big Ed. The Squire center was edging up behind Big Ed. Frank reached him, put a hand on his chest and said, "Let's talk about this."

The two officials jumped into the middle of it then. They were pushing players back. One of the officials got Big Ed by the arm and pulled him aside. "What's this about?"

"You saw it," Big Ed said. "He cut the Shooter's leg from under him. He could have broke his back."

The official looked down at Cort.

Cort wasn't out, but he wasn't fully awake either.

The Shooter limped over to the official and said, "How about an injury time-out while I see if anything's broken?"

The official still hadn't done anything about the fists Big Ed had thrown. Usually a fight meant automatic ejection from the game. But now the official seemed confused; he looked at the Shooter's numbed hands and blew his whistle for the time-out. The Shooter put an arm around Big Ed and turned him toward the bench. It was then he realized that the crowd was silent, shocked into holding its breath.

"Ed, I appreciate that back there, but I think we ought to mix you in with a few blacks so nobody'll know who threw those punches."

"Smart-ass," Big Ed said.

The team doctor met the Shooter at the bench, and over his protest led him off the court and down the tunnel to the trainer's office. He was there for around ten minutes. Nothing was broken and the feeling came back into his hands—from numbness to a burn and sting. When he came back on the court, he saw by the clock there was still a bit more than four minutes left in the final quarter. The Crackers were up by ten points. That was a surprise. They'd been playing a few points under the Squires when he left.

He sat down on the bench next to Coach Thorn.

"How do you feel?"

"Good enough to play," he said.

"We got them," Coach Thorn said. "I've never seen them like this, playing this mean."

Standing, Coach Thorn made the sign for the time-out. The Cracker players came to the bench and Big Ed looked down at the Shooter, a fierce gleam to his sweating face. "You gonna sit on the bench all night, Shooter, or do you want some of that blood?" The Shooter stood up. "I'll drink what you're having," he said.

The phone rang in the Wardlaw suite. Vince got to it before Al could reach it.

"Judge Tate would like to speak to Mr. Wardlaw," the man on the other end of the line said.

"Just a minute." Vince turned and nodded at David's questioning look. David passed him on the way to the phone. Vince sat down on the stool next to Helen. "Judge Tate," he said to Helen.

"He's supposed to be a frightening old man," Helen said.

"Scared the hell out of me the couple of times I've seen him," Vince said.

The call lasted only a minute or two. Wardlaw came back to the window. "The committee settled on the Whitehall site."

"How did Judge Tate know that?" Vince asked.

"He knows everything." Wardlaw looked down at the court. "He wants to see me tonight. He said he had an idea, but he didn't want to talk about it on the phone."

"An idea about the Convention Center?"

"He didn't say." Wardlaw turned and looked at Helen. "You haven't met Judge Tate. How'd you like to come along with me?"

"I'd like that. Do I need my steno pad?"

Wardlaw grinned and shook his head.

"You won't need me?" Vince asked.

"Not tonight," Wardlaw said.

At the left end of the bar counter, Pete Kendall whooped and clapped his hands. "Look at the Shooter go!"

Vince looked down at the court and saw the Shooter on a three-on-one break. The Shooter was filling the center lane; and when the ball came to him, he was free and the shot was his. He remained in the air, seeming to hang there, and punched the ball back to Big Ed who was coming down the left lane. Big Ed dunked it.

The game ended a minute or so later. The final score was: Crackers—108, Squires—97. It was the final game of the season against the Squires and the first time they'd beaten them all season.

"Looks like you might have a team there," Vince said to Wardlaw.

Vince rode the elevator down to the ground level with Frances Wardlaw and Pete Kendall. Just inside the door, before they stepped out into the cold night, Vince asked, "Where are you two headed?"

"I'm giving Frances a lift home," Pete said.

"But we don't have to go straight there," Frances said.

Vince saw the surprise on Pete's face, his first realization that Frances wasn't about to be treated like a high school date. While Pete was still absorbing this, Vince said good-night, left them and went to a phone.

Angela answered on the second ring.

"Vince here. You busy?"

"I was getting ready to cruise a few bars," she said.

"I've got a bottle and a little passion left. Not much but a little."

"Anything's better than having to hustle on a cold night like this," she said.

"You know how to make a guy feel good."

"Bet on it," she said.

"Be right there." He put the receiver back, stood at the window and looked out at the street. It was Saturday-night thick, the traffic, and he thought of all the people out there, going here, going there, going God-knows-where. And of his own life, of Timothy and Joyce, the weights that made him hump-backed. Of the years gone, sloughed off like old skin. And of bright promises not kept.

The vomit locked in the back of his throat. He dropped the half-filled coffee cup in the trash receptacle on the way out. The cold outside in the parking lot struck him, and he sat in the car shivering for a few minutes before he was ready to drive away.

⚜ ⚜ ⚜

Dressed in white shorts and a t-shirt, Big Ed came down the aisle between the lockers.

"Shooter, I didn't get my hundred points tonight. That means I might have to go without some trim."

"I gave you two of mine."

"You mean that diddly volleyball pass?" Big Ed grinned. "I saw it coming—I almost pissed in my jock."

"Got to have quick hands," the Shooter said.

"Oh, shit, yes." Big Ed tilted his head and looked at the bruises and the fat lip the Shooter had. "How you feeling?"

"I'll make it to my bed, I think." The Shooter got the Spanish leather coat from a hanger and stepped back. "I'll get you the other ninety-eight points next game."

"You do that, farm boy, and we'll get along."

"It's a promise. And let's have a drink sometime."

"Tonight?"

"Can't," the Shooter said. "Got this girl waiting and she's prettier than you are."

"Rain check then?"

When he reached Entrance A, he was surprised to find Edna alone. "Where's your cousin?"

"He couldn't wait," she said. "It looks like you're going to have to give me a ride home."

"Planned it that way, huh?"

She smiled. "I thought you'd notice that."

"But not right away?"

"Of course not." She took his arm. "Among other things, I could use a drink."

"We'll talk about those other things later. First the drink"

"No." She'd been matching him stride for stride. Now she pulled on his arm and stopped him. "First I want you to know my last name."

"No reason," he said. "You got the tickets, didn't you?"

"I felt ... well ... strange."

"Serves you right," he said.

"My last name is Dunn."

"Edna Dunn." He walked on and she matched his stride. "Would that be the Dunn of The Peachtree State Bank?"

"Yes."

"I think I'd better switch my checking account."

"You'd better," she said.

"First thing Monday morning."

He took a quick step or two and whirled and blocked her way. She closed her eyes and lifted her face. He kissed her on her cold and wind-flushed nose.

CHAPTER FIFTEEN

"Judge Tate is in the library." The old black man who answered the door wore a shiny black suit. In cut and age, it looked like one the judge might have passed down to him ten years before.

"Thank you, Will."

Will helped Helen with her coat and then came over and took David's. When he was close to Wardlaw, his voice dropped so that Helen could not hear him. "It's past Judge Tate's bedtime."

"We won't stay long," Wardlaw whispered back.

Will nodded. "You can go right in the library, Mr. Wardlaw, and your lady too."

The library was a large room. Except for one wall on the side that had French windows that led out to the garden, all the walls were filled to the ten-foot ceiling with books. Once, when he was left in the library alone for half an hour, he'd spent his time looking through several shelves. He'd found battered books that went back to the judge's undergraduate days at Yale. Mixed in were the latest biographies, works on history and recent novels.

"Come in, David," the judge said from the far right corner where a strong lamp burned. The judge was in a soft leather chair. On a table at his elbow was a glass of sherry. He was dressed as he usually was, except this late at night he'd exchanged his suit for a smoking jacket.

"I've brought a lady with me," David said. "I hope you don't mind."

Judge Tate used the armrests to push himself to his feet. "Of course, I don't mind. It's a rare thing to have a beautiful lady in my home and I'm very grateful."

After the introductions, Helen said, "I think I've talked to your secretary several times. You see, I'm David's secretary."

"Mr. Wardlaw is very lucky in his secretaries," the judge said.

"It's not luck at all," David said. "I selected her with care."

Will had entered behind them soundlessly. Now he brought over two chairs and placed them so that David and Helen would face the judge.

"Will," Judge Tate said, "I think our guests might like something to drink."

"Yes, Judge."

"I'm having sherry, but I think we have stronger spirits in the house as well."

"We have quite a collection, Judge," Will said.

David and Helen decided that sherry would be fine.

When Will was gone, Judge Tate looked at David for a long moment, as if assessing him. "It looks like plan 2 or 3 . . . or is it plan B and C?"

David nodded.

"What would you say your loss will be?"

"I don't think I'd call it a loss," David said. "It's not like losing money you already have. It's not even like the paper profits that vanish when the stock market falls." He smiled. "It's more like money you dreamed about while you were asleep. It would be pleasant if it were there when you awoke, but not shattering if it isn't."

"The source of my information seemed to think you showed some weakness in refusing to deal with . . . shall we say, the opportunists? He said it was the first sign of weakness he'd detected in you."

David shook his head. "I could deal with their petty greeds, but not their larger ones."

"I don't understand," the judge said.

"It was a matter of a secret tape recorder," David said.

"I see." There was still a puzzled look on his face, but the judge could make his guess.

Will brought in a tray on which there were two glasses and a decanter of sherry. He placed the tray on the table and poured sherry for David and Helen. When he stepped away, Judge Tate said, "I think that will be all for tonight, Will."

"Judge…" Will began. He dropped his eyes and looked at the floor.

"I know," Judge Tate said. He looked at his watch. "In twenty minutes, I'll be extremely rude to my guests and drive them right out of the front door."

"I'm sorry, Mr. Wardlaw, ma'am," Will said.

Judge Tate watched him out of the room. He shook his head slowly, a warm smile on his face. "Will has been with me twenty-five or six years," he said to Helen. "Sometimes he's worse than a wife."

"He doesn't bully you," Helen said.

"Not in front of guests," the judge said. He sipped his sherry. "Now what do you do with the Boulevard land?"

"Nothing right away. If the Convention Center had been built in the Boulevard area, the whole development might be completed in five or six years. Without it, it might take ten or fifteen years. It might not be finished in my lifetime. The land rush is over now. It's waiting time."

"You appear to be taking it well, David."

David shook his head. "Tomorrow morning I'm going to wake up with a headache and second thoughts. Tonight, I don't feel that way at all. Let me tell you a story, Judge. When I first moved to Atlanta, before I decided to go into the real-estate business, I saw a man buy a piece of property that didn't have any apparent value. It was a matter of about twelve acres and there wasn't anything I could see going on around that tract that would warrant buying it. I didn't see any way it was going to become important or greatly increase in value. After a time, I got around to asking him why he bought it. You know what he said?"

Judge Tate shook his head.

"He said they were going to make a lot of everything in the world *except* land. According to him, there just wasn't any way in the world to create any more."

"What does that mean in terms of the Boulevard land?"

"That I can wait and my son can wait and his son can wait. Sooner or later there'll be some special need for the land. The short-range view is always easy. The long-range view is a bit more difficult."

"You seem to have an over-surplus of patience," Judge Tate said. He got up slowly and stretched. "I haven't wasted my whole evening. I've made a few calls."

"Judge," David said quickly, "you know how I feel…"

The judge stopped him by lifting his hand. "I've been asking questions, only questions. It seemed odd to me that all of you were locked in, on a single track. Perhaps it took an outsider to realize it."

"Realize what?"

"As soon as it became obvious that the State would be willing to put up the thirty-five or forty million dollars to build the Convention Center, all of you seemed to lose your imaginations."

"I don't understand, Judge."

"The Convention Center doesn't have to be built with State money."

"A commercial undertaking?" David asked.

Judge Tate nodded.

"It's a lot of money."

"The moment someone offers to finance the Convention Center as a commercial project, the State will find better things to do with the thirty-five or forty million dollars."

"It's worth considering," David said.

"Without committing you at all," Judge Tate said, "I've taken the liberty to make a few inquiries. Worldwide Consolidated might be willing to take a long-term lease on one floor of the Convention Center for exclusive control of the catering and beverage concession. That would include cafeteria, restaurant and bar services. They'd prefer one of the top floors, but I said that would depend, of course, on the design." He walked to a telephone table across the library. He returned a moment later with a thin sheaf of pages from a note pad. "I've made some notes. Park-Beatherd might be interested in a jewelry and gift shop in the Center. Hertz, auto leasing. A book shop. A men's store. A dress shop." He passed the sheaf of papers to David. "I suspect that you will hear from some of these during business hours on Monday morning."

David looked at the pages and then put them in his pocket. "Thank you."

Judge Tate sat down and lifted his glass and sipped the last of his sherry. "I hope I haven't presumed too much."

David shook his head. "If you weren't such a damned good lawyer, I think I'd hire you to work on planning with me."

"If I were younger, I might take it." He turned to Helen. "And my first project would be to steal Miss Morris from you."

"I'd quit if I couldn't work with you," Helen said.

"David, from now on when you visit, I want you to bring Miss Morris with you."

"It's a promise," David said.

"And now," Judge Tate said, "I'll have to run you out or Will'll pout all day tomorrow."

David and Helen said their good-nights. They'd reached the library door when Judge Tate called David back. "One more thing, David."

David said, "See if you can find our coats, Helen," and crossed the room again. When he stopped in front of the judge, he saw that the old man was looking past him, toward the library door.

"I didn't know about Miss Morris, David," he said.

"There's nothing to know. She's nice, but it's all business."

"An old man has some rights," the judge said. "I'm going to use one of those rights now and step over the line." He paused, as if selecting his words carefully. "I think you know how much I cared for Mrs. Emily?"

"Yes," David said.

"Don't waste the rest of your life."

Helen returned. She stood in the doorway with both coats over her arm. David turned and looked at her, and Judge Tate saw the look that passed between them. "Good-night, David," he said, and then louder, "Good-night, Helen, and you come and see me."

Helen said she would. The judge stood and watched them meet in the doorway and then go out of sight beyond the door. He heard, a few moments later, the front door close. Seated again, he drew the tray toward him and poured another half glass of sherry from the decanter.

He was surprised a minute later to see Will crossing the room toward him. "I thought I told you to go to bed," he said.

"I had to lock the front door," Will said, "and I had to make sure you'd keep your word."

"After all these years?" Judge Tate shook his head mock-wearily.

"Being visited this time of night by a lady," Will said, "and at your age."

The two old men looked at each other and laughed, the judge's laugh high and thin, Will's a low, warm rumble.

"We don't have to stay in Atlanta," Ethel Ann said.

Harley didn't answer her. They were in the living room and the TV set was tuned to the Saturday Night Movie. He was straining to pretend an interest in the western that he really didn't feel. There was a bottle of Michelob on the table in front of him and a glass in his hand.

"The offer from Denver seemed reasonable enough," Ethel Ann said.

"I turned it down," Harley said, without taking his eyes from the TV screen.

"I know the offer from New York is still open."

He turned and stared at her then. "How could you know that?"

"I just do."

"Can you honestly see us living in New York? Or living in New Jersey and me riding the train or the bus in every day?"

"It's almost twice as much money," Ethel Ann said.

"Do you know what living expenses are up there? You know how many people you have to pay off just to get an apartment up there?"

"Is that the real reason?"

"No," he said. "We live in Atlanta and that's it."

"Is it worth it … after today?"

"Yes, it is. Oh, I know how you're feeling. You've decided that I lost a big battle today and I ought to get mad and leave town. The real truth is that the wrong battle got fought today." He put his glass aside and lifted the cold hand and placed it on her neck. "The real question wasn't whether the Convention Center ought to be built here or there or somewhere else. It was whether the Convention Center ought to be built at all."

She shivered under the cold hand. "I had a feeling you were thinking some dark thought today."

"You know what this is all about? You know who really wants a Convention Center?"

"No."

"Downtown merchants. They see the short-range dollar in it. They see hotels overflowing and new ones built. Bars all over town without an empty chair or an empty glass in them. Restaurants with waiting lines and bulky reservation lists every night. Stores selling god-knows-what to people from all over the country."

"What's wrong with that?"

"On the surface, nothing," Harley said. "It's easy money, with ten or fifteen thousand new people coming into town every few days. Expense-account money and a bit of mad money thrown in. All spending money like it's a sin to go back home with more than two dollars in their pockets."

"I still don't see..."

"It's the short-range view that bothers me. It's inviting those ten or fifteen thousand people in and not realizing that those people aren't going to do one damned thing to improve the quality of life in Atlanta. In fact, it'll go down about ten notches."

"But, Harley..."

"You remember the last time the Shriners were in town? Thousands and thousands of them. It was hot as hell, in the summer, and they had parades three days in a row. Well, a little black lady I know got off work at two in the afternoon and she waited at the bus stop for an hour and a half. It seems all the buses got tied up in the rerouted traffic downtown and just couldn't get through. When a bus finally showed up it got almost to town and then got rerouted from Peachtree to Courtland, and there was such a traffic jam on Courtland that it took almost an hour to go twelve blocks. Well, it just happened three Shriners and their wives got on the bus, and they were drunk and loud and obscene and were bitching about how everybody in town was ripping them off. And here was a busload of people who live in Atlanta all year and pay taxes, and they'd been waiting in 90-degree weather for more than an hour for a bus. The amazing thing was that the whole busload of people didn't get up and beat the shit out of those Shriners."

"That's an isolated example."

"Maybe, but just wait until they've got a Convention Center."
Harley poured the last of his beer into the glass and got a sip.
"Or, if it'll make more sense, take that spare bedroom we've got
upstairs. Why don't we rent it out? We could get a hundred dollars out of it ... easy."

Ethel Ann's face had a puzzled look. "Of course," Harley
said, "with a stranger here in the house there'd have to be some
changes. We'd have to keep our doors closed all the time and we
wouldn't be able to walk around in our underwear. And we'd have
to put up with that stranger coming in at all hours and being in
the bathroom when we wanted to use it. But, on the other hand,
we'd have that hundred dollars a month, even though the quality
of life in this house would go to hell."

"I can see that, but it doesn't have that much to do with the
Convention Center."

"Sure, it does. After the Convention Center is built, don't be
surprised if another thousand prostitutes are recruited from somewhere to handle those out-of-towners. Don't be surprised if the city
has to hire more police because the mugging rate goes up. Don't
be surprised if the city doesn't end up providing better service to
visitors from Bridgeport, Connecticut, than to people who live in
Atlanta all year round." Harley tossed back the last of the beer and
tapped the glass on the table. "Back to that spare bedroom again.
Now, here's this stranger living in our house, and you really get
to like that hundred dollars a month. First thing you know you're
giving him a clean towel every day while I have to use one for three
or four days. And you're fixing his breakfast now, and he's getting
two eggs and I'm just getting one. And just to make sure he's happy
and doesn't leave, you start taking him to bed about once a week."

"Harley, that's silly and ..."

"Of course, it is." He put an arm around her and pulled her
against his shoulder. " 'Cause first of all, that stranger wouldn't
be in your bed but once before I'd kick his ass out in the street. A
hundred dollars don't mean that much to me."

"You always were a jealous type."

"You can bet your butt on that." He kept his arm around her. A loud burst of gunfire from the television set drew his attention. The showdown in the center of the western town was beginning and he watched it while Ethel Ann watched his face.

After one drink and a dance at Richard's, a huge hard rock place near Monroe and Eighth, the Shooter leaned across the table toward Edna. "That music hurts my bones, the ones that aren't already bruised from the game."

"We can leave," she said.

They plowed a path through the crush of hip and semi-hip to the doorway and out into the cold and windy parking lot. The wind sucked the breath out of them. He took her hand and they sprinted to his XKE. When they were inside, he looked over at her. "What now, lady?"

"What?"

"Your place or mine?"

In the slash of half-light from the street he saw that she hadn't taken the question as a light one. "Are you tired, Eddie?"

"Usually I'm not. Tonight, I got beat on some."

"You could drop me at my place," she said. "We can try again another night."

"We could go to my place," he said.

"Not if I have to arm-wrestle you."

"I promise."

"Then your place."

On the elevator at the Madrid Apartments she said, "If that doorman looks at me one more time like that, I'm going to kick him in the crotch."

"How?" He hadn't noticed anything special about the way the doorman had acted toward her.

"Like I was one of your playmates," she said.

"Aren't you?"

"Not that way."

The elevator doors opened and they walked down the hall to his apartment. Unlocking the door, he said, "I'll pass the word down so it gets to him. When you see that tall girl, act like she's the Queen of England." He swung the door open and stood aside to let her enter. "Would that be better?"

"Better," she said.

"A drink?"

"I'd like some coffee."

"I've got a new gadget," he said. In the kitchen he got a bag of coffee beans from the refrigerator and a new electric grinder from the cabinet above the stove. He plugged in the grinder and threw in a couple of handfuls of the coffee beans. While he ground them briefly, she stepped around him and got the kettle and filled it with tap water. He put a filter in a new Tricolette coffeemaker and spooned the ground coffee into it. He turned from the stove and found Edna seated at the kitchen table.

"Coffee's coming up," he said.

"You having some?" She opened her purse and got out a cigarette. She held the cigarette and looked at him. When he hesitated, she waved the unlit cigarette at him.

"Oh." He got up and found a book of matches. "Am I going to have to light all your cigarettes?"

"Most men I go with do," she said.

"I'm not most men you go with," he said. He dropped the book of matches on the table in front of her and watched her light the cigarette.

"No, you're not. You don't have manners."

"Manners?"

"Yes, common, ordinary manners," she said.

"We don't have schools for manners up in North Carolina."

"You need them."

"In North Carolina, most girls can light their own. They've got hands and fingers and sometimes they even open doors for themselves without any trouble."

"It's not a matter of that."

"What is it a matter of?" he asked.

"Respect," she said.

"Hell, I respect you. I respect you a lot. And it doesn't have anything to do with whether I light your smokes or not." Behind him the water in the kettle began its tumbling roar. He moved away from her and poured the coffee into the filter.

"If you have any respect for me tonight, it's a thousand percent more than you had for me last night."

"I thought about you some," he said. "I thought about how you weren't like some of those other girls."

"Are you being honest with me, Eddie?"

"Sure I am," he said.

She smiled at him then. It was an odd smile, warm and at the same time a bit sad. The smile caught at him, choking him in a way he'd never felt before. I'd better watch myself, he thought. That isn't the way it's supposed to be. I'm supposed to con you and you con me and we end up using each other for as long as we like and then we let the con slide away and we see each other as we really are. And then it's over.

"That's a step in the right direction," she said.

"If it'll make you feel better, I'll start carrying matches and I'll open some doors for you."

"And that's a major concession?"

"Isn't it … for me?" He grinned at her, and the smile she gave him this time didn't have the sadness in it. Instead it had a tenderness, and he felt that the breath had been forced out of him and a kind of pain clawing at his throat.

"Is something wrong, Eddie?"

He shook his head. He couldn't talk. He covered himself by turning to look at the coffeemaker. He saw that most of the water had settled through the filter. He got down two cups and placed them on the table. When he looked at her, he saw that she was studying his face.

"Are you sure?"

I think I am going to like this girl, and it scares the shit out of me, he thought. It's not supposed to happen to me. "Struck by your beauty," he said.

"I'm not beautiful, not even pretty," she said.

"It must be soul then," he said.

"Eddie, that's a nice thing to say."

"Call me Shooter," he said.

She shook her head. "Not me. Your other girls can call you that if they want to, but I won't."

The Shooter didn't ask her why. He nodded and got the coffeemaker from the stove and poured two cups of coffee. It was shifting, he was the one off-balance this time, and he wasn't really sure that he was against it altogether. The other girls were fading in his mind, and if he wasn't falling in love it was a very good carbon copy.

Vince swung his legs over the edge of the bed and stood up. His knees buckled slightly. He locked them and walked stiff-legged over to the ice bucket. He tossed in a couple of ice cubes and a splash of Glenlivet. "So, what's bothering you?"

"Nothing," Angela said. "Yes, something. You don't seem to be very happy."

"Is that right?"

She scooted across the bed and, placing a pillow against the head of the bed, sat up. Her shoulder was back, lifting her breasts. "Fucking ought to be fun."

"Isn't it?"

"Tonight, it's what I call sad fucking. Like you're thinking of something else or someone else."

"You can tell all that just from fucking?"

"It's my trade," Angela said.

"Or craft or art."

Angela gave a short, coyish bow of her head. "Thank you."

He walked back to the bed and stopped with his knees touching the side of the mattress. "You're welcome." Just from looking at her, hearing her voice, he could feel himself lifting and stretching out. "You see?"

She laughed and fell forward. She crawled on her hands and knees until she reached him. Still on all fours, she lifted her head and caught him in her mouth. Under the touch of her mouth and the flick of her tongue he could sense the last stage, the turning stone-hard. He lifted his drink and sipped at it. When he looked down, the short blonde hair was shaking with the forward and backward tilt.

And found himself thinking of Helen. Maybe that was why she thinks of this as sad fucking. All this mail being delivered to the wrong address. All this. All.

Angela released him from her mouth and fell back.

Vince placed the glass on the night table and fell on top of her, pushing himself past the valentine hair shape and deep inside of her. Her hands came up and caught him at the waist and pulled him deeper as she kicked her legs up.

"Come on," she hissed at him, "be happy, and if you can't be happy, be nasty, mean, shitty, crappy, nasty…"

And though he couldn't feel the happiness, he could feel the strong pull of her; as he rocked toward the faraway and inevitable explosion, some of the sadness seemed to blow away from him and pass. But it will come back, he thought, it will come back. As soon as this small death is over. That soon. Just that soon.

❧ ❧ ❧

"The real drawback to the commercial financing and construction of the Convention Center is the high square-foot cost of auditoriums and meeting halls when compared to structures built for other purposes. It is not so much the fact of high initial cost but the matter of low returns on that investment. For example, a theatre-type seat in a convention hall where a conference is being held might, for the sake of argument, bring in one dollar a day when the overall rental of the hall is broken down into parts. This same seat, in a movie theatre where a popular film is being shown, might be occupied four or five times during a day. The movie theatre and the convention hall might cost about the same in terms of the per-square-foot costs, but the movie theatre might return twelve to fifteen dollars a day on that investment as compared to one dollar in the convention hall. Related to this is the assumption that the movie-theatre seat might be used three hundred and sixty-five days a year while the convention-hall seat might, even with the best planning, only be used about a hundred and eighty days a year."

Helen looked up from her steno pad. "I think it's beginning to make sense now, David."

David nodded. "The loud outcry of the theatre owners in the 1950s when they were being hurt by television was that they make whatever profit they did on the sale of candy, soft drinks, popcorn and ice cream. I think we can use this as our key. We will assume that the necessary meeting halls and conference rooms, these rentals, will do little toward retiring the initial cost involved in construction. A tie-in with other enterprises such as bars, restaurants, shops and franchises might go some way toward counterbalancing the relatively low return from these meeting spaces. The second possibility is the utilization of this space during the other one hundred and eighty-odd days of the year when this space is not being used for conventions.

In line with this, I believe it might be worthwhile to spend a few minutes on the multipurpose theatre design research being carried out at Yale. That is, the manner and method of changing, mechanically, the properties of a theatre to suit the presentations."

David looked up at Helen. "Six copies, please. And note in the proper place that the meeting will be held in the conference room at ten on Monday morning."

"You want me to type this now?"

David shook his head. "Monday morning, early, is fine. I'll call everyone tomorrow and give them a rundown on the problem so they can mull it over until the meeting. The memo is just to define it again for the purposes of the meeting."

"And to give you a chance to define it for yourself," Helen said.

"You know me too well." David pushed back his chair and stood up. He stretched. He left the desk and walked over to the window, ignoring the model of the Boulevard projection below it, and looked out at the midnight streets. Helen closed her steno pad and placed it on a corner of the desk and followed him. David said, "I didn't want to hurt the judge's feelings. It wasn't that any of us ignored the possibility of commercial financing. Rather, it seemed a problem without a solution."

"Is it still ... without a solution?"

"Perhaps. But let's try it as an exercise, a way of discovering what kind of brain trust I've got here in the office."

"And if you can't solve it?"

"We pass it up." He made his slow turn from the window, his face still reflecting the darkness and the cold outside. "I don't know any other lady who would go out for a drink and let herself end up taking dictation."

"I don't mind."

"You ought to." He put a hand on her shoulder and turned her. "I think we ought to have one drink and call it a night." As she walked with him toward the kitchen he said, "Judge Tate admired my taste in ladies tonight."

"He wasn't at all the terror he'd been made out to me."

"He didn't say it. I've gotten so I can read him. He loved Emily quite a bit. I think he saw Emily in you."

"Oh, no." It was almost under her breath, an exclamation she might have wished she'd held back.

"I know that might not be a compliment," he said evenly.

"I know it was meant as one."

In the kitchen, David got down a bottle of vodka and the bottle of Glenlivet. Helen placed a bottle of tomato juice on the counter and, still not looking at him, filled two glasses with ice cubes.

As he mixed the drinks he asked, "Why isn't it a compliment?"

"It's because a woman doesn't like to think she was hired or liked or whatever because she reminds a man of someone else. It's a matter of ghosts."

"Is that what you thought he meant … or what I might mean if I said you reminded me of Emily?"

"Yes," she said.

"I knew you were sensitive …"

"But not that sensitive?"

He finished mixing a Bloody Mary and passed it to her. Then he poured a shot of scotch over the ice and looked down at it for a long moment while he swirled the ice and scotch together. "I loved Emily for more than twenty years, and I think there's some secret place in me that still tries to keep part of her alive even now."

"I think I know that," she said.

"But I think if a girl walked into this office on Monday morning who looked exactly like Emily and who seemed like Emily in every way, I don't believe I'd do any more than look at her in complete surprise."

"Then what did Judge Tate? …"

"By approving of you, he was saying that he saw the same light in you, the same strength, the same dignity." He looked up from the glass. His eyes touched her face and slid past. She was open to him, vulnerable, and she showed him more than he'd ever seen of her before. He found he was a little frightened and more than a little touched.

"All that in me?" She laughed nervously. "I didn't know all that was in me."

"That's the beauty of some things," David said. "The one having them isn't even aware they're there."

"You're embarrassing me."

"I know. And, for the first time, I don't really think I care."

"What are you trying to do to me, David?"

"I think, in some rusty and out-of-fashion way, I'm trying to edge up on you."

"Why?" She raised the Bloody Mary and drank.

"Why am I edging up on you?"

"No, why tonight? Why not last month and last week or yesterday?"

"It was Vince," he said. "I thought you'd given up on yourself. It scared me."

"And tomorrow, when you're no longer frightened?"

He shook his head. "It won't be like that."

"Can we take some time and be sure?"

"As much time as we need." He drank half the scotch in one swallow and carried the glass back to his desk. He dialed the number that connected him with the driver in the underground garage. He said, "We'll be down in a few minutes." He turned and found Helen close to him.

"Do you know what Vince said about you? That if you loved me, you'd build a shopping center on me."

"Vince has a warped perception," he said. He smiled. "Perhaps a building *around* you."

Helen placed her glass on the desk and, eyes on his face, waited until he finished the last of his scotch. "We don't have to be all that slow," she said.

ABOUT THE AUTHOR
AND THIS BOOK

The original version of this novel, entitled *Atlanta*, was published by Popular Library in paperback in 1975, mid-way through the twelve-book run of Ralph Dennis' Hardman series of crime novels.

The book was inexplicably packaged by Popular Library as a sprawling potboiler similar to bestsellers of the day written by Arthur Hailey, Harold Robbins, John O'Hara and Irwin Shaw. There was nothing subtle about the ploy. The blurb across the cover screamed:

"A city aflame with the passions of today — the most enthralling blockbuster novel since AIRPORT and HOTEL."

But *Atlanta* was nothing like those books, and Ralph wasn't like those authors, so the novel disappointed the readers the publisher was trying to attract and didn't reach the audience that would truly appreciate it: crime fiction fans.

Atlanta was essentially a novel about conflicted "fixer," a ruthless lawyer of dubious morality hired by a real estate titan to quietly and efficiently make problems go away with bribes, cover-ups and persuasion.

Once again, Ralph was sabotaged by his publisher's bad packaging and promotion, as he had been with the Hardman series (which were marketed as numbered men's action/adventure novels like *The Executioner* and *The Penetrator*).

But Ralph also sabotaged himself. His skill was writing lean, evocative prose that moved a story along at a brisk pace without a wasted word. But in *Atlanta*, perhaps in an effort to bulk up the number of pages to Hailey-esque proportions, he filled the book with rambling descriptions and lengthy, irrelevant backstory that dragged the pace down. But the original manuscript was even longer, as Ralph revealed in a letter he wrote in May 1975 to his friend Wesley H. Wallace, chairman of the department of Radio, Television and Film at the University of North Carolina, Chapel Hill:

"*Atlanta* is a book I didn't want to do, but Popular Library kept raising the advance money. It was written for a godawful series of books … *Saturday Night in San Francisco, Saturday Night in Los Angeles, Saturday Night in Milwaukee*…and mine was to be *Saturday Night in Atlanta*. When I finished it, the manuscript was 375 pages. It was too long and I was sick of it. They cut 75 pages and two whole characters out themselves. But the series was such a disaster that they decided to bring my book out apart from it and try to get their money back. Without telling me, they brought it out as *Atlanta*. In fact, I didn't know it was out until a friend saw it on the shelves at Brentanos."

Atlanta was a commercial failure and disappeared into obscurity. Ralph returned to his Hardman series and the kind of writing he did best, though he was ashamed of the books and longed to be taken seriously as a literary writer.

What he didn't believe, and most critics at the time didn't either, was that crime novels are serious, literary writing. Lean prose isn't a sign of superficiality and setting a story in a world of crime doesn't make it any less emotionally, spiritually, psychologically and culturally meaningful than so-called "literary fiction."

This new, retitled edition is a substantial revision of Ralph's original manuscript. Unnecessary exposition was cut and scenes were tightened to improve pacing and sharpen characters.